WHY ME

WHY ME

TRAGEDY, COMEDY, LOVE AND ADVENTURE

JOHN BOLSTRIDGE

authorHOUSE

AuthorHouse™ UK Ltd.
1663 Liberty Drive
Bloomington, IN 47403 USA
www.authorhouse.co.uk
Phone: 0800.197.4150

© 2013 by John Bolstridge. All rights reserved.

No part of this book may be reproduced, stored in a retrieval system, or transmitted by any means without the written permission of the author.

Published by AuthorHouse   12/10/2013

ISBN: 978-1-4918-8762-2 (sc)
ISBN: 978-1-4918-8763-9 (e)

Any people depicted in stock imagery provided by Thinkstock are models, and such images are being used for illustrative purposes only. Certain stock imagery © Thinkstock.

This book is printed on acid-free paper.

Because of the dynamic nature of the Internet, any web addresses or links contained in this book may have changed since publication and may no longer be valid. The views expressed in this work are solely those of the author and do not necessarily reflect the views of the publisher, and the publisher hereby disclaims any responsibility for them.

Contents

WHY ME 1

THE JOKER 91

FOR THE LOVE OF BRANDY 257

THE DAY TIME STOPPED 387

THIS STORY IS DEDECATED TO THE LIFE
OF A WONDERFUL WOMAN

TRAGICALLY TAKEN FROM THIS WORLD ON
03/06/2010

BY METASTIC BREAST CANCER AND
CLOSTRIDIUM DIFFICILE COLITIS

MARGARET ELIZABETH STEPHANIE BOLSTRIDGE

AGE 54 YEARS

BORN 19/12/1954

WHY ME

This is a true story about the life together of Margaret Bolstridge nee Ward, and John Bolstridge

We start story of John Bolstridge, after he had just gone through a marriage breakdown after finding that his first wife had cheated on him with another man. Only one week before he is going to Emigrate to New Zealand, with his wife and two small children. This knocked him for six his whole life fell apart around him, and he moved back into his mum's house with him already selling his home.

The time is approaching Christmas and one day after he had finished his early shift at work, went into the local pub for a drink. Sitting at a table near the window sat two of his work colleagues, he brought his pint and went over to them and asked if he could join them. They straight away told him to join them and started talking about work and general small talk.

John asks them what they were doing that afternoon, Margaret one of the girls tells John that they were going down Town to have their hair done. John asks them if they would like a lift, because he had his Capri outside. The girls look at each other and tell John that would be nice of him.

They finished their drinks and start to go to Johns Capri, once outside Margaret tells John that he had a nice car. For his Capri was a 2 litre 2 door hatchback.

On the way into Town the two girls sat in the back while John sat in the front, he looks in his rear view mirror and asks them if one of them would like to go for a drink that night. Well they both giggle and did not answer John.

He pulls up in Town outside the hairdressers and he pulls the front passengers seat forward so they could get out, the first girl gets out, while Margaret inches across so she can get out. She puts her hand on John's chair while she was still in the back and said.

"What time tonight then," well John is knocked back with this and murmurs.

"How about the shop at the top of Melbourne Road 7.30, pm."

Why Me

"OK 7.30 see you John," he just sits there and watches them go into the shop. He just couldn't believe that she said yes, well the drive back home is all smiles and singing to the music on the car radio.

Back home he tells his Mum about Margaret, well John's Mum asks.

"This Margaret is she the one that lives on Forward crescent."

"Yes Mum."

"You have a nice girl there her Mum is called Margaret to, very nice family."

"Thanks Mum," John smiling at is Mum with the reply that she gave him. That afternoon he was watching a little T.V, but all the time John had one eye on the clock then back to the T.V.

Well the time was approaching 6pm then John couldn't stand it anymore and decided to start to get ready to meet Margaret.

He's in the bathroom showering, shaving and generally dusting himself with aftershave and deodorant, well he smelt like a King. He looks at his watch and its approaching 7pm.

"God look at me anyone would have thought that I have never been on a date," it's probably because he had been married for 7 years. 7-20pm John goes to the front door and gives one last look in the mirror, when his Mum comes out of the lounge.

"Are you off now John," his Mum smiling at him looking into the mirror. He turns round and tells her.

"Thanks Mum, wish me luck."

"Away with you son you look a million dollars you enjoy yourself you deserve it," his Mum brushing his shoulder. John opens the front door steps out and looks back and thanks his Mum. He starts to get into his Capri with his Mum looking on, she is thinking to herself that what he had gone through that he deserved to find happiness.

Chapter 1

the Date

John pulls up at the shop at the top of Melbourne Road, and he starts to get nervous. He is saying to himself what if she does not turn up; boy I'm going to look a plonker. When he suddenly looks in his rear mirror and sees Margaret is approaching, well the look on his face at seeing her walking towards the Capri.

Long black hair short mini skirt and long knee length boots, she looks really fetching. This was the norm of dress in the year of 1977 he just could not take his eyes off her.

She opens the passenger's door and says "hi" to John, she starts to sit down and when her back hits the seat it goes fully reclined. Well Margaret is flat on her back lying in the back and her legs just flaying in the air in the front, well poor old John comes straight out with.

"Not yet love we have only just met," well Margaret is in tears with laughter with what happened. All John is doing is apologising profusely.

He tells Margaret.

"That he had not fully clicked the seat back that afternoon when he dropped them in Town."

"That's ok John where are we going."

"Well do you fancy a ride to Derby, a few drinks not too many for me and take it from there."

"Let's go."

They drive of down Aspley Lane and head for the Boulevard that leads to the A52 to Derby, after about 15 minutes they are well on their way going down the A52. Margaret turns to John and tells him.

"You're quiet you haven't said a word," well this threw John because with him concentrating on his driving he had not said a word. All he did was look out of the window and see cows in a field some standing and some sitting, he just came out with.

"Look at all them cows in that field." Well Margaret just looks at John with a smile and a giggle, touches his hand on the gear stick. John looks back at her and smiles back not long and they are pulling up in Derby, park up and go into the first pub.

They get their drinks and go and sit in a booth so they are on their own, John looks at Margaret and start to apologise about his quietness on the way there.

He tells Margaret he thinks it is because he has been married with two children, Margaret puts her finger up to John's lips this stops John in his tracks she tells him.

"Don't forget John your wife worked with me and I know all about you, I will admit in some small way I've fancied you for some time." She removes her finger from his lips leans forward and gives John a kiss fully on his lips. Well John had this feeling running round his body, and gently puts his hand on Margaret's face moving forward and returns the complement by giving her a longer kiss. They are both linked and it seemed to last forever.

They part and the look on each other's face was if they had known each other forever, in fact if the truth is known this is the time they both fell in love with each other.

John Bolstridge

The night goes well and about 10pm, John asks Margaret if she would like to go back to Nottingham and go to a nightclub.

"What ever John, lets go." They both head back to the car and start to make their way back, this time John is more comfortable with Margaret and it was lots of small talk on the journey. After about half an hour they are back and head for the nightclub, once inside its dancing and long sessions of kissing and cuddling. Margaret with the hard drink while John was on soft drinks, they are truly engrossed in each other when Margaret tells John that it was strange that the feeling she has seemed to tell her that it would be ok for her to make love to him, well John tells her.

"I have the same feelings", within the same breath he tells her. Would you like me to book a Hotel in Skegness for Saturday and come back Sunday?"

"Hope you will make it a double room," Margaret lifting her eye brows and giving a cheeky smile.

At about 3.30am Margaret tells John that they had better start to make their way home, it 's about 3.50am when they turn onto Fulward crescent when Margaret tells John to pull over.

Why Me

"But you live a little further up," John looking at where Margaret lives.

"Yes but just wait," well in the next minute Margaret's Dad comes out of her house and starts to ride away on his motor scooter for work.

"You can see why, I would have walked straight into Dad, you can just imagine what he would have said."

They sit there and they are all over each other, well Margaret is getting aroused, and John is too they both pull away from each other and it is if they were saying to each other. God roll on Saturday, Margaret leaves John's car and tells him she will see him at work on Thursday. They both are off that day Wednesday, for both of them worked at the weekend and it was their day off. They both work in the hosiery trade, unknown to them but they will work most of their working life together.

Friday night and they arranged to meet in their local for a drink, and all the talk was about their trip to Skegness tomorrow. Margaret asks.

"What time in the morning are we going?" John thinks and suggests.

"That we ought to go about 7am; you know miss a lot of the early morning rush hour traffic with people going to work."

"Fine by me." Margaret grabbing hold of John's hand and just looking straight at him with glassy eyes, it's if they were filling up with tears. Well John notes this and asks Margaret if she was alright.

"John I've never had this feeling before about anyone, I know that I am truly deeply in love with you. It's funny I have only known you for 4 days but it feels like I have known you all my life, I LOVE YOU JOHN." John looks Margaret in the eyes, and tells her.

"You might not believe this with me coming from a broken marriage, but the truth be known I feel the same way. I wish you had been my first wife but I cannot because then I would not have had my two boys. I love you to, that first sight of you on Melbourne Road. I think from that moment on I worship the ground you walk on. They start to kiss and the look in their eyes at what they had said to each other, Margaret knew that she had to change the situation or they both would have attracted other customer's attention to them.

"Get away with you my knee length boots and mini I know what you were thinking." Margaret gently smacking John on the arm, well this changed the atmosphere and they carried on talking about the trip and things they were going to do.

Saturday morning and John is up and readying himself for the trip, he goes outside at 6am checking the oil and water on his car. At about 6 20am it was time for the off he drops his overnight bag in the boot and starts to head for Margaret's home.

He pulls up outside Margaret's house and it's if she was watching from the window for John to pull up, and she is straight out. Smiling at John, he opens the boot and she puts her suitcase in the boot.

"Blimey Margaret we are only going for the night, not eloping."

"Well you never know what might happen if it rains at least I've a choice of clothes."

They settle down and it was off to Skegness just after Lincoln they pull over and into the café car park, they go in the café and order a tea and coffee then Margaret asks John.

"Where are we stopping tonight?"

"That's a surprise wait till we get there."

After about 30 minutes they head back to the car to finish the journey to Skegness. It's 9.30 am when they pull into the Hotel car park they get out and John takes the suitcase and bag and head for reception, well when Margaret sees that it was the County Hotel she stands there gob smacked.

"No way are we stopping here, how you can afford it."

"Just leave it to me and you enjoy being pampered."

Once inside they go to reception, and John tells the person on the desk that he had a room booked for Mr&Mrs Bolstridge. The receptionist looks in the book and tells him.

"That's right Sir Sea view top floor bed and breakfast, would you like a paper sent up with your breakfast."

"Yes please the News of the World."

Well Margaret stands and cannot believe all she was hearing, the receptionist rings a bell and a bellboy comes to take their cases and to escort them to their room. Margaret whispers to John when they are heading to the lift.

"Have you won the pools."?

"No it's just a little something I wanted to do, you know I've just sold my house and I got a decent offer."

They enter their room and to their surprise it had a four poster bed, John tips the bellboy and he leaves them alone. When he had gone Margaret is looking at the Sea view.

"Come and see this John," he walks over to Margaret and they both look out of the window. After a couple of minutes they both look at each other and they are suddenly standing kissing each other, when John starts to gradually walk towards the bed. Margaret stops him and tells him that they should wait till that evening.

"Ok Margaret what time are we going to bed 4pm," John with the biggest grin on his face, Margaret taps him and asks what we are going to do.

"Do you fancy going for a walk round Skegness first, but after we have had breakfast here."

"Fine but are you sure about breakfast here, it would be too expensive."

"Don't worry about that; let's make the most of it while we can." Well all decided about the day, they start to refresh themselves up, about 9.50am and they are ready for breakfast. They go down to the restaurant and are escorted to their table by a waitress.

It's full English for them and Margaret already feels like a Princess with all the pampering that the waitress was showing her. They finish their breakfast and start to head for the days fun round Skeggy.

They start by walking along the promenade heading for the clock tower at the top of the prom that leads to the Main Road through the shops of Skegness. They are looking in all the shops window with all the gifts and souvenirs of Skegness, they come to the part where the road branches off to the left you have chip pan alley a famous street in Skegness renowned for the abundance of chip shops. By the time they have walked the street and back up the Main Road back to the Tower it is well past 1pm, they both decide to head for the front and have a bite to eat on the Seafront.

After Lunch they sit on the sands with it being a very warm and pleasant day, blue skies light breeze. At 4pm they start to head back to the Hotel to start to get ready for the evening fun around the Skegness pubs.

They are back in their room and they start to shower and put on their clothes, John with blue jeans and white tee-shirt. Margaret starts to put on her blue mini skirt white silk top and knee length boots, she stands there and asks John what he thought. Well poor old John stands looking at her starts to pat the back of his head and tells her.

"You look very fetching and a million dollars, I will have to take a cold shower to calm down." Margaret smiles at him for the compliment.

7pm and the first drink is in the Hotel bar, then off round the bars in Skeggy. At about 11pm they decide to head back to the Hotel for being residents of the Hotel they can stop in the bar, and then John tells Margaret.

"Yes and it will keep all the wolves off you tonight, you look gorgeous Margaret."

The time is approaching 12 midnight, and John looks at Margaret and asks her.

"Are you ready to turn in, it's been a long day."

"Yes let's go up."

They are in their room and start to get undressed, just like any couple the first time always seems a little embarrassing, they slip beneath the sheets and are soon kissing and cuddling. It must have been a good half an hour when they decide to have their first sexual contact.

(This part of the story I will not go into intimate details with this story being based on true facts, it does not take a genius long to know who Margaret and John are in this story, yes the Author, so please just use your imagination.")

They are totally engrossed in each other and Margaret tells John.

"That she was truly in love with him," John caresses Margaret pulling her close to him and tells her.

"That she is the only one for him that he to loves her so much."

The next day it was a day round the funfair and relaxing on the beach till early afternoon when they started to head back home.

3 months have passed and John one morning received a letter confirming that the housing association that he wrote to about a flat in Bloonwood had wrote to tell him the good news that he was a successful candidate for one of the flats, well he was straight out to the top of the garden. At the front gate leading to the road standing waiting for Margaret to

Why Me

go by to go to work, with it only being 7.30am. John was on the afternoon shift.

Unknown to him that Margaret also had some news for him; he spots her walking down the Road and Margaret waves at him and goes hurrying towards him. She is shouting to him that she had some wonderful news, at the same time John is waving the piece of paper and punching the air. Margaret stops in front of John, throws her arms around him and stands kissing him. They part and they both talk at the same time in excited voices. John tells Margaret to go first.

"I have had the test back from the Doctors and they have confirmed that I am pregnant," John replies.

"I don't believe it," well Margaret takes one step back at not believing what John had said. He sees the look on Margaret's face and straight away tells her.

"No not that silly, look at this that came this morning," John gives Margaret the letter.

She stands reading it then her face lights up.

"My God that's imposable here is me worrying what we are going to do when the baby arrives and you give me the answer," once again they are kissing with the joy this time with the good news on both sides. Then Margaret suddenly looks at her watch and tells John.

"Blimey look at the time I will be late if I don't hurry." She starts to hurriedly walk off leaving John standing there, he shouts out.

"Hey you slow down you have a good excuse now, see you later Margaret." He stands there with hands out front and making the shape with his hands of a pregnant woman. She looks at him and blows him a kiss.

Over the next few weeks they are shopping for furniture and a range of carpets to be fitted in their new flat.

Margaret over the next 8 months is starting to experience pain she is on her own one morning with John on the early shift and her waters break; she is on the phone to tell the midwife who arranges for an emergency pick up. Margaret stands outside the flat and not long after the ambulance pulls up, one of the medics comes walking to Margaret and ask if she knew were Margaret is. Margaret tells him that it's her.

Well the ambulance men cannot believe it for the first thing he did was look down at Margaret's Belly.

"I know what you're thinking but all the way through the pregnancy I've been small."

"That's Ok love let's get you to the Hospital."

John is informed about Margaret and not to panic for they have told her that it will be later that night before it is due. That night Margaret gives birth to a baby Girl, they are both over the moon.

Within 3 weeks they have decided to call her Mandy.

When Margaret goes to register Mandy she only goes and registers both of them to get married on the 24th February 1978. When she arrives home John is sitting reading the paper, when she pulls the paper down and shows John Mandy's Birth certificate, and also straight out with.

"And also we are getting married on the 24th of February."

"Fine let's hope it's a nice day."

"So you don't mind what I've done," Margaret not believing what John has said.

"Look love I would marry you anyway, but I better do one thing to put it right," Margaret confused and asks John.

John Bolstridge

"What thing," well John drops the paper and stands and goes down on one knee and grabs hold of Margaret's Hand, and asks her.

"Margaret will you do me the honour of becoming Mrs Margaret Bolstridge, for I love you so much, will you be my wife."

Well Margaret straight away is in tears at what John had said and tells him.

"Yes I will." The day comes and all went well at the marriage, after it was back to the Barley Mow on Basford Road for the reception.

Over the years Margaret and John love seemed to blossom you could tell that they were truly soul mates, over the next 35 years they were in work all over Nottingham. Knitting firm, after that fish and chip shop, then they had 9 years in different jobs and finally they both landed jobs for one of the top retailers on the high Street Marks&Spencers

They took Holidays in the Canaries and family holidays to Florida, Mandy also married and for her before the wedding she knew her Mum and Dad would not be there for her for she was marrying in Las Vegas U.S.A. She knew that her Parents couldn't afford it, (WRONG.)" For Margaret that day was the most wonderful day that she neither would nor miss for the

Why Me

World, she told her a week before Mandy was going to America that she and her Dad were going to Lanzarote.

But unbeknown to Mandy they had booked a holiday to Las Vegas, no way on this Earth were Margaret and John going to miss their only Daughter's wedding.

The day before Mandy's weddings Margaret and John go to Mandy's Hotel on the strip in Los Vegas, that she was stopping at they go to reception and ask for Mr and Miss Yates room number.

But even when they explained the reason they would not tell them for security reasons, all they could do is get reception to phone the room and if they were in they could speak to them. Well they accepted, and the receptionist phoned Mandy, their luck was in for Mandy answered the phone.

Well John answers the call and Mandy is surprised to hear her Dad's voice, he tells her that he and her Mum wanted to wish them luck for tomorrow. Then Mandy asked where you are phoning from Dad home, well John just tells her.

"No we are down in reception at your Hotel," when he said this the phone went dead. He looks at Margaret and he is about to tell

Margaret when all you could hear coming from the casino was, "Mum; Dad."

Mandy and Lyndon are running towards them, anyone would have thought that there was a fire. Mandy throws her arms around her Mum and she is crying, Lyndon shakes John's hand and then Mandy with her eye liner running with all the tears gives John a kiss and cuddle. John tells her.

"No way would I miss not giving you away."

The wedding went well and they all had a great time.

Chapter 2

In the beginning of 2008 Margaret worked for one of the biggest retailers on the UK High Street Marks&Spencer, John works there too. It's if all their working life they had followed each other into work together.

One night Margaret and John are in bed small talk and in general kissing and cuddling, when John starts to fondle Margaret's Breast. His hand is just at the top of her right breast around the cleavage when he feels a small lump; well his hand is on it straight away and he tells Margaret.

"Have you felt this love," well Margaret pulls John's hand away and she feels for herself after a moment she just tells him.

"That it was just a piece of gristle, nothing to worry about love." John thinks no more of it and they are soon back to what they were doing.

After about six months they are in bed and once again John starts to fondle Margaret's breast and the same again his hand makes a beeline to where he felt the small lump, well this time it was a little larger.

"God Margaret it's grown, that small lump of gristle," the same reaction from Margaret she once again pulls John's hand off and tells him.

"What are you worried about I had my Mammogram in February and I had the all clear."

This was a free test that their work does for all their female employees every year.

John in a small way was reassured.

The year of 2009, March, one night they are in bed and they are both kissing and cuddling, when they start to make love, once again it's if John wanted reassurance and he felt her right breast, well this time he is straight up and sitting looking at Margaret for when he puts his hand in the same spot the so called gristle was the size of a small egg.

"This is not right it's definitely got bigger."

"It cannot be anything serious for you looked at the results on my Mammogram all clear, stop worrying."

Why Me

Well John lies back in bed and he's in catch twenty two, for every time he feels her breast and the lump seemed to get bigger. But on the other hand something is telling him he must be wrong with what Margaret had told him. Then in the August Margaret's Mum dies. Margaret only just losing her Father less than a year ago. John notices that the top off Margaret's cleavage it was turning red, he points this out to Margaret and once again she goes on the defence.

"John please stop pestering me over it I will go to the Doctors after Mums funeral." All goes well at the funeral and John is on her case again, all he gets back is the same from Margaret.

"Not now don't forget we are off to Florida with Mandy and Lyndon and our two grandchildren Jamie and Ben," Jamie is 8, and Ben is 3.

They have the time of their life, pulling in all the Theme Parks and meeting Mickey Mouse, Donald Duck and the rest. It is now the last week of November Margaret asks John to pick her up from work at 5pm, and they will go for a drink in the Nags Head. This is Margaret's and John's local; they meet all their friends there.

John pulls up outside the Staff entrance at 5pm, and sees Margaret coming down the stairs; he opens the door for her.

"Had a good one then love."

"Good one I'm ready for that drink," Margaret telling John.

They pull up at the Nags Head Park up and start to walk to the pub, John notices that Margaret is dragging her left leg.

"You ok sweetheart you're dragging your leg."

"Tell me about it, it came on this morning." They go into the Nags and sit with their friends and it was small talk all-round.

Chapter 3

Second week of December and John is on the early shift, at work the time is coming up to 12.30 pm he had only 30 minutes to go before he goes home. He's backstage when one of Margaret's friends comes up to John and asks.

"Hi John is Margaret alright she had not come in today, and she had not phoned in."

"She was alright when I left her this morning." John is a little concerned, he notices the time and he heads towards the cloakroom to change to go home.

He pulls up on the drive and opens the front door, and shouts straight away.

"Margaret you there love," from upstairs Margaret shouts.

"Up here love," well John is straight upstairs and goes into the bedroom and sees Margaret, straight away he can see that something is wrong for Margaret is crying.

"What's up love," John sitting on the bed and stroking Margaret's Hair.

"I woke up this morning and I tried to get out of bed but my leg is completely dead, and I am having trouble lifting my left arm."

"That's it I'm phoning the Doctor for a home visit."

John goes back downstairs and rings the Doctors, he is connected to the Doctor and tells the receptionist the symptoms and could he have a Doctor. Well the receptionist tells John.

"I've an appointment at 5pm could you make it in."

"No I've told you my wife is completely unable to move," with John's voice sounding alarmed the receptionist tells him.

"That there will be Doctor Rose at 4.pm for a home visit."

At 4pm, John is looking out of the window and sees a car pull up, and up the drive comes Doctor Rose. John is straight to the front door to greet the Doctor.

"Please come in Doctor my wife is up stairs first room to your right." The Doctor goes upstairs to see Margaret and John waits downstairs.

After 30 minutes the Doctor comes down and tells John that in his opinion it looks like your wife has a trapped nerve, keep her in bed and comfortable and it should heel or come out of the spinal cord on its own. John thanks the Doctor and shows him out. He is straight up to Margaret.

"Do you need anything love."

"No I will be alright, wont I John." Then Margaret bursts into tears.

"Come on now Margaret where is my strong young lady, I will phone up work and tell them that I will be off to look after you."

"Please don't John I will be alright until you get home." That night John is down stairs and it was one of those nights with all that had happened, it was if he had a bad feeling about this.

The next day it was up early and off to work, all Margaret's work friends were asking how she was it was getting to much for John that he wanted to say I will put up a bulletin in the Ladies clock room.

John Bolstridge

John is thinking that in a few days time they were supposed to be going to Mandy's for Christmas, that afternoon he goes upstairs and he puts it to Margaret.

"What are we going to do about going to Mandy's, there is no way you can go like that."

"You try and stop me I'm not letting a trapped nerve stop me from seeing my two boy's open their Christmas presents on Christmas day."

Then there is a knock on the front door and John goes to answer it, at the door it is Margaret's brother Andrew, who was told about Margaret's trapped nerve and wheels in a wheelchair.

"I thought you might need this, my farther in-law does not need it anymore." Well John thanks him and asks him in for a drink.

"No thanks John I've got to get back I'm taking Pam out this evening. John thanks Andrew, then Margaret's brother leaves. John goes back upstairs and sits with Margaret.

"Well I think it will be ok for you," John telling Margaret.

"Why's that," she asks.

"Well your brother just called and he has left you a wheelchair so you can go."

"Is that who was at the door," Margaret asking.

"Yes and I know what you are going to say next and the answer was no, he was taking Pam out tonight."

Couple of days go by and it was the day before Christmas Eve, John came home and finds Margaret sitting on the sofa.

"How the hell did you get there," John looking at her with that look of surprise.

"Shuffled down on my bottom, I was getting bored lying in bed." John asks her if there is any change in the feeling of her leg and arm.

"No not any," reply's Margaret.

It's 4pm Christmas eve John is helping Margaret into the car for the stay at Mandy's for Christmas, it was a struggle for both of them with Margaret with no feeling down one side. But after 10 minutes Margaret is in and belted up, John puts the folded wheelchair in and it was off to Mandy's.

John Bolstridge

At Mandy's the same thing trying to help Margaret out John helps by lifting the left leg and placing it onto the floor so she can put her good leg on the ground, so Mandy and John can lift her up and into the wheelchair.

Chapter 4

CHRISTMAS

Once inside Mandy's Margaret is on the sofa and the look of relief of making it too her Daughters house, and into the room comes Jamie and Ben.

"Santa's coming tonight," Jamie trying to climb onto Margaret's knee. Mandy stops him and tells him that his Nana is not well so be gentle and look after her, Jamie nods and Little Ben goes up and starts to stroke Margaret's leg.

Margaret with the biggest smile on her face, strokes Ben's hair and turning to John and telling him that she would not miss this for the World. The night goes well a few bottles of beer for John and wine for Margaret and Mandy, Lyndon is working till 8pm, and will not be home till 9pm. Margaret and John retire at 10pm, and when they are in bed John tells her that they ought to recall the Doctor after Christmas.

"For it is not right for a trapped nerve to take all of one side." Well Margaret tells John.

"To leave it just let it lie."

Poor John just laid there with eyes open and looking out of the window with all the stars shinning bright, and he is thinking what more can I do. If I suggest something she jumps down my throat, the truth be known I think John is frightened at what might happen.

6 am. And the boys are up and going round to make everybody get up for Santa's been and left a load of presents under the tree.

Well it was all up and into the lounge last one in his Margaret in the wheelchair, the boys are shouting.

"Come on Nana let's start," well they take it in turn to open their presents. Jamie first.

"Wow look at this Nana." Jamie putting an X box on Margaret's lap.

"Very nice we can play with that later; you must have been very good for Santa to leave you that." Well just like an 8 year old he tells her.

"Yes Nana I've been very good," well Mandy's straight in.

Why Me

"Oh yes we know," Mandy looking at her mum with her eyes up lifted and a grin on her face. Next it was Bens turn with him only 3 he was more interested in the wrapping paper and boxes.

The morning goes well then Margaret asks John to help her to the toilet, straight away he is up and wheels her to the bathroom. Once inside he helps her onto the toilet and leaves her, there is one thing about Mandy's home it is a bungalow after about five minutes there is a crash and Margaret shouts out. John and Mandy go quickly to the bathroom, poor Margaret is in tears for she had slipped of the toilet seat and fell between the wall and the toilet. She is telling them that she could not stop it, with her not having any feelings in her left side, John and Mandy help her up and Mandy pulls her jimjams up. Margaret sits there crying.

"Come on Mum you couldn't help it."

"I know sweetheart," Margaret holds Mandy's' hand and tells her.

"I'm frightened Mandy."

"You will be alright Mum," Mandy trying to stop herself from crying, John comes back into the bathroom and Margaret asks. If he would take her back to bed, for she would like to rest for awhile.

Margaret tucked up back in bed, and John comes back into the lounge were Mandy is on her own for the boys are in their room playing with their new toys. Mandy goes up to her Dad crying and puts her arms round him, John trying to comfort her and Mandy is saying.

"Mum's going to be alright Dad."

"Come on now sweetheart you know your mum's a fighter, and don't worry after Boxing Day I'm on the phone to the Doctors without telling your Mum. It's time we got to the bottom of this."

At about 2.00pm Margaret calls for John to help her up for Dinner, once in the wheelchair she is pushed into the kitchen where the table is set for Dinner. Margaret is all apologetic for not being able to help prepare Dinner with her.

"Don't you worry Mum; it's nice to do it for you for once?"

The day goes off well Christmas dinner with all the trimmings crackers and wine for the girls and beer for the two men.

After dinner it's off back to the lounge, and the rest of the day watching games the boys were playing on their X-box.

Boxing Day after lunch John and Margaret give their goodbyes to the boys and Mandy and Lyndon, it's a struggle for John to get Margaret in and out of the car. At home at the bottom of the stairs John helps Margaret upstairs.

Margaret's good right foot on the first step while John puts Margaret's left foot on the second step, so Margaret can then lift her good right foot onto the next step.

After 10 minutes she is settled in bed and John goes back downstairs to the lounge, he sits there and he has all these bad thoughts of what Margaret is going through.

It got to a point where he tells himself to pack it in, for it was frightening him.

Chapter 5

THE TRUTH COMES OUT

The next morning after Boxing Day John is up and on the phone at 8pm to the surgery.

"Good morning Mr Bolstridge here I'm phoning about my wife Margaret we had a house call before Christmas and the Doctor said that she had a trapped nerve, but at the moment my wife cannot move her left side and is bedridden. I would like a Doctor to come and see her." The receptionist tells John to hold and she comes back and tells him.

"Mr Bailey will be there at 2pm, is this convenient?"

"Fine that would be alright."

"That's it it's now booked, and thank you for calling Mr Bolstridge."

Precisely at 2pm, the Doctor pulls up and goes to the door; there to greet him is John.

"Come in Doctor Bailey I'll show you to my wife's bedroom."

John escorts him up and stands there while the Doctor sees Margaret.

Good afternoon Mrs Bolstridge what seems to be the matter then?" Margaret tells him that she has no feeling down her left side.

The Doctor pulls the sheets back and sees Margaret lying there with her arm across her body she looks like, when you see someone who has had a stroke. Then the Doctor asks.

"Please could you stand so we can see you standing," then John interrupts and tells the Doctor.

"Doctor Margaret will not beadle to stand because she has no feeling down her left." But Margaret starts to try to rise with the Doctor helping her up, she stands there and the Doctor lets go.

Then Margaret falls and neither Doctor nor John can help, and she falls and on the way down bumps her head on the chimney breast with a sickening thud.

Well John is fuming and at the same time going to his wife's side telling the Doctor.

"I bloody well told you she could not stand."

Poor Margaret had blood coming down the side of her head were she hit the chimney breast, the Doctor stands there and felt very humiliated at what had happened then he tells them.

"It looks like she has had a mini stroke I'll arrange an ambulance to take her in." Forty five minutes later and the ambulance pulls up, the two ambulance men take a small chair upstairs to Margaret.

"Hello Mrs Bolstridge, let's have you in the chair and off to Hospital." The ambulance man smiling at Margaret, and trying to make her feel more at ease.

"Thank you," Margaret smiling back at the ambulance man.

They manage to get her downstairs and into the Ambulance. John also comes with a small suitcase with Margaret's things within it.

They arrive at the Hospital and she is put onto the ward, John tells her that he will go while they assess her and tells her to give him a ring later. Margaret gives John a kiss and tells him that she will ring. By the time John leaves the time is 4pm, he goes down to the Nags Had for a drink with some of his friends who come in after they finish work.

Everyone who comes in asks him how Margaret is and they are all took back when John tells them that she is in Hospital.

Then into the bar comes Stuart, he is a very close friend of John and they sit talking all about Margaret and John tells him about the large lump on her right breast, all the time John is saying I hope it's not Cancer. Well Stuart tries to comfort John by telling him.

"Come on now John stop worrying wait till they examine her and do tests, then you will know." John smiles at Stuart and tells him he is right. John stops for an hour then gives his leave telling he better go he has to get the cook book out for tea, John smiling at them.

"Well don't burn the water."

"Don't worry any sign of things going wrong and it's down the chippy." John waving when he went out of the door. Back home he opens the door and locks it behind him and he stands there and it is the first time he had been alone, he starts to make dinner and decided to just have faggots mash and garden peas.

At about 8pm the phone rings and it was Margaret.

"Hope you have had something to eat." she asks John.

"I'm just about to dish up faggots mash and garden peas."

"Sounds nice, anyway the reason I rang is to tell you that they have taken x-rays and they put me on a machine that you go inside while you are lying down."

"You mean a body scan; it takes a 3d picture of your body." John tells Margaret.

"You can visit 2pm till 4pm, then 6pm till 8pm." she tells John.

"After I have finished work I will be there at 2pm."

"That's fine and don't worry if I'm not there, they said they would like to-do more tests tomorrow."

"Ok sweetheart you look after yourself." Margaret then said,

"I will see you tomorrow then John I would like to have a rest now with all the tests and prodding that I've had."

"I love you more each day John."

"Same for me, I love you to sweetheart goodnight and God bless." They both put the phone down and then it hits John again, the feeling of being alone.

That night is one of the longest and lonely nights all John seemed to do was toss and turn, with all the events that had unfolded and happened that day. He's up early and to work, the day seemed to go quick with him doing his job, at 1pm he's off and to the Hospital.

Margaret is in bed and she tells John,

"That this morning they took her to radiotherapy, and they gave her a session and that I will need to have 5 more."

Then into the Ward comes a nurse and comes to Margaret's bed.

"Would you both come with me the Doctor would like to have a word with you."

John helps Margaret into the wheelchair and then he follows the nurse pushing Margaret, they come to the room and the nurse opens the door and they go in. The first thing John notices is that there are two nurses and one is holding a box of tissues, the Doctor tells John to come and sit down.

Then the Doctor starts to put x-rays up on the screen for Margaret and John to look at, she then starts to tell them.

"Please look at the lungs on the X-ray you will see this light patch," Then she changes the slides.

"Also look at the light patches on the Brain; they are admiralties.

Then the Doctor tells then that they will not know till they have a biopsy done. I've arranged for this to be done tomorrow. With what they were told Margaret asks the Doctor.

"Oh my God I'm not going to die am I?" Then the Doctor asks.

"What do you do for a living?"

"I work for one of the top retailer's Marks&Spencer."

"Well you won't be going back there for a long time."

Margaret and John cannot believe what they have been told Margaret with her good hand grabs John's hand and just squeezes, they are escorted out of the room and back to the ward. Margaret gets back into bed and just looks at John.

"Don't forget love your friend at work she had just been given the all clear and she had breast Cancer."

"Yes I'm going to fight this, you mark my words" with this they both felt a little better.

Over the next week Margaret is continuing with her radiotherapy, on the third session of radiotherapy Margaret is in bed and she can lift her arm and move her fingers, she is over the moon and cannot wait till John comes.

2 pm and John walks in to the Ward, Margaret see him and with her left arm lifts it and in a slow way waves at John.

"That's your bad hand Margaret."

"Yes and just before you came I could wiggle my toes." she starts to cry and out stretches this time her both arms for John to comfort her.

"Come on sweetheart you're my big fighter."

"I know John but you don't know what a relief it is starting to get my feelings back, God knows what I would have done if they told me that I will be paralyzed all my life."

John with a tissue is wiping away the tears from her eyes.

"That's your bad arm you lifted when I gave you a hug," Richard not believing what he just seen.

"Yes it was in the night and then I could move it a little, it looks like the radiotherapy is working." Over the next week Margaret each day has more feeling and finally she can stand and is starting to walk.

It is just over a 2 weeks and she is told that she can go home and that she will be contacted over the next week with what treatment she will be having. It is now the end of January and John is on the way to pick her up from Hospital, they have been given a wheelchair till Margaret is back to normal movement.

John comes into the Ward and tells Margaret.

"Boy you are looking radiant sweetheart."

"I think it's because I'm going home." They both go outside and there is a taxi waiting, after ten minutes they pull up at their home and John helps her out of the taxi he goes to get the wheelchair for Margaret but she tells him.

"No let me do it this way." Margaret goes walking with John behind her and slowly walks up the path to the front door. She stands there and bursts out into tears.

"What's up sweetheart?" John holding her arm.

"Nothing it's what I've just gone through, I can not explain what it felt like not being to move your left side."

Once inside it was like they had just come through a nightmare and now it was back to normal. The next 2 days Margaret starts to get more of her feeling back when a letter comes from the City Hospital, she opens the letter and starts to read it.

"Dear Mrs Bolstridge could you please phone and let us know if you could attend Mr Chang Cancer Clinic on Monday the 3rd of February 11am. 2010. Also in the letter is an appointment on ward 2 for her first course of chemotherapy, at 12.30pm. Margaret looks at John and shows him the letter.

"Looks like you are going to start your fight again sweetheart." Putting his hand out for

Margaret to hold, they both stand smiling at each other.

Monday comes round and John is now off work to look after Margaret, they go by car and they both sit in the waiting room of Doctor Chang clinic. The first thing they notice is the amount of patients that were there, it has already been decided that when she had seen Doctor Chang that John could go home and wait for her to ring him. With the treatment takes an hour and a half to administrate.

11.20 then a nurse calls out their name and takes them and sits them in a office and tell them that Doctor Chang will be along shortly, 10 minutes they sit talking when the door opens and Doctor Chang enters.

"Good morning Mrs Bolstridge," then looks at John and asks.

"Is this your Husband," Margaret tells him.

"Yes this is my husband John." All the formalities out of the way doctor Chang opens Margaret's folder, sits looking at then he lifts his head and tells them.

"We have had all the tests back and the biopsy results I'm afraid that your condition is

Why Me

Secondary Breast Cancer, and it had spread to the Lungs and Brain." Margaret and John just sit there and did not say a word, just a loving glance at each other, and then Doctor Chang tells them.

Chapter 6

THE TREATMENT

"What I would like you to do is sign you up for a new chemo treatment that had just come out, you see Cancer cells split and multiply that is why you have a large lump on the breast. But his new chemo attacks the cells and they do not know how to split. Therefore killing the cells off."

Margaret tells Doctor Chang.

"Give me the paperwork let's get it in me," Margaret a little excited about what Doctor Chang had said.

They come out and she tells John that she will be off for the appointment for her first chemotherapy. John tells her he will see her to the Ward and that he will know were to pick her up when she phones. Safely at the ward John leaves Margaret and tells her he will see her later.

Why Me

Within two hours and John receives the call to pick her up, time he gets there it is 3.30pm. Margaret stands there waiting for John; he sees Margaret and the first words are.

"Are you alright love?"

"Yes fine it took about an hour and a half; you should have seen the number having it done. It certainly opens you eyes to see how many people in Nottingham alone have it."

Then Margaret shows John all the pamphlets and leaflets that they gave her, and then she shows John a thermometer. That she had to take her temperature every four hours and if it goes over 37 she will have to let the Ward know straight away.

"Let's go for a drink on the way home, it would be nice to see some of our friends, I've not seen them for a month."

"OK sweetheart lets go," at the Nags Head at Bobbers Mill

everyone who was there are all over Margaret asking how she was and it was nice to see her back on her feet she held nothing back and came straight out with her condition Telling them that she had Secondary Breast Cancer.

The girls were really taken back at what Margaret had said and asking all sorts of questions, John came to the rescue and asked them.

"Please not too many questions she would like a drink not an inquest."

"It ok John I don't mind," with what John had said they start to change the questions. After about 2 pints they decide to go home, over the next week Margaret is checking her temperature and it is ok. But she cannot eat every time John brings her food she just picks at it, John notices and asks.

"You have had nothing now for a few days what's up."

"Everything tastes like cardboard."

One week goes by then one night at 6pm Margaret checks her temperature and it is 35, she tells John and she tells him she will check it at 8pm.

At 8 pm it is now 37, Margaret looks at the card that they gave her and the phone number to ring, she rings and after the call tells John that there is an ambulance on the way.

"Not again John starting to look concerned."

"Don't worry sweetheart I'll be alright."

The ambulance arrives and takes her back to the City Hospital; John tells her that he will see her tomorrow at 2pm.

"Ok sweetheart love you."

"I love you too." he standing watching them putting Margaret in and driving off, John turns and the next door neighbour sees him and asks.

"Hope everything is alright,"

"Yes thanks for that it's Margaret she has a high temperature they are taking her in for observation."

The next day John arrives at the Ward and Margaret is not there, he suddenly starts to get bad thoughts he is about to turn and go to reception when Margaret comes through the door with one of the ladies that was in one of the beds in the Ward. She sees John and smiles she helps the lady back into bed and goes over to John, at the same time looking at another lady in bed and tells her. Don't worry Mary I'll make sure the nurse knows about your dressing.

"Bloody hell Margaret you're supposed to be poorly yourself." John telling Margaret this was typical of her always looking after others and not feeling sorry for herself.

John asks about her temperature and she tells him that all through the night they checked her temperature every hour.

"This morning I was that sleepy that I fell fast asleep after breakfast and did not wake till 11am."

"Did you have any breakfast," asks John.

"A little toast I mentioned it to the nurse and they told me as long as I am drinking liquids that I will be alright."

Margaret spends four days in hospital and then they let her go home, John comes to pick her up and Margaret is doing the rounds going from bed to bed saying her goodbye's and telling some not to worry that they will soon be home.

Out of ear shot John tells her.

"Anybody would think that you were the nurse."

"Away with you John." Margaret gently tapping him on the arm. The end of February comes and she still had not had anything to

Why Me

eat, just bottle after bottle of Lucozade drinks and pop.

And to top it off she had developed diarrhoea, she tells John that she as had it for over 3 weeks, and then she received a letter to attend for her second chemotherapy in 3 days.

John takes her and the same he drops her off and waits at home for her to ring after the session Margaret rinks and John picks her up, the first thing John asks.

"Was everything alright," Margaret tells him.

"Fine no problem, that night Margaret tells John that she is feeling the effects of the treatment and would he mind if she turned in.

"No sweetheart you go and get some sleep, unknown to John over the next 3 weeks Margaret never came down. John is starting to get concerned and tells Margaret that he is going to report it to the Hospital, Margaret did not want him to-do this.

"Look Margaret it cannot be right it's coming up to 2 months and I've seen you eat nothing, you cannot go on like this." John goes and tells the Hospital all about Margaret being in bed for so long and not eating, she is again remitted and she is not happy with him doing this.

They put Margaret in the ambulance she completely ignores John when he is saying, see you later.

That night John feels guilty but something keep telling him that he had done the right thing, the next day John goes to the Ward and asks were Margaret is. They tell him that she is in an isolated room and escorts him to her room. He goes in and the first thing he asks.

"Are you mad with me sweetheart at what I have done."

"Not now I know you're thinking of me," come here give me a kiss. John feels a lot better and Margaret tells him what they have done.

Chapter 7

"They have put me on a drip and so I do not dehydrate and you should see this, Margaret pulls back the sheet a little and shows John a pipe they had inserted down below John straight away tells her.

"They have shaven it has well."

"Yes and you can get rid of any thoughts in your head."

"If I would" John blowing a kiss at Margaret.

That certainly changed the mood and they smile at each other, John is holding Margaret's hand and she tells him.

"I think all this trouble I'm getting is because of the chemotherapy I've had." One thing that never occurred to both of them was why she is isolated, after a week Doctor Chang comes and sees her and tells her that when she feels better they will give her the third dose of treatment. Margaret asks if she could go home, Doctor Chang looks at her chart and tells her.

"I can see you are ready, ok but any changes you must report straight away.

Margaret is over the moon with what he told her, once home they start to get all sorts of equipment. One man comes and puts up another banister on the stairs so she had two rails to help her upstairs, then a bath handle so she could get in and out of the bath. Then a chair with a bowl in the seat so she could do her business in the night, time they had finished she had everything she needed. John tells Margaret.

"There is something about the National Health the home help side is very good."

Time stands still for no one and over the weeks Margaret is losing weight at an incredible speed, and she is getting weaker by the day.

John himself with the strain of doing everything for her, and looking after the house, is feeling rundown.

Margaret on one of the rare occasions comes down and sits on the settee, John tells her.

"You look terrible sweetheart."

Why Me

"You try having Chemotherapy, and see how you feel after."

"I know love but to go so long without food, it's May now and all you have had is drinks and a little toast." Just then the door bell goes and John answer, he open the door and a district nurse stands there.

"Good morning, my name is Jane and I have been told to call on one Mrs Margaret Bolstridge."

"Please come in Margaret is in the lounge," the nurse goes in and into the lounge and introduces herself to Margaret.

She takes all Margaret's details and tells her that from now on she will be calling on her to make sure all her needs and well being are looked after. This sounds a relief for John with finally getting some help.

Most nights Margaret wakes John that she needs the toilet; she tells him that she feels weak and help her onto the chair. After she had finish John empties the bowl and the smell and the watery contents make John heave, he knows that if he did not do it no one else would. This shows what true love will make you do for your love one, it is now the last week in May and on the Wednesday night Margaret is by now feeling really weak.

The time is approaching 2am in the morning when John feels something warm on his leg and the smell he knew what it was.

He gets out of bed and turns the light on, goes and cleans himself then helps Margaret onto the chair and changes the bed sheets and helps her back into bed. He goes and puts the soiled sheets in the washer and starts it up, by the time he had done it was 3.39am. He just is about to get into bed and Margaret asks if he would help her onto the chair, once again she uses the chair and again John helps her back into bed. Cleans the bowl and by now it is 4am.

Friday the district nurse comes and sees Margaret, John tells her that she was upstairs, and then she drops a little bomb shell.

"You know it is Bank Holiday on Monday and we will not see you again till next Thursday, well John tells her.

"What about me she is getting weaker by the day, I want a Doctor to see her." the nurse tells John that she will phone one to come.

Within an hour a House Doctor comes and sees them, she is Doctor Bailey, and John takes her up and he sits while she looked at Margaret, they sit all three of them then Doctor Bailey asks Margaret.

Why Me

"What one thing that she would like to happen?" Margaret tells her.

"We have two lovely grandchildren and every Christmas we go up to my Daughters and spend Christmas, but this year I was poorly and I missed it." Well what the Doctor tells them knocks them backwards.

"Why not have it now, put up all the trimmings and have Christmas dinner." Margaret nor John answered her, not long after and the Doctor left. Margaret lay there and tells John.

"What the hell is she on about Christmas now, what with me having this cardboard taste and feeling like I do.? Yes I would love it, and I don't think so."

With the district nurse doing nothing and the Doctor, John is back in catch 22 all on his own again.

Saturday night John is in bed and about 10 o'clock Margaret tells him that she has terrible back ace and tummy ace, John gets her a couple of paracetamol tablets and she settles down again. 3 pm and again John wakes and he is wet, this time it was all over him and he gets out of bed and again into the bathroom to clean himself up, back into the bedroom and once again he has to get her up. Margaret is totally out of it and when John is putting her into the chair she suddenly shouts at John and her face is close to his ear and said.

I HATE YOU, HATE YOU. He slowly puts her into the chair and the mess; first he is trying to get Margaret's bottoms off then her top. And Margaret said nothing, he takes the dirty clothes and puts them in the wash basket Again cleans his hands and then starts to clean the bed, he turns the bedding over remakes the bed and helps Margaret back into bed. The rest of the night all he can here is the sound of Margaret in his mind saying I Hate You, Hate You.

Sunday morning he is at his lowest still with the words ringing in his head I Hates You, Hate You. Gets up and said to himself.

"That's it"

He is on the phone to the Hospital and tells them that his wife had a bad knee and Breast Cancer and she had a fall and cannot move. He is put through to the Ward, and they tell him that an ambulance is on its way.

John just sits there and just looks out of the window; he just looked like he was in a trance, 20 minutes pass and an ambulance pulls up and takes Margaret to the ambulance. Margaret with eyes shut said nothing. John

Why Me

gives the ambulance driver her overnight bag, and when they were shutting the door John tells her he will come and see her tomorrow.

John goes to the Nags Head, and is drowning his sorrows, everyone asking about Margaret and John just tells everyone that she's not well and back in Hospital. And he keeps repeating the words I Hate You, Hate You.

Back home he closes the door behind him and the silence hits him it's 9.30, and John a little one too many retires to bed.

He is in bed and the feeling of loneliness hits him, it was a good thing that he was a little tipsy for he dropped off and did not wake up till 8am.

Chapter 8

(THE LIGHT GOES OUT OF JOHNS LIFE.)

10 am. And John drives to the Park and Ride, and catches the medi-link bus to the Hospital. He arrives and goes to reception and he is told where Margaret is. He goes into Margaret's room and the difference in her; she is sitting and looking better she smiles at John and said hello to him. Then she tells him.

"I've had a little breakfast this morning." John smiles and asks.

"Margaret last night when I tried to sort you out you told me you hate me, you don't do you love." Margaret looks confused at John and tells him.

"Don't be silly I would not say that to you I love you to much come here." Well Margaret's arms out stretched puts them round John and they are holding each other very close, then she notices that John is shaking. Pulls away gently so she can see his face and John is sobbing.

"Hey come-on now, what's the matter." Margaret looking concerned.

"Sorry sweetheart it's all the trouble we have been going through, it's just come to a head I suppose." John touching Margaret's face then kissing her.

They sit there in general talk and Margaret tells John.

"If that happens again what she did, that she can not remember saying anything not to take it to Heart."

The time is approaching 12 noon when into the room comes Mr Chang with about 6 other consultants and he smiles at Margaret and picks up her chart, and then looks at Margaret and said.

"Good morning Mrs Bolstridge," then he pulls back her top a little and shows the lump to the others and talking in medicals terms telling them what it was and what treatment they were using.

"I've just been explaining to my colleges, the lump and what treatment we are using,

I'm pleased to tell you Mrs Bolstridge that the results of your X-rays show that the chemotherapy is breaking the cancer cell down, in layman's terms they do not know how to split.

Therefore they are dieing, so let's get you back on your feet and get the 3rd chemo into you. Dr Chang smiling at Margaret.

She is over the moon with what Dr Chang had told her.

"Thank you Dr Chang." Margaret smiling at the Doctor and his colleges, John holds Margaret's hand and they are both smiling at each other, it's like having a great weight lifted knowing that they are on the road to recovery.

Dr Chang gives his leave and he and is cortège leave. Well Margaret is straight away looking at John and she suddenly starts to cry.

"Hay come on now." But Margaret buts in and shaking her hand tells John?

"I'm not crying just happy at what he had said." They sit there for an hour just kissing and in general small talk, then at 1.PM A House Doctor comes into the room and asks.

Why Me

"Could I have a word with your Husband Margaret?"

"Why yes, please be my guest."

The Doctor smiles at John and asks him to follow him; he goes to a room down the corridor, opens the door and asks John to take a seat.

"I've some bad news about Margaret; your wife is in the final stage of Termination." John sits there and he thinks that he had the wrong person.

"What do you mean final termination, Dr Chang was only here an hour ago and he told us the chemo is working. You must have the wrong person."

"I'm afraid not you see we have had all the tests back and they show that her Kidneys are failing, there is nothing we can do I'm so sorry." John just sits there and did not say a word to the Doctor; it's if his whole World had just collapse around him, after about 3 minutes the Doctor asks him.

"Would you like me to break it to your wife?"

"NO she would go insane with all that had happened, what are we are looking at 6 months 3 months."

"Within the next few days, we will do our up most to keep her comfortable; we will give her something that will help her to keep her dignity to the end." All John wanted is for him to stop, it is if everything is going wrong and the feeling inside him is building up.

"Is there anything that I could do for you?" The Doctor asks.

"No I would like to go back to my wife."

The Doctor shows John out and he goes off walking down the corridor back towards Margaret's room, he is wondering what he is going to tell Mandy. He pushes the door open and smiles at Margaret, Margaret looks at John and she asks.

"What's up now?" John straight of the top of his head tells her.

"You're not going to believe this, but you have a Kidney disorder."

"Well it's probably with me having Diarrhoea for so long."

The time is approaching 4pm and Margaret turns to John and tells him that he better go for he looks like you could do with a pint, and he has to cook and do the house work when you get home."

"OK sweetheart I will see you in the morning, have a goodnight." He leans forward and gives her a lingering kiss, touches her face and looks straight at her and smiles.

"Boy wait till I get better, I'll make it up to you." Margaret lifting her eye brows in a suggestive way. John goes to the door turns back to Margaret and tells her.

"I love you." Margaret answers back.

"I love you to now make haste all you will miss the Medi-link."

Once outside he is looking up Mandy's mobile number He knows she had finished work, dials it and the tone starts to ring.

Mandy answers the call and knows who is phoning.

"H'I Dad is everything alright."

"Where are you?"

I'm with Sharon we are on our way to see Mum."

"I don't know how to tell you this, and you must promise not to tell your Mum."

"OK Dad."

"It's your Mum, (John stops for a moment, then comes straight out with it) your Mum is going to Die within the next few days."

Then it hits John for he knows he had done the wrong thing, for he can her is Daughter hysterical on the phone.

"Please sweethearts don't, be brave." Mandy calms down a little and tells her Dad.

"I will stop with Mum tonight; I will phone Lyndon he will look after the boys, God Daddy my Mum."

"Don't sweetheart it's hard for me to, let's just hope that there is a light at the end of the tunnel. Please keep your hopes up we still have her with us."

John by now is well down he just does not know which way to turn; he goes for a drink and he tells all his friends in the pub all about Margaret. Some of them were crying and saying My God

How will you manage John?

"We will cross that bridge when we get there."

John drinks about two pints and tells them that he was off home, on the way home he feels just like a zombie, he's just thinking of

Margaret. He comes to his front door and puts the key in and opens the door shuts it behind him, then it hits home for he knew from now on this is what it will be like, he flops on to the stairs and just sits there with hands on his head.

All the time all that had happened in the last 6 months are going round and round in his head. Unknown to him it must have been 45 minutes, when he finally decides to move.

That night he is in bed and the loneliness hits home he is holding the sheet on Margaret's side of the bed and he is still turning over and over again all that had happened.

Finally he grabs Margaret's pillow and puts it between his legs and puts his arm around it, it's as if he was with Margaret and after an hour he drops off to sleep.

The next day Wednesday he was up and getting ready to go to the Hospital, when Mandy phones.

"Daddy are you on your way yet,"

"No but will be in a few minutes, why is everything alright with your Mum."

"Yes fine I was just phoning to make sure you were alright."

"Fine sweetheart, will be there in about 40 minutes."

Back at the Hospital Margaret was sitting up and talking to Mandy, when all of a sudden she tells Mandy that she was feeling a little sleepy. She lay back on the bed and she had gone to sleep.

Not long after and John walks into the room and sees Margaret asleep, he looks at Mandy and asks.

"Your Mum looks peaceful, and then Mandy stretches out her arms for her Dad to comfort her, he holds her and she starts to cry.

"What's the matter Mandy?"

"It was Mum she just laid back and fell asleep, the nurse came in and told me that she had gone into a coma, oh Daddy I'm frightened."

"John holding Mandy just looks at Margaret."

Then into the room comes one of the nurses and tells them.

"That if Margaret had any close relatives like Brothers and Sisters to phone them and tell them if they wish they can come and say their goodbyes."

Why Me

Well John tells Mandy that he was going to sit outside for just the other side of Margaret's room there was a balcony with benches, with it being the 3rd of June it was a fine and sunny day.

Mandy is on the phone and telling Margaret's two Brothers about their Sister, they both tell Mandy that they will come and see their Sister.

Before long the room is full of Margaret's Family all saying to her to have faith, all Margaret is doing is the death rattle, for she is well out of it.

The time is approaching 4pm and John and Mandy are now on their own, sitting with Margaret.

John asks Mandy what she was going to do, she tells him that she was going to stop with her Mum, John tells her.

"I cannot stay here and watch your Mum die, please understand sweetheart." He sits there holding Margaret's hand. Then Mandy tells her Dad.

I understand Daddy if you want you go, I will be Ok with Mum."

"Thanks sweetheart." John stands and kisses Margaret on the side of the check and telling her he will see her in the morning, kisses Mandy and leaves the room.

Outside he sits at the bus stop and he just cannot think it was as if he was in some kind of dream and he will soon wake up.

He goes to the Nags Head and sitting with his friends who he has told them about Margaret. He has had about 4 pints and the time was 5.05pm, he sat there with his friends around the table when is mobile goes off.

He answers and it is Mandy.

"Daddy Mum has just passed away, she did not suffer and now she looks peaceful. I'm going to go home and I will phone you later, love you Daddy."

"I love you to" John hangs up and looks at his friends.

"Everything alright, John." Asks one of his friends sitting at the table.

"Margaret has just passed away." John just looking around the table with a blank face.

At this point John just finishes his drink and tells them that he will see them later and leaves.

Chapter 9

THE FUNERAL

John is back home and this is the first night of many that he will have he close the door and the feeling is very strong of being alone, he goes to the fridge and opens a can of beer, he just sits down and the phone rings he picks it up and on the phone is Mandy.

"Are you alright Daddy?"

"Yes sweetheart just having a beer."

"The reason I have phoned is to ask if you would like to go and register Mum on Monday at the Registration Office."

"Whatever about 10.am."

"That's fine and at the same time we will put in a claim for you, you get £2.000.00 towards the funeral costs."

"Who pays that, are you sure?"

"Yes with Mum in full time employment it is paid by the Pension Service."

"OK then will see you Monday." They say their goodnights and hang up.

John is just sitting down again and the phone rings again, it was one of Margaret's work mates. After about an hour John must have had about 20 phone calls so in the end he just pulled the phone line out and went back to having a drink, he is well on the way and at about 10.30 pm, decides to go to bed.

This is going to be one of the longest nights for him, all through the night he is just thinking about Margaret and all that had happened, over and over again. Then he looks at the clock and it was 6.am, he just tells himself that he has had enough and to get up.

He is down and just sits there looking straight out of the window, the dawn course is starting and he can see the Sun starting to shine on house chimney tops and he gets up makes a cuppa and cereal and goes and sits in the back garden on the decking. By 7.am the Sun is up and starting to feel warm, it looks like it's going to be a fine summer's day.

The whole of the weekend John is having more to drink than usual, all of his friends are giving their condolences to him and asking all sorts of questions, in away John is glad when he comes home at lunch time goes in and locks the door for the next time he will open it is when his Daughter comes Monday.

First thing Monday Mandy comes and she kisses her Daddy and they embrace each other, Mandy tells John that they will go to the City Hospital to pick up the cause of Death and take it to the Registry Office, then go and fill the forms out for your claim. Then go to the funeral care at the CO-op on Aspley Lane.

"Let's hope there is enough time." John says smiling at Mandy.

"Come on Daddy lets go."

Just after lunch and they have it all sorted bar the Funeral, so the next stop is the Co-op. They arrive and are escorted to a table and the Funeral Director starts by showing them coffins. They both decide on a white one, they take all the details and then they tell John and Mandy that it will take place on Thursday 17th June 2010 at 11am. Pick up at Margaret's home, in one Hearse plus one Limousine and then onto the Bramcote Crematorium.

In the Main Chapel then after Mourners returning in Limo to the Nags Head at Bobbers M ill, the Service to be Conducted by Minister

Joan Barks. All sorted John and Mandy come out, John turning to Mandy as they walk to the car and says.

"God they are thorough all that detail," John looking at his watch with the time approaching 4.pm, he asks Mandy if she would like a drink.

"Yes I think I need one after to-day."

They jump in Mandy's car and head for the Nags, when John starts to tell Mandy.

"There's one more thing to do, and that is see Glen in the Nags about the wake on the 17th." They pull up and go into the Nags lucky enough Glen is on and John asks if he could do the Buffet for a 100 people on the 17th.

"No problem John, just tell me the price for the Buffet you would like to spend and I will sort it for you, and there will be no charge for starting early and me putting on extra staff, it's the least I can do for Margaret."

"Thanks for that Glen, that's well appreciated." John shaking Glen's hand. Mandy only stops for one for she had to be back to take over from Lyndon, for he has to go back to work that evening and she had to get back for Jamie and Ben.

Why Me

"OK sweetheart love you and give my love to the boys." John kissing Mandy.

"Will phone you tomorrow, and I love you to." Mandy leaves and John carries on drinking with his friends, at about 6.pm John gives his leave and heads for home. Every time he gets home and closes the door that feeling is getting stronger and stronger, of being alone.

"God I hope this feeling doesn't last long." Then he tells himself to stop talking out loud there is no one here. He makes dinner and sits and watches Sport on the box

Chapter 10

THE DAY HAD COME

The morning of the 17th John is up and is telling himself that he has no need to get ready yet with it being 7.30 am; he is having breakfast watching the news on the box. At about 9.30am he starts to ready himself into the bathroom shower shave and general smartening himself ready for the day. He stands looking in the bathroom mirror and he is saying to himself. God I will be glad when it is all over with. In a small way I think its fright of this his last time he will be with Margaret.

Slowly at 10.30am Margaret's Brothers and members of the family start to turn up, they are in John's house and are all congregating on the decking out the back. The time is approaching 11.00am, when someone comes up to John that Margaret is coming. They all start to go outside were they can see Margaret coming in the Hearse with the limo following.

John locks the front door and goes to the Hearse and puts his hand on the window, it was if he was saying his private word to Margaret.

Everyone starts to get into their cars to follow the Hearse and the Limo, John sits in the Limo with Mandy and Lyndon the boys have not come with them being at School. It's not the sort of thing that you would let so young boys do. The Hearse pulls away with the Limo, and out front walking with his long walking stick is the Head funeral director. He walks to the end of the road, and then gets into the Hearse; it's a fitting tribute to the deceased.

They make their way up Aspley Lane and there must have been 20 cars following, when they arrive at Bramcote Crematorium there must have been well over 100 people mostly from Margaret's work place. For a top Retailing business on the High Street they had brought in bolster Staff to cover Margaret's Funeral so her work colleagues could attend.

The Hearse pulls up and John and Mandy with Lyndon stand while they get the coffin out of the Hearse, slowly they walk into the large Chapel of rest. With Margaret out front and the rest follow. They all start to take their seats and by the time everyone was inside there is standing room only.

John Bolstridge

Mandy places a framed photo of Margaret on top of the centre of the coffin of her Mum.

(The same photo at the beginning of the story.)

All settled then Minister Joan Borks begins.

"We are gathered here to celebrate the life of Margaret Elizabeth Stephanie Bolstridge, born on 19/12/1954, Margaret all her life was devoted to others, in her teens she did voluntary work at the mentally impaired and other institutes only thinking of others and not herself.

Many of you here today have been touched by her kindness, all her work colleagues, always seeing to their needs and not once considering herself. Margaret enjoyed Holidays abroad with John, visiting the Canaries Lanzarote and Florida with her two Grandsons Jamie and Ben, the highlight of her life. John has asked if he can read to you about Margaret so I invite John up to the pulpit to address you."

John stands and goes to the pulpit and starts by telling the congregation about the first time he met Margaret.

"Well it was our first date and in the evening I met Margaret at the top of the Road on

Melbourne Road shops, for our first date. When Margaret came along I opened the door for her and not realising I had not fully put the front passenger seat back after someone had got out with it being a two door car. Margaret got in and the seat went flying back into the fully reclined position, with poor old Margaret's legs flapping about in the front and she was lying flat out in the back."

Well this brought a round of laughter when John told them."

"That all I said was not now love we have only just met."

Then John asks them if he could read out an anniversary card out that he sent Margaret while she was in Hospital in February, he lifts the card up and shows the congregation.

You will see that Margaret joined in with all the fun, going round Disney trying on all the fancy cartoon hats and in general enjoying her life with her Family.

The card is done from my Heart and you will have to excuse the spelling that is a draw back with me having little education and being dyslexic.

But those going back to the Nags Head after can look at the card or after the funeral.

John Bolstridge

John holds aloft the card for all to see.

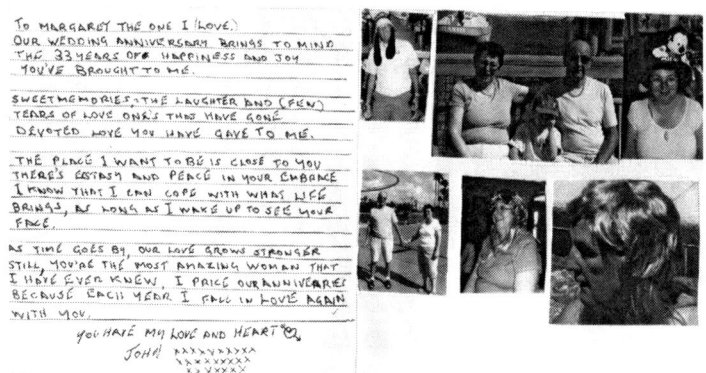

The photo was taken in 2009 when we went

To Florida and the words are.

> "To Margaret The one I Love.
>
> Our Wedding Anniversary brings to mind
>
> The 33 years of happiness and joy
>
> You've brought to me.
>
> Sweet memories, the laughter and (few) tears of love one's that have gone
>
> Devoted love you have given to me.
>
> The place I want to be is close to you

Why Me

> There's ecstasy and peace in your embrace
>
> I know that I can cope with what life brings,
>
> As long as I wake up to see your face.
>
> As time goes by, our love grows stronger
>
> Still you're the most amazing Woman that I have ever known.
>
> I price our anniversaries because each year I fall in love again with you.
>
> You have my love and heart.
> John xxx.

While John was saying the verse he was looking at the photo on Margaret's coffin, one or two of the Ladies were shedding a few tears.

The Minister Joan Borks stands and reads from the bible and at the end they all clap for the life of Margaret.

They gather in the garden of remembrance looking at all the flowers and passing John and giving thire condolence, everyone that went by John is telling him that the whole shop must be there, they reassured him that there is bolster Staff to cover for it. Even the Manager of the Store attended, and then it was off to the Nags Head for the wake.

One or two sat outside and John went round all of them, he approaches Mandy who sat outside and when her Dad came up to her she burst out into tears, all she was saying is.

"It's so unfair; Mum was the World to Jamie and Ben, more tears.

"Come on now sweetheart you have to go and pick the boys up from school, you don't won't them to see you like this."

The wake goes on all afternoon; at about 7.pm John leaves for home a little weary with all the beer, he opens the door of his home and the same feeling of loneliness. He stands there and he just cannot understand why he has never broken down since he lost Margaret.

The months roll by and everything seems to fall in place he received payment from the Department of Pensions, of over £2000.00 and from work Death in service payment of thousands, he paid the house off and other outstanding bills that Margaret left. But still the feeling of loneliness is still there.

He is drinking a little more than usual; all his mates in the Nags are always there for him. Then one Thursday night he is at a very low point he has had well over 8 pints, then he suddenly gets up and just waves at his mates and tells them that he is off.

Back home he is trying to open the door with the key and finally gets in, he shuts the door behind him and he nearly falls into the lounge with him not to steady on his feet. He goes into the kitchen and into the pantry where he keeps his box for his car. In front of him he sees the tow rope.

"That will do." He picks it up and starts to make a hangman's noose, there is one thing that he was good at and that was knots.

He makes the perfect hangman's noose and puts his hand in it and pulls and it tightens on his arm. With a smile he goes with the rope dragging behind him upstairs.

He looks up to the loft trap door and goes and gets the loft ladder that he keeps in the bedroom lobby hold. Takes them, and then unlocks the loft hatch door. Then he puts the rope over the beam and adjusts it so the rope stops about 3 feet after the trap door.

He sits with his legs dangling through the loft hatch takes the rope and puts it around his neck, all the time he his saying.

"I miss you so much sweetheart I just cannot go on."

Then he edges forward and he is just about to fall when from behind him he hears.

"What are you doing Daddy?" He looks back and sees Mandy standing there, he tells her.

"I love you're Mum that much I cannot go on without her."

Then Mandy said.

"What about these two you are there only Grandparent that they have left." Then he hears the voice of his grandchildren.

"Grandpa, are you alright." He looks back and sees Jamie and Ben holding their Mums hand and smiling at him, he realises that he is making a mistake and just when he is trying to go backwards he slips and FALLS.

Down he goes and if by a miracle he puts his elbows out and they stop on the hatch side, he is trying to pull himself up but a combination of his age and strength he cannot do it.

Why Me

He knows that if he relaxes he will fall and it will be all over, but by chance he puts his legs out and they reach the bathroom wall. He presses back so he is supporting himself so his hands are free. With his hands free and he takes the rope off his neck, and then falls through the hatch and lands on the landing.

He sits there and all of a sudden he burst out into tears, the flood gates have opened and all the months that he did not cry have all come together. All the time he is saying I love you sweetheart that much, and then a voice in his head tells him.

"And I love you more then you can imagine goodnight sweetheart."

He is straight on the phone to Mandy, and tells her that he loves her more each day, and to give his love to the boys.

That night he had a good night's sleep, and the truth be known this was the night he was on the road to coming to terms with the loss of his wife.

THE END

Always remember in times of sorrow look further than your eyes can see, for you are never alone in times of need, there are always loved ones there for you.

Life is precious look beyond the self-pity that you are feeling and love will come and comfort you.

THE JOKER

This story starts with a young 19 year old who had just completed his college work with a burning ambition to be a stand-up comedian, is name Paul Young. Sitting in his local one night the time was 8.30.pm. When the landlord gets up onto the stage he taps the microphone and asks for anyone in the pub who would likes to come up and do any songs or any other form of entertainment. Well Paul's hand is straight up, and calls for Bob the landlord to come over.

"Bob I will give you a little turn if you like."

"Fine what will it be?" Bob asking Paul.

Paul tells him in a quiet voice comedy, well Bobs eyes light up and tells him.

"That when all have refreshed their drinks he will announce him."

Not long after and the landlord is back on the microphone.

"Ladies and Gentlemen will you put your hands together for Paul Young, who is going to entertain you with a little bit of comedy. Come on now a big hand for Paul."

Well they are all cheering and whistling and Paul gets up and takes the microphone of Bob.

He had not started when you know the pubs heckler starts.

"Come on Paul, get a move on me has not got all-night. Well Paul knowing him thinks to himself, let's shut him up.

"Ho it's you Jimmy, don't like saying this but you're wife you cannot say she is fat for last night just before I shagged her, she was laying on her front with that big fat arse in the air. All I did was slap the thighs and ride in with the wave, Paul moving forward as if he was trying to shag her. Well everybody's in tears bar one, yes that's it Jimmy, he just sits there murmuring.

Then Paul starts,

"Sorry about that, Right did you here about the Irishman who brought a new bath, the salesman asks if he would like a plug with that, why replied the Irishman, is it electric." There is laughter from the audience,

Why Me

"Little Lad said to his Dad, suppers burnt, why said Dad, Chip shops burned down."

"You always can tell when the mother in-law is coming, the entire mice jump onto the traps."

"Dad what's a vampire, shut up and drink your soup before it clots,"

"Dad what's a werewolf, shut up and drink you milk before it clots".

Paul's going down well, the landlord is well impressed with Paul, because his tills are ringing and the customers are well into the entertainment. Paul himself is well into it and he can not stop, so he sees his drink on the table and his mouth is starting to go dry. He tells them that he will take a break and have a drink, and if you won't more just let the landlord know. But just before I go here is one more.

"What's pink wrinkled and hangs out your underpants," All the girls are shouting your PRICK," well Paul's straight in, "NO YOU'RE MUM." Well all the audience are in uproar, and as Paul gives a wave and leave the stage, they are all clapping whistling and shouting more.

Paul picks up his drink and goes to the bar, Bob sees Paul and just when one of the bar staff is about to refresh Paul's drink, Bob is straight there.

"I will see to that," he takes over and fills Paul's glass and takes it to him.

"Here you are Paul that one is on me and anymore you require, if you give me another half an hour there is £30.00 init for you." Paul stands there not believing what Bob had said, and just tells Bob.

"Fine by me, just give me a few minutes to have a drink" Paul sits making small talk with one or two of his mates, when one asks Paul.

"Were did you get the jokes from."

"It's just what you pick up; you know when you are with your mates and at work."

"Don't know how you can remember then, and the way you put Jimmy down that was professional. You know the same when you see the comedians on the TV, they always win."

"Yes that's because the comics always have the microphone so he is always going to be in command," Paul answering him. Then Bobs up and telling the entire customers if they are ready for more laughter.

Why Me

"Fill your glasses folk because in a few minutes Paul Young is back on stage," well this brought a big cheer and cat whistles. The function room is even fuller, it's if the word had gone round that there was a good act on. Bob once again is up and announcing Paul. Paul rises and waving to the audience, goes back up on stage passing Bob and shaking his hand.

"Hello again," he looks up and said to them.

"Where the fuck have all you lot come from, anyway were do I start, Ho yes my Dad was teaching the dog to talk, he sat it on sandpaper and asks the dog how it felt, the dog said rough rough." More Clapping.

"No wait my Granddad and Nan where in bed and Nan asked Granddad have you put the cat out, Granddad said why who has set it on fire. MORE, the audience are shouting.

Well Man goes to a pizza hut and asks for a pizza, the Man behind the counter, asks do you wont it cutting into six. The man replies no four I could not eat six." They are in stitches when someone shouts out give us a dirty one, well there is thunderous cheering and Paul looks at Bob the landlord, well Bob nods his head in approval.

Well don't blame me, seven dwarfs in a bath, one was feeling grumpy, so grumpy got out" well they are shouting not that kind, well Bob smiles and said.

"Only kidding, did you here about the Blind man at a faith healing meeting, sat next to Paddy and the blind man ask Paddy what was happening? Well Paddy tells him that a man on crutches had gone on stage to the faith healer, and then the blind man asks what is happening now. He's thrown one crutch away yes yes, what's happening now. He's thrown 2 crutches away yes yes, what is happening now. Well Paddy turns to the blind man and tells him. "HE'S FELL FLAT ON HIS FUCKING FACE." That brought a better response, they are shouting for more.

"Did you here about the Vicar and is faithful wife, well every time he is in bed with her and he feels a little frisky, she keeps pushing him away and telling him not till I've hear from the Lord. Well poor old Vic is getting a little fed up with being rejected and after about a week sees a tramp walking by the vicarage. Excuse me would you like to earn a fiver the tramp is straight in, what do you want me to do. Well the Vicar tells him to sit up that tree near his bedroom window and every time I shout out Lordy Lordy up above is it time I had a shove. You just shout out YES.

Well that night the Vicar starts to feel is wife when again she rejects him and the same, not till I hear from the Lord. Well Vic is straight in Lordy Lordy up above is it time I had a shove, the tramp shouts out YES. Well his wife straight away legs open and he gets a good shag.

This goes on for about three weeks and the tramp is getting fed up with it, so one night when the Vicar shout out lordy lordy up above is it time I had a shove. Well the tramp shouts back. "CUNTY CUNTY DOWN BELOW, IN IT TIME I HAD A GO."

Well the whole audience are completely in Paul's hand, some are sitting with tears in their eyes and others are clapping and charring. Before Paul realise he already has gone over his time he looks at his watch and tells them, O.K. one more and I will let you refresh your drinks.

This man walks into a bar with an octopus under his arm, well when the Landlord sees him asks what the hell have you there. The man tells him that it was his talented octopus. The Landlord said "talented, what can it do," well the man tells him. "Play any instrument." The Landlord tells him." I bet it cannot play that piano." "How much," said the man. "£10 pounds," said the Landlord, "you're on." The man puts the octopus on the piano seat, and it starts to play allsorts of music, classic modern. Well the Landlord gives the man is £10 pounds, then thinks, then he tells the man. "£40 pounds that he will not play the next item."

"Bring it on," the Landlord goes and get some bagpipes and throws them on the floor. The man puts the octopus on the floor.

After twenty minutes not a note well the Landlord stands there and tells the man, "you owe me £40 pounds." The man replays "wait till it cannot FUCK THEM, HE WILL PLAY THEM." Well the audience are in stitches; Paul tells them that was it and waves to them as he left the sage.

Well they all are clapping cheering, banging their classes on the table. Bob the Landlord can not believe the reaction that Paul was getting goes over to Paul and trying to tell him over the noise to come in tomorrow night to see him. Well Paul nods his head and sits down to finish his drink.

After about twenty minutes everyone with drinks all in start to shout for Paul, Paul looks at Bob and Bob nods and you can tell what he was saying, well Paul gets up and goes back on the stage with his pint, puts it on the table and raises the mike to his lips.

Why Me

Well let's get it on the road again. Did you here about the two men shipwreck, they are swimming away from the sinking ship. After swimming for 3 hours they see land and start to head for it, but when they are dragging them self's up the beach they see this great big native with the biggest chopper in his hand. He tells them that this was his island, and they had better start to get back into the sea and swim away.

Well one of the men tell him that they will die if they go back in, the native thinks for a moment and tells them. "OK if you wonted to stay you will have to do one think."

"What is that" asks the man, "well you will go north and pick 100 of your favourite fruit, and the other to go south and pick his favourite fruit. Come back and answer one question then you can stop. But if you come back and fail the question or laugh, I will chop off your head with my chopper."

Well the men set off and after an hour the first man comes back with 100 grapes, the native tells him. "That he had to shove them up is arse without laughing, well the man starts and he gets up to 99 he is just going to shove the last one up when he bursts into laughter. "What you gone and done that for, now I have to chop your head off."

Well the man answers. "Turn round and see my mate he's come round the corner with 100 fucking coconuts." well more laughter, Paul looks at his watch and it is well past 11.30pm. He tells them that one more and he is off for the time is late and he needs a drink.

Man in wheelchair is pushed to a river were there is a faith heeler dipping people into the river; the man in the wheelchair goes to him. And the faith heeler pushes him in and out the other side, someone in the audience shouts was he cured. No said Paul but he came out the other side with two new tyres and 2 new wheels. That's all folks hope to see you soon. Paul comes of stage and doing something he really likes is given one of the biggest send off the pub had ever heard.

He is straight down sitting at his table and downs the pint in one gulp; some off his mates were tapping him on the back. Paul standing to get is last pint thanks them.

On the way out Bob the landlord shouts to him not to forget about tomorrow night, Paul waves to him and said is goodnight. On the way home it was a slow walk for the cool air seemed to cool him down, he was completely wet through with sweat. He's home about 12.15am is Mum shouts asking if it was him,

"Yes Mum it's me, I'm all-in see you in the morning."

"Night Paul is Mum answering."

"Night Mum."

Chapter 1

The next morning Paul is up and it's that feeling you have when you are off work and it is Saturday, he goes into the kitchen and his Mum is doing breakfast.

"You were late last night Paul." Paul's Mum frying the bacon and sausages.

"Yes Mum boy you are not going to believe this in Conrad's Bob asked if anyone would like to do a turn, and he gave me £30.00 for just standing and telling jokes."

"You're not telling me you had £30.00 for doing that," Paul's Mum putting the breakfast onto Paul's plate.

"Yes Mum and he told me he would like to see me tonight, what for I don't know." Paul getting tucked into his breakfast.

Then into the kitchen walks Paul's Dad,

"Morning all, everything alright," Paul's Dad coughing and sitting down.

Mum starts to pour Dad a cup of tea and telling him all about Paul's evening at Conrad's.

"£30.00 for what, you're still not into that game, you know that it is a dead end, you will never make it, I mean a young lad like you should be up at the printing firm I work for, and there is some dame good money to be earned."

"Yes Dad but its if something that is inside me, it's if I've got someone inside me pushing me on." Paul's Dad sits there just shaking his head.

That night Paul goes to Conrad's and he see Bob and tells him that he told him to pop into see him, what will it be? "Pint of mix Bob" (pint of mix is half a bitter and half a mild in the same glass.) bob gets the drinks and comes and sits with Paul.

"Do you know Paul last night was one of the best nights I've had for a long time, my takings were through the roof?

What I would like is give you a Saturday spot, let's say 3 sessions so the punters can refresh their classes. What would you won't?" Bob smiling at Paul, well Paul did not know what to say with him saying how much did he want. Bob sees this and tells Bob.

"OK what about £150.00 then we see how you go, if it's a success then I will have another look."

Well Paul sits there and he is saying to himself £150.00 for an hour and a half, he would have to work half a week for that.

"Ok when do you want me to start?"

"Next Saturday I will run the posters off and put them up."

"Fine first session 8.30pm."

"No problem," Bob out stretching his hand for Paul to shake, all the formalities over and Paul just sits there wondering what had happened.

Couple of drinks then Paul is off home, he cannot wait to get home and tell is Mum and Dad.

He goes in and his Mum and Dad are sitting on the sofa watching TV, Paul is straight in and tells them you are not going to believe this.

"What" asks Paul's Dad? Paul tells them about the work at Conrad's and the £150.00.

"£150.00 for what, your kidding us."

"No Dad that is the price agreed, we handshake on it" well Paul's Dad just looks at Mum and shrugs his shoulders.

Paul asks them if they are going to come and watch him perform, then he realises that there is smut and swearing.

"Dad looks at Mum and they tell Paul.

"Ok we will come,"

"But I must tell you with it being a pub atmosphere that there is swearing and smut," well if you could have seen Paul's face.

"You're kidding us with all those people looking on," Mum looking at Dad,

"Don't you worry dear just cover your ears and hum, till it's over, she is telling Dad."

Paul can not believe what his Mum had said.

"Well I now know where I get the funny side of me from." Paul smiling at his Mum.

"Away with you Paul I'm looking forward to your Dad taking me out."

His Mum turning and looking at her husband, all that he does is grump and said.

"Well I hope it's going to be worth it." Then Paul tells him.

"Don't worry Dad it's free beer all-night, so go and enjoy it."

Well this certainly changed the face on Paul's Dad, he just stands there with the biggest grim you have ever seen on his face.

Over the next few days Paul is up in his bedroom in front of the mirror practising the moves and jokes that he is going to tell, and looking on his computer at jokes over the years that he had saved.

On the Friday night Paul goes into the Conrad's pub and sees the poster that Bob had put up, there in bold letters are Paul's name he looks at the poster and starts to read it out.

Saturday night come one come all see the new comedian to hit the big time one.

Paul Young. Starting at 8.30pm.

Don't be late.

Comedy to rock your socks off.

Come early to grab you seat.

Happy hour, 7.pm till 8.pm.

Well Paul seeing this suddenly gets butterflies; it's if this is going to be his first time. He just stands trying to tell himself. "Come on now it will be no difference than last time.

Well Paul only has about 3 pints he his convincing himself that he had better be off and start rehearsing for tomorrow.

Back home he is straight up stairs and the note pad he had written the jokes he was going to tell on Saturday night he just stands in front of the mirror and over and over he goes with the jokes.

At about 10pm Paul's mum shouts up to him and asks if he would like a little supper. Paul shouts.

"Yes please Mum down in a minute."

He comes into the kitchen and his Mum asks Paul.

"Tomorrow night will there be somewhere for Your Dad and I to sit, and what time will it start."

"Don't worry about hat we have the table next to the stage reserved for me, and the show starts about 8.30pm."

Why Me

"Did you here that Dad, we will feel like Royalty."

"I and I will not have far to go for a pint." I think Mum is starting to get a little excited about tomorrow night.

That night Paul is in bed and over and over again he is going over the routine he is going to do, he is clock watching and the night seemed to be the longest ever.finnaly he drops off and he is up at 8.30am.

Chapter 2

Saturday is mainly relaxing and watching sport on the box, at 5.00pm, he goes and starts to get ready for the big night. And every minute that goes by he seemed to be getting a little nerves and he notices that his hands are starting to shake. He looks in the bathroom mirror and his reflection looking back at him seemed to be telling him to calm down.

"I know, blimey I was up there last week and all went well, you daft sod."

This brought a smile and he starts to get ready.

He's back in his bedroom and into the wardrobe he is looking at all his cloths.

"What will it be." He's pulling out his suit putting it up to himself and looking in the mirror. "No it's a pub Saturday night." Then he has a thought, pulls out his light blue jeans white T-shirt and his short leather coat. "Yes this will do, I look like a Rocker."

Why Me

At 7.p.m. he tells his Mum that he was going to take a slow walk to Conrad's so he can rehearse his jokes.

"OK Paul Dad and I will be there at 8.pm."

"OK Mum see you later." He walks out off the front door and closes it behind him. By the time he reaches Conrad's the time is approaching 7.45pm. Just when he is going through the door he sees the poster with his name and the butterflies start again, and when he opens the door they are almost coming out off his mouth for to greet him is a packed room already. Well when some of the regulars see Paul walk in they are clapping and wolf whistling, this made the rest who did not know his do the same.

Paul waves at them and, putting his thump up to some and shaking hands. He goes to the bar and is greeted by Bob.

"Well Youngman you have made an impact already," Bob smiling at Paul and asking what his drink is."

"Usual Bob Pint of mix."

At 8.15pm he sees his mum and goes and takes them to the table that was reserved for them he sits with them and before he knows it is 8.30pm, he sits there waiting for Bob to introduce him, it was if he is the condemned man waiting for his fate.

Up onto the stage gets Bob, and on the mike.

"Good evening and welcome to Conrad's on this Saturday night and I 'am sure before the night is done you will all be in stitches. So let's have a big welcome to our own comic PAUL YOUNG." All the audience are Wolf whistling and cheering and clapping, when Paul starts too go on stage,

"Evening and thanks for the warm welcome, can you give a big hand for my Mum and Dad who are here." Paul pointing to his Mum and Dad. They are all clapping and Mum stands and gives a wave.

"Right lets go, what do you call an Indian Scot, Hawkeye the new.

Well the audience give a sigh at the first joke when Paul's Mum stands and shouts out.

"FUCK THAT SORT OF JOKE LETS HAVE SOME GOOD ONES."

Well if you could have seen Paul's Dads face it was a picture, all the audience were clapping and cheering, at what Paul's Mum had said.

Why Me

(Unknown to Dad Paul and his Mum had practised that so it got the audience off on a good note, well it did the trick.)

"Mum" Paul looking at her and saying.

"OK, here we go, you're in for a bumpy ride."

"Indian says peace on, White man say peace off."

"If you piss down my back don't tell me it ante raining." The audience love it and Paul's Mum is giving one or two load two finger whistles.

"Big John Wayne is on his death bed with all his family around him, his youngest Son is sobbing his socks off." "What's up?" Said. John.

"I've seen you kill cowboys and Indians in films and Japs and Germans in War films, but I have never seen you have a wank." "OK" said John," just as he was on the final stroke, the Doctor walks in.

"What the hell is going on." said the Doctor. Big John said.

"I've come for my Boy." Well that sure brought a smile and laughter all-round.

OK one more and I will take a small break while you refresh you glasses.

"Did you here the one about that chap who slept with the German Woman and he tells her to mark him out of ten while they had a shag, well the bloke turns her onto her belly and lifts her up so she is in the kneeling position and tries to slip it in, but it goes up her arse and he is going at it hammer and tong, she shout out.

"NINE NINE, well the bloke had the biggest grin on his face."

"For all you thick fuckers nine in German means NO. SEE YOU SOON."

Paul puts the mike down and goes and drinks his beer and gets them in. all the audience are giving him a big send off. He sits back with his Mum and Dad, and the first thing is Dad is straight in.

"Paul did you here your Mum she was disgusting."

"No Dad Mum and I practice the whole think; it was part of the show to get the audience going."

"He sits there and the look he gave Mum.

Why Me

"God you telling me you have been stewing on it till now, I wish some times Paul I did swear." Mum giving Dad the eye, he just sat there and smiled back at her.

"Anyway dear what are you going to do in the second half?"

"Well I was thinking of doing a quick round of short jokes and leave the best till last." Paul and his Mum talking, then Dad said.

"Sorry I was not to know."

"Dad just forget it we still love you." Mum touching Dads face and smiling.

Paul sits there when Bob gives him the nod for the second session, he sees this and looks at his Mum and Dad, and said.

"Here we go again."

"Go on Son break a leg." This time his Dad telling him.

"Thanks Dad here I go." He is up and back on stage, he picks up the mike.

"Are you ready for my next session?" Paul walking around the stage.

All the audience are clapping and cheering, its deafening.

"Right this session I would like you to all join in, and no hecklers if you do I will bring you down like you have never experience." Them Paul looks at Jimmy." Jimmie shouts out.

"You're right Paul, if I were you don't." then Paul starts.

"Right the first, what does Bob Marley like in his doughnuts." All the audience shout out.

"With jam in."

"You have got is lets speed it up."

"How do you get four elephants in a Mini, two in the front and two in the back."? How do you get four Hippo's in a Mini, you can not because there is four Elephants init." They start whistling and cheering.

"Sign in a canning Factory, eat what you can and can what you can't.

Why did Bruce Lee have time of work? He had Kunk flu.

How did the cat find out he was a father, she sent him a litter." They are all cheering laughing and shouting more.

"What does an Essex girl have in her knickers, NEXT. Why did the skeleton not cross the road, he had no guts.

How many men does it take to decorate a room? It depends how thin you slice them. Bum bum." Over twenty minutes he is reeling them off, when he tells them a few more and I will let you fill your glasses for the final session.

"Come on shout the answers out he we go, what do you call a cow that's had an abortion? A decalfinated. What do you call an Irish sheep singing, a Ronan Bleating?" Paul has gone on for over forty minutes; he looks at his watch and tells them.

"OK I will have a break and see you in a few minutes, don't miss the last session." He walks off to an eruption of cheers and applause.

He goes and sits down with the sweat pouring of him all is T-shirt is wet through, his Dad passes him a drink, and he gulps it down.

"Your good Son I take it back you could make a living out of it. How the hell can you remember all those jokes?"

"Thanks Dad it just comes to me it's if I am reading of the top of my head, it's hard to explain.

On or two customers are going over to Paul and really giving him loads of credit for his act, they all seem to say the same question, how do you remember them all.

Paul tells them. "It's hard but I get there, thanks for your comments."

Bob the landlord comes over to Paul and tells him that he has never seen so many customers in on a Saturday night, and then he asks what will be your last act.

"Well hopefully they will be in the mood for a little slut." Paul with a smile on his face. Bob rubbing Paul's back that will do for me, good look when you start.

Paul gets up and is back on the stage with a wave, all the audience are cheering and really giving him a big hand. Hello lets get this session fucking rolling.

"Do you know I came and seen Bob this afternoon at Conarads and on the corner there was this little Lad and he was crying, I said to him what's the matter with him. He said." "Grandpa got burned this morning."

"Don't worry little boy, he will soon get better." "He fucking well won't, they don't mess about down at the crematorium."

Two pieces of tarmac go into a Bar and order some drinks, when the doors burst open and a red piece walks in and barges pass the other two. Telling them to get out of the fucking way. And demands to be served straight away, they other two start to argue with him. When the Barman tells them to cool it, for the red piece is a bit of a cycle path.

The audience are loving it and shouting for more.

Hear about Quwasey Modow, he was lying at the bottom of the tower. When Esmeralda comes down from the tower, Quwasey said," I think you misunderstood me when I asked you to toss me off.

This man went to the Doctors and tells him have you anything for wind, he came out with a ball of string and a kite. Well they are all getting aces in their stomachs with all the laughing, when Paul tells them.

"Let's all refresh our glasses, but don't be long, for when I've my pint I will be straight back on." He comes off and finishes his pint and up to the bar, Bob comes over and fills his pint and tells Paul.

"That was a good idea look at them ordering more than one drink." Paul is back on stage with his pint and puts it down.

"1500 Irish men go for the same Job and are given a test, the test is maths, the last one goes in and the question is what's 3+7.The man puts down 87, comes out and tells his mate that he had the job. "How come." said his mate, he answers "I was the closest."

"Man goes to the Doctors with a strawberry stuck up his arse, the Doctor tells him not to worry he had a little cream for it."

"Rent collector on his first day, comes back to the office and tells them. Most of my customers must be Chine's, when I knock on the door all I get is. Chin tin."

"Nun marking a Darts match, Man first dart treble twenty, second dart twenty third dart hits the Nun she drops down dead, his opponent shouts out one Nun dead and eighty."

"Woman puts her hand down a Scotsman sporran and said." It's gruesome. I said the Scotsman, put your hand further down and it will grow some more."

"Indian says peace on, white man say peace off."

"I was walking my dog along the Promenade when my dog fell into the water; this big German jumps into the water and pulls him out. Are you a vet?" I asked him." I'm fucking soaking." He said.

The time is close to midnight and Bob looks at Paul and put his hand across his throat to tell Paul that is it.

"OK folks I've enjoyed your company and will see you soon."

Paul starts to walk off the stage with them giving him a standing ovation.

He sits down and the sweat is well showing, his Mum asks him.

"Are you alright son, you look well and truly done in."

"Yes Mum just will have one more drink and we will get a Taxi home." Paul stands and goes to the bar, Bob see him and comes over and fills his glass and telling Paul that he will square up with him tomorrow. Paul is about to turn round when he is approached by one of the customers.

"Hello my name is James Doyle I'm from the BBC Talent Scout unit, could I have two minutes of your time."

"Yes so long as it's only two minutes, I've got to take my Mum and Dad home." Paul looking apprentice at him.

"I know it's late but could we meet up tomorrow lets say 10.30am."

"Fine at my home then my address is." Paul gives him all the details how to get there.

"Well see you then Good evening Paul, look forward to meeting you tomorrow." With this he gives his leave and goes.

Paul sits back down and his Dad asks.

"Who was that Son?"

"Just a bloke from the BBC, he's coming to how house tomorrow morning to see me."

"The BBC, you r kidding us."

"Well you will meet him tomorrow." Paul smiling at his Dad, and finishing of his drink. They start to get up and depart waving at Bob on the way out, outside there is a Taxi waiting and they get in and it was off home. Once inside their home Paul flops onto the lounge chair and tells his Mum and Dad that he was all-in His Mum tells him.

Why Me

"You go and get some rest, you were brilliant tonight." His Mum planting a big kiss on his cheek. Then his Dad tells him.

"Son I take it back you are really good at this comedy lark and I hope you will go far. We both love you very much." Paul looks at them both and thanks them and goes to bed, giving them both a big kiss.

Next morning Paul is up and in the bathroom, the time is 10.o-clock splashing water on his face and trying to wake himself up.

"God it's if I have never been to bed." When his Mum shouts up.

"Paul is you ready for some breakfast."

"Yes Mum down in a minute." He starts to fresh himself up and starts to go down the stairs and into the kitchen, is Mum sees him and straight away said.

"Here is my talented son come and sit down and I will get you your breakfast."

"Thanks Mum." She is straight in telling Paul that last night he was fantastic, and then she asks.

"This fellow you are meeting what time did he say he would be here."

"At 10.30 am." Well if you could have seen Paul's Mum she no more looks at her watch and sees it was 10.10am.

"WHAT my God get your own breakfast." She was off rushing here and there, hover out in the front room and everything.

Well Paul just sits there and nods his head, with Dad just the same nodding his head, when Mum comes back into the kitchen.

"Come on move your self's, I wont it to look spotless when he comes."

"He is only coming to see me not inspect your home." Then the door bell rings and Mum is first to the door, she opens it and standing there is James Doyle.

"Good morning my name and I.D. James Doyle, I've come to see Paul Young."

"Come in my home is your home." Mum bowing and showing him into the living room, and at the same time picking up the hover.

"Just tidying up Sunday morning, you know what I mean." Paul's Mum picking up the hover and telling him that she will get Paul, exiting the room smiling at James Doyle. Paul comes into the room and seeing him puts out his hand to shake it.

"Good morning Paul you have is a charming Mum."

"Yes she is a one in a million, what it is you won't to see me about."

"One of my Nottingham colleges came into Conrads the first time you preformed you comedy act and phoned me and tolled me all about you, and that this was your first time. You see we are starting a new young talent show, to be shown on a Saturday night prime time to attract more viewers and I would like you to appear on it."

"You mean you won't me to be on the telly, what about getting there and things."

"Don't worry about all that, we will sort it. What it consists off is 16 acts then two are alimented each week, and before you ask that you could not stop that long. It is filmed over two days, 3 programmes the first day then on the second day the others and at a later date the final life on a Saturday nig."

Paul sits there and can not take all of it in, in the kitchen Mum and Dad are ear wigging through the kitchen hatch and are looking at each other and they can not believe what they are hearing. With Mum saying to Dad.

"How Paul on the B.B.C."

Back in the lounge James Doyle asks Paul.

"Would you like to be included on the show?"

"Right on put my name down." Then James Doyle pulls out the paper work for the contract, and starts to read it out to Paul. Then he gets to the part of the contract about money. If you make it to the final the payment will be £15.000, before he could finish he is interrupted by Paul's Mum and Dad with them both standing in the hatch and saying.

"How much." James Doyle looks at Mum and Dad standing with mouths to the ground.

"If you would like to join us I'm sure your son Paul would not mind." He had not finished and the door opens and they are both in and head for the settee, with Mum bowing as she went by Mr Doyle.

"You will excuse my Parents; you understand it's the age thing you know. Paul looking at his Mum and Dad, all they do is smile back at him.

"Carry on don't let us stop you." Mum looking at Mr Doyle.

"Right also you do know that there must be no bad language with it being before 9.PM. Only clean jokes."

Why Me

"No problem it will be jokes like. "Did you here about the Lone Ranger and Tonto riding hard all-day and into town they come and pull up at the saloon, well Silver the Lone Rangers horse is covered in sweat. So the Lone Ranger tells Tonto.

To take his blanket and waft it up and down and run round my horse to cool him down, while I go for a drink." "Yes ke-mo sah-bee." The Lone Ranger had been in the saloon for 10 minutes when this cowboy comes in and said "who owns the white horse outside. The Lone Ranger tells him that it was his horse, the cowboy tells him.

"You've left your injun running."

Well Mum and Dad are in tears, but all Mr Doyle does is look at his Mum and Dad and tells Paul.

"Yes that will be fine; you seem to have this control over people, looking at Mum and Dad" He looks like his whole family had been killed. He starts to put his paper work away and tells Paul.

"That the show is in 3 weeks time and at the end of the week he will receive all the details. With this he rises and is saying his goodbyes to Paul's Mum and Dad and Paul shows him to the door, he shakes Paul's hand and wishes him all the good look at the show. Paul stands there watching him go and he gets to the gate when he suddenly said to himself.

"You've left your Injun running." Well Mr Doyle is buckled over with laughter and you could still here him halfway down the road.

Paul closes the door and just stood in the doorway, he seemed to be saying to himself, I must be dreaming. When his Mum and Dad come up to him.

"My Son on the Telly waits till I tell everyone."

"Mum I have not won yet."

"You will win Son, you're brilliant." Even Paul's Dad comes up to him and shakes his hand and then hugs him.

"Good luck Son I'm with you all the way."

"Thanks Dad, I think I will go and have a shower and get ready to go and see Bob at Conrads." Paul departs and goes to have a shower and, when he was finished just goes back into the bedroom and flops on the bed. All the time he his laying there and he just can not comprehend all that had happened over the last week, he is saying to himself me on the Telly. I'm just trying to get into it and look at me.

Why Me

He shakes his head and the time is 11.30 come on then super star get ready.

He comes down stairs and shouts to his Mum and Dad that he will see them later. He closes the door behind him and heads walking towards Conrads. Well you should have seen it when he walks in, there are only about twenty people in but when they see Paul they all start to clap him.

He just waves and smiles at them, Bob see Paul and come over to him.

"What will it be Paul pint of mix."

"Fine Bob and a packet of plain crisps." Bob brings his drink and also a packet with his earnings from last night, when Paul tells him.

"Bob I had the man from the B.B.C round this morning and in a couple of weeks they wont me to go down to London to appear on a New Talent show, it is only for a couple of days so it should not affect my job here."

"That's Fine would you like to do half an hour next Saturday, you see I've this singer Richard Taylor Country and Western. You on first say 9.15pm to warm them up and he will do the last hour between 10-11.pm."

"Yes fine by me."

John Bolstridge

"Same wages you have for last night, you will bring them in."

Paul goes and sits down and he has a sneaky look at what was in the packet, well when he sees £300.00 for last night he can not believe it, he just looks back at Bob. All that Bob does is smile and puts his thumb up to Paul. This is when he realises that Bob had told him same as last night, well Paul just sits there and puffs at the thought of getting £300 for one session.

The week ahead all that Paul is doing is to start to put together some jokes for Saturday night, midweek and he goes to Conrads and he sees the poster.

Saturday Night 28th August.

The one and only Richard Taylor
Country and Western singer.
ALSO
THE ONE AND ONLY
PAUL YOUNG (comedy)
Look out for him on the BBC SHOW
Young Talent programme starting in
September.

Well Paul sees the poster and is well impressed, he is saying to himself.

"It does not take long for Bob to get the news."

Chapter 3

That Saturday Paul is at Conrads and the same as last time he his dressed in his leather jacket blue jeans and white T-shirt, the time is approaching 8.15pm and already the pub is rammed.

It's if they are all waiting for Paul, well Bob looks at Paul and asks.

"OK now Paul." Paul nods and Bob is up on the stage.

"Ladies and Gentlemen welcome to Conrads this Saturday night we have two great acts for you tonight, the first up is your very own Paul Young. Let's give him a Conrad's welcome." Well the cheering and banging of glasses and wolf whistles is deafening, and on to the stage comes Paul.

He must have been there two minutes and they are still at it so he jumps in.

"Fucking stop, blimey anyone would have thought that some one good had walked on." Well again they are all at it whistling and cheering.

"Have you been told about me being on the Telly in two weeks, on the BBC I hope you all vote for me." Well they are all shouting YES-YES.

"Ok Ladies and Gentlemen lets get this rocking before my time is up, let's get going by telling you the Worlds ten greatest FUCKS.

1. "What the fuck was that?-Mayor of Hiroshima.
2. "look at all those FUCKING Indians!-General Custer.
3. What a place to plant a fucking tree!—Marc Bolan.
4. That's not a real fucking gun!-John Lennon.
5. Of course I'll fucking beat Tyson 'Harry!-Frank Bruno
6. I thought I could smell fucking petrol!-Nikki Lauder
7. Watch him, he'll have some fuckers eye out!-King Harold
8. Who let that fucking woman drive!-Space shuttle Capt.
9. No fuckers going to know!—Richard Nixon
10. Where's all that fucking water coming from!-Captain of the Titanic."

Why Me

What a start they are in stitches, then Paul shout are you ready for more.

"YES" they all shout. Paul wipes his brow with the lights on the stage making him sweat. Ok here we go again for some more quickies.

"What's the maximum penalty for bigamy, Two Mother-in-laws?"

"Wife, I've made the chicken soup darling, Husband. Thank fuck for that, I thought it was for us.

"What do you call 20 long eared mammals hopping backwards in a line?

A receding hare line."

"A man drove is car off a cliff; he was testing the air brakes."

"What part of France has got more than one toilet?—Tolouse."

Paul had gone well over his time and Bob catches his attention and puts his hand across his neck to tell Paul to cut it off. Paul sees this and tells the audience that he will give them one more and then he is off.

"A teacher is teaching her class maths when she asks Johnny a question, if you had 10 apples and Mike takes five what are you left with. Johnny replies A FUCKING FIGHT." Then Paul waves to the Audience and leaves the stage with the utmost clapping and cheering. He goes to the bar and once again Bob thanks him for a wonderful act, and at the same time looking round and seeing all the customers.

The time is approaching 9.30 and it is time for the main event at Conrads and Paul had noticed that the concert room was emptying fast, Bob shouts to Paul to get back on stage well Paul is up and straight on the mike.

"Where the fuck are you lot off, is there Bingo somewhere, or have you got to get home before the ten o clock horses get you. Well this certainly brought laughter from the remaining lot. Them Paul starts to tell one or two jokes and would you believe it they start to drift back in, Bob walks by and tell's Paul to carry on for another stint and he will see him right.

"An Irish man goes to the local carpenter and asks him to make him a box one inch wide and forty foot long, the carpenter asks what the hell do you wont that for. The Irish man tells him so I can send my Mum a washing line in the post for her Birthday."

"A man walks into the butches shop and asks him if he had a sheep's head, the Butcher tells him no it's the way I brush my hair."

"Did you here about the stupid man who went to his dentist, and asked if he could put a wisdom tooth in for him."

"A man walks into a pet shop and tells the pet shop owner, you said this cat was good for mice. But it has not caught one. The owner tells him. Well I think it is very good for the mice. Said the pet shop owner"

Then Paul tells them just a minute, he steps of stage grabs his pint and goes back on stage taking a sip.

"That's better hope some kind sole puts me one in, Paul with a big grin on his face."

"Right lets change them round, I know you like dirty ones." They are cheering Paul and clapping out load.

"How do hedgehogs fuck, very carefully?

"Bacon and egg walk into a bar the barman said, YOU TWO CAN FUCK OFF WE DON'T SERVE BREAKFAST IN HERE."

"How can you tell a Gentleman, He always takes the pots out of the sink before he pisses in it?"

"Young girl had a road accident as a paramedic tends to her she is asked, where are you bleeding from. The girl answered fucking Essex."

"That's all folks lets here it know for to-nights singer Richard Taylor."

With this Paul leaves the stage and the room is full again and it is too late to move on so they stay and listen to the singer as he starts to sing his first song. Paul goes up to the bar and is greeted by Bob.

"Thanks for that Paul you sure made them come back and made it a success, I will see you tomorrow and settle up, Paul is just going to ask for another drink when Bob tells him that he had 15 pints in.

"What were from," asks Paul."

"You should know you ask them to buy you a drink and they did." Bob smiling at Paul while he pulled him is drink.

Chapter 4

That Sunday Paul comes into Conrads and sees Bob at the bar, Bob comes over to Paul and hands him his wages, Bob telling Paul.

"I've had a little extra for the job you did keeping them in last night."

Well Paul looks at the packet and his eyes light up for he only had over £400.00 in the packet.

He can not believe it and looks at Bob; all that Bob does his put up his thumb and smile.

Over the next week all that Paul is doing is working out a plan for the show on the Telly, he sits on his computer and printing a routine off at what he proposed to do. He goes and shows it his Mum who sits and looks at it. After about an hour she looks up at Paul leans over and kisses him on the cheek.

"If you use this I think that you will have know problem, how are you feeling Son about the whole thing."

"Don't really know Mum, it's if I'm on a different Planet, you know one minute I'm struggling and the next I have to be on the Telly. It's if I won't someone to say stop the World I won't to get off."

"You will be alright Son the way you have preformed and what people have told me, YOU'RE A WINNER." She is shedding a tear and Paul sees this, he puts his arms round his Mum and kisses her and telling her.

"Thanks for being there for me."

The rest of the week Paul his rehearsing in front of the mirror, when suddenly his Mum shouts up to Him.

"Paul in the post there is a letter to you from the BBC."

Well Paul comes rushing down the stairs and in front of his Mum opens it.

> Dear Mr Paul Young.
>
> Please find enclosed all the details of your visit to the Central studios of the BBC, and the details of your accommodations for your two day stay in London.

Why Me

Also incorporated are the times of the rehearsals and phone numbers to contact when you arrive. If you have any questions, Please don't hesitate to contact the number provided.

Yours Sincerely
Carol Simcoe.
(Head of Programs.)

Well Paul stands there and is Mum is saying.

"What does it say? All Paul does is show her the letter and stands there frozen just looking straight forward. Well the same for his Mum she to reads the letter and just stands there, when all of a sudden Paul said.

"This Is It I'm off tomorrow to be on the Telly."

You will be fine my Son, you will have them eating out of your hands."

The show is being recorded on the Thursday and Friday, with a change of plan the Final is scheduled for the 15th of October, with the finalist appearing on that day with the audience phoning in to choose the overall winner.

Paul will go down on the Tuesday and the first rehearsal is for 10.am Wednesday, all that day Paul is sorting his cloths out what he will wear for the shows and things he needs to take with him. Suit case packed and he tells his Mum that he will go and have a drink with the lads in Conrads that night before he is off to London Tuesday.

In Conrads all Paul's mates are asking allsorts of question on the show that he is gong to do.

"Hold on one at a time, for a start don't forget that this is all new to Me." then Bob leaning on the bar asks Paul.

"I suppose if you win that will be it for us at Conrads."

"On your bike Bob this is my home and my base, if I did hit the big time and this is if, Conrads will always come first. You will have to build a bigger concert room." Paul smiling at Bob.

"Thanks for that Paul what will it be."

"No more Bob I'm trying to get through all the beer from the weekend brought for me." Then Paul has an idea.

"Bob get my mates a drink will you they deserve a little reward for all the support and you lot don't forget to vote for me if I get through to the Final on that Saturday.

Why Me

"When's the final Paul." Asks one of Paul's mates.

"You will know I think the whole town will know when it is."

Paul about ten gives his goodbyes and tells them that he was off, for it was an early start for him in the morning. Well it was like royalty leaving everyone in the pub were shouting and wishing him luck down London.

"Thanks everyone see you when I get back." With a wave and smile Paul leaves. On the way home all Paul is thinking is what if I don't come anywhere, what are they going to think of me, well a little voice in his head tells him you are good don't worry you will win. With this Paul smiles to himself and it is if there was an extra stride in his step.

At home it was off straight to bed with him catching the 6.30am inter-city express to London. 5.00am the alarm goes off and Paul straight away is up and into the bathroom, he dresses and down he goes at 5.30am, when he opens the door to the living room the first thing that hits him is the smell of bacon. And would you believe it there was Paul's Mum in the kitchen doing Paul a full breakfast. Well when Paul goes into the kitchen he sees his Mum in dressing gown preparing breakfast, the first thing Paul said.

"Mum it's too early for you."

"No way is my boy going out of this house without a full breakfast inside of you."

"Thanks Mum." And would you believe it into the kitchen comes his Dad, all sleepy and trying to wipe the sleep out off is eyes. They all have breakfast and at dead on six-o-clock the door bell rings and Paul knew it was his taxi for the train station. At the front door Paul kisses his Mum and hugs his Dad and heads for the taxi waiting, he turns and looks at his Mum and Dad waves and gets into the taxi.

The taxi pulls away with Mum and Dad waving at it, Mum turns to Dad and said.

"He will be alright dear wont he."

"Yes Mum he is a winner, lets go back to bed." They both watch as the taxi turns the corner and disappear; they close the door behind then and go back to bed.

The taxi pulls up at the station and Paul gets out the taxi, the driver wishes him luck for Paul was telling him about is trip to London and that he was going to be on the telly.

He is standing on the platform when over the platform speaker comes the announcement of the arrival of the 6.30am express train to London.

Paul boards the train and sits on a table seat so he could use the table to look at his script of what he intended to use on the show. The train pulls out and it has only one stop on the way with it being the express and stops at Leicester, at Leicester the train pulls into the station and this young Lady board with her brief case and computer. She sees Paul sitting at a table seat and sees that there is room on the other side of the table for her and the computer, she asks Paul if anyone was sitting there and Paul looks up to her and tells her to help yourself.

The train pulls out of the station and is soon up to speed for the rest of the trip to London. After about 30 minutes Paul looks down and sees music sheets and she seemed to be humming to it as she looked through the paper work. Paul asks.

"Are you in an orchestra, I could not notice the music sheets.

"No I'm a singer; I am off to London for a talent show at the BBC."

"You kidding me, I'm a comedian I to be off for the same show." Well they both can not believe it

"My name is Paul Young." The girl tells Paul.

"My name is Carol York, please to meet you." They end up in small talk and are surprised for they are in the same Hotel. Then Paul asks her.

"Would you like me to buy you dinner tonight in the Hotel; we could keep each other company." Carol thought for a moment and said to Paul.

"Dinners paid for in the Hotel." Paul smiling at her said.

"Well I am a comedian." She gently taps Paul on the hand and tells him.

"You've got a date." After an hour and 50 minutes the train is pulling into London, they share a Taxi and book into their Hotel. At reception they can not believe it for they have been given rooms next to each other.

When they had booked in they were just going to go and unpack before the rehearsals when they are approached by a Lady holding a clip board. She asks them if they were part of the New Show that is being held at the BBC.

"Yes my names Paul Young and this is Carol York." She ticks them both off the lists and asks them.

Why Me

"Are you an item."

"No" Carol telling her.

"We met on the train coming down here." She looks at Paul and smiles at him.

"Very well when you have unpacked had something to eat, could you meet me here at let's say 10.15am for the short journey to the recording studios. We have a mini bus provided, anything you would like to know."

Paul turns and said.

"Yes when we were booking in the flea's were jumping up and looking at what room we were in." Paul smiling. Well if you could have seen her face it was a picture. 10.15am and it was back down to the reception for the off for the studio's at the BBC. All the contestants were gathered and the Lady with the clip board comes up to them all.

"Good morning all I'm your host Miss Frances, I will be looking after you for your stay here and at the studios, if there is anything you would like to know just ask, please follow me to the mini bus." Well they all felt like school children and Paul was saying to Carol.

"Come along Carol no doddering you don't won't to go and up set Miss Frances." Paul walking waddling along with his hand pointed down, well they all were laughing at Paul when Miss Frances turns sharply and sees Paul.

"I see we are going to have trouble with this one." Miss Frances looking at Paul in a stern way. They all board the mini bus and it was a short drive to the BBC, once they arrive they are shown all the production crew and the main Director of the show. He explains all about the show and they start by having a draw for who will be going first and so on.

One by one their names are pulled out and Paul just stands there waiting for his name then Carol's name is pulled out and then the Director tells them.

"Now the last name, Paul Young." Well Paul turns to Carol and said.

"Blimey the last one."

"Yes and I'm second to last, boy we are in for a nerves time at recording waiting for our turn." The day is all about places and the singers are shown how to work with earpieces inserted so they can here the tune that they are singing to, for the rounds there is no live orchestra, only in the final witch is live.

Then Paul is called out, he approaches and for the first time he feels what it will be like to face the cameras on the floor, he is told that there is no live audience only dubbing laughter, he his told that he to will hear it through is hearing piece. Then the director points to the spot where the 4 judges will sit for the rounds, and then he tells him that the final is judged by the phone-in and the one with the most votes win. He then tells him.

"I will leave you for a few moments so you can acclimatise yourself for the rounds starting tomorrow."

Well Paul stands there and all that he sees is the cameras and the judge's seats, he is saying to himself.

"God I've never done this before just on my own." He can feel the butterflies starting to come and the nerves creeping in when from behind Carol comes up.

"It looks daunting Paul." Well Paul jumps out off his skin with a load scream, that could be heard all-round the studio.

"God you made me jump Carol."

"You're telling me." Carol looking round and seeing everyone looking. She smiles at them turns back round to Paul grabs his arm and telling him.

"Let's go and have a cuppa." They sit on the sidelines with a drink and Paul looks at Carol and asks her.

"Would you have dinner with me tonight?" Carol looks at Paul apprehensively and said.

"What the same we had last night in the Hotel."

"No go out and have dinner, you know somewhere in London."

"Thanks Paul, yes I would but we can not be late for it's the big day tomorrow." All sorted and it was back to rehearsing for the first 3 rounds, tomorrow.

Chapter 5

Back at the Hotel Paul and Carol are in the lift on their way to their room Paul suddenly pulls Carol to him and plants a kiss onto Carol just when the doors open on the lift at their floor, they are still kissing when a customer waiting to get on the lift suddenly coughs and they part. They both come out off the lift Carol in front and Paul looks at the gentleman waiting to get into the lift and Paul tells him.

"We are actors just practicing our moves for tomorrow." Winking at the man and blowing him a kiss, Paul walking off smiling.

The time is 6.30pm Paul and Carol are off for the dinner date, they are going to a pub and steak house. They find a table and Paul brings the drinks and sits next to Carol. All the talk is about the show tomorrow and Carol tells Paul.

"Hope you don't find me rude or anything but would you be upset if we had an early dinner and go back at least for 8.30, I would like to practise for tomorrow before I turn in." before

Paul could answer she holds Paul's hand and tells him.

"That when this was all over she would like to carry on with the relationship with him for she is having strong feelings towards him."

"No problem Carol I myself have the same feelings." They both lean forward and are in a full embrace and kiss.

They have an early dinner and they are both back in the Hotel and head back to their room, when again they are in the lift in full embrace and once again the lift comes to their floor the doors open. And would you believe it the same man is waiting for the lift. They are leaving the lift and Paul tells him.

"Hard work this practicing lark." The man just shakes his head and enters the lift. Paul is in his room and he is looking at the routine he his going to use when he hears Carol singing, he just stops dead and just listens to her, she has this voice that seemed to keep you enthralled. The song was a slow love song and after Paul was clapping and shouting bravo, in a soft voice. He was telling himself that she will go all the way with a voice like that.

Paul carry's on looking at the script when he notices the time is 10pm, he then turns in and all that seemed to be on his mind was Carol

Why Me

and not the show. Most of the night he is tossing and turning, when at 6.30am he pulls back the sheets and said.

"That's it I'm up; I can not stand it anymore just laying here." He showers and starts to put his clothes that he is going to go in on the show, into a case he dons his suit and he is ready to go. The time is 7.15am when there is a knock at the door he opens it and Carol asks him if he is going to go down and have breakfast. He tells her yes and they make their way to the restaurant, on the way Paul comments on her singing last night and tells her that she was good and should be fine today.

"Thanks for that Paul, are you getting nerves now the day had come."

""Funny that but no, it's if I'm not going to go on. You know the feeling that it is not happening."

"Lets hope you don't get those when you are about to go on." Carol holding Paul's hand and squeezing it. 8.30am they are all there the whole 16 contestants when into reception comes Miss Frances.

"Already for the big day, don't forget the 6 that are eliminated, to see me back here at 6.30pm for your final statements on expenses before you leave." Miss Frances looking at Paul and smiling, Paul looks behind him and then back at Miss Frances.

Carol is giggling at Miss Frances.

They all board the bus and it was off to the studio, when they arrive the first thing they notice is the entire camera staff crew and the four judges with paper work all studying the contestants. The producer tells them all to go and get ready for the start for it is scheduled for 9.15am start.

Dead on 9.15am the host of the show was up and onto the floor and welcoming all the viewers to the brand new talent show, he announces all the judges and tells the viewers all the rules and about the final programme. When they the viewers will be the final judge with their vote.

He announces the first act Darrel Woods who is singing Rock and Roll.

He comes on and just like Elvis he is swinging his hips and making a real fool of himself. Well by the time he had finished and the judges had told him what they thought, I don't think he was in the running.

Halfway through the contest Paul turns to Carol and tells her it must be sweltering out there under all thoughts lights for the heat was even back there. 14 contestant's gone and it came to Carols turn. The show host calls out for a big hand for Carol York from Leicester. Paul tells her sing like you did last night.

Carol goes skipping on and stands on her spot, she can here the clapping die down and the music starts, well her voice seemed to even have the judges attention and she sings it perfectly in tune. After she bows and the clapping and whistling she hears in her earpiece, she smiles again and bows. Well the judges were overwhelmed and the comments she received from them she was a sure winner. Off she came and Paul notices the sweat on her back.

"Boy Carol is it that hot out there."

"Yes but you are so enthralled in the song you don't notice it." Well before Paul had time to answer her he hears the show host.

"Ladies and Gentlemen lets give a good welcome, for your last contestant Mr. Paul Young." Well Paul with hearing this is straight out onto the stage, he is dressed in the same leather·coat white T-shirt and blue jeans that he had on at Conrads. He to is off running on and straight away looks round the empty studio and the look on his face is if he was looking at a packed studio.

"Good evening and look at all you lot, wow who's come on, wow it's me I'm from Nottingham and I would like to start by. Did you hear about?

Robin Hood when he asked Maid Marion."

"Ah Marion," cried Robin Hood. "Let's go deep into the forest, fair damson. "Damson" she replied. "You mean Damsel; a Damson is something in a jam."

"We haven't been deep into the forest yet." Quote Robin. Bum-bum.

"Why do squirrels swim on their backs, so their nuts don't get wet?"

Paul can listen to the laughter in his earpiece.

"There were two men standing at a bus stop when a bus comes along the second man ask the first man. "Do you won't this bus," the first man replies. "No I've no were to park it."

"Is camping loitering within tent?"

"Hitchhiker standing by the roadside card round his neck asking for a lift, no arms one leg and three eyes, a motorist pulls over and said, "eye eye eye you look armless hop in."

"Have you ever notice the sign's they put up, the other day I was going into the General Hospital when the sign on the gate said. Guard dogs operating here. I can just see it now two dogs in gowns one saying "scalpel woof woof, swab woof woof."

Paul can here the laughter in his earpiece, he giggles and then said. But just before he starts he here's one more than that is it in his earpiece.

"Well it's been lovely talking to you, just before I go did you here about.

The man that travelled the lengthens and breath of the country telling everyone he was rich and famous, when he was actually a penniless nobody. He was a mobile phone."

Goodnight and God bless. Paul stands and waves to the empty studio with all the clapping and whistling in is earpiece.

The judges all give him a good score telling him that he was truly a professional and he should go far. One judge even told him you are a natural at this game. Again Paul thanks the judges and leaves waving at the so called audience. Carol claps and plants a kiss on Paul telling him you are through.

John Bolstridge

"Thanks baby." The compare comes back on and starts by telling the viewers that they are know ready for the two who are leaving the show.

Yes you have got it the first to be alimented is the Elvis singer and one other, second round starts and they have to go through it all again.

Paul and Carol are through this and the last round, at the end of recording they are well and truly exhausted. Paul and Carol just look at each other and they are saying to each other, two more rounds and that will be it we will be in the final.

They are met by Miss Francis at reception and the first thing she does is look at Paul and said.

"Off home are we then" With a big smirk on her face.

"Actually no both me and Carol are through." lifting his hand to his mouth and giving a cheeky cough into it. Well her face was a picture it was if all her hopes and ambitions had come crashing down.

That evening Paul and Carol are having a relaxing drink in the Hotel bar when Paul asks her what she was going to sing tomorrow.

"If I get through the first round the second round I'm going to sing the Whiney Huston song I will love you so." What about you Paul have you anything planed. He thinks for a moment and said.

"No just come out with more or less what I have been doing."

They dine in the Hotel and are on their way back to their rooms and Paul stops outside Carol's room and they are embraced in a loving kiss. Paul looks at Carol and asks.

"Let's go into your room."

"No Paul lets wait I have this feeling that if I give into you now it will put me off tomorrow, please be patient. I love you so much that it hurts."

"Sorry Carol but I love you too; break a leg tomorrow lets both get into the final."

"Thanks for understanding Paul." She puts her arm round Paul and it was one long and lasting kiss. And would you believe it the same man they seen in the lifts is going to his room.

"Goodnight hopes you both do well tomorrow." Well Paul and Carol just look at each other and are totally taken back at what he had said.

John Bolstridge

The next morning it was the same routine 8.30 at reception the last 10 contestants are gathered. And in to reception comes Miss Frances.

"Good morning all to day you will know that four of you will be eliminated, please see me here at 6.30pm before you depart. And once again she looks at Paul. Paul this time gives her an Irish jig.

"Come along now stop this tom foolery and go to the mini bus." Paul walks pass Miss Frances; head bowed and in a childish voice tells her.

"Sorry Miss Frances." Looks up and gives her a cheeky smile. She tries to give him a clip round the head but Paul is to fast for her. After the fun and games with Miss Frances it was onto the bus and off to the studio. Today they seemed to be a more rush about things at the studio when they arrived into the studio the director is shouting for lights to be altered and in general talking to the back room boys.

Carol and Paul are standing together when the man they keep bumping into at the Hotel comes walking by with headphones round his neck and smiles at them when he went by and into the sound both in the studio.

Well Paul and Carol just look at each other with that look of misbelieve. Just like yesterday they are told when they will be on, this time Paul is on fourth and Carol sixth.

Before long and Paul is called out onto the stage and introduced to the judges and the pretend audience. He chats for a few moments then turns to the so called audience and tells them to put their hands together for, Paul Young.

"Thank you and good evening did you here about the little old lady who lived on the top floor of a block of flats, she was out one day shopping when the gasman knocks on the door. A voice from inside shouts

"Who is it?" The gasman replies.

"It's the gasman come to read your meter." Unknown to the gasman it was the parrot inside the flat that was answering him and once again shouts.

"Gasman come to read your meter can you open the door please."

"Who is it." shouts the parrot.

"It's the gasman can you let me in please."

John Bolstridge

"Who is it?" Shouts the parrot. Well this had been going on for an hour and the gasman's face was getting redder and he starts to hold his chest, knocks again and said.

"Can you please let me in it's the gasman come to read your meter."

"Who is it?" Shouts the parrot well the poor gasman drops dead on the door step just when the old lady comes round the corner and said.

"Who is it?" From inside the flat the parrot shouts.

"It's the gasman come to read your meter."

Paul can here laughter from his earpiece, and went on to tell them about the Lone Ranger and you've left your injun running. Well the four judges are in stitches and the camera crew, he tells one or two off his best jokes.

"Worried man goes to his Doctors and tells him that he thinks he is shrinking. The Doctor calmly replies calm down you will have to be a little patient."

"A boxer goes to his Doctors and tells him that his insomnia is getting terrible." The Doctor replies, "try counting sheep." The boxer replies.

"That's no good every time I get to nine I get up." Then in his earpiece he hears the Director telling him 2 minutes left wind it up.

Boss to worker, "why are you late to day." Worker replies.

"There are 8 people in how house and the clock was set for 7."

"Two goldfish in a tank one said, "How do you drive this."

With this Paul thanks them all for there time and he hopes to see you in the Final. He stands waving to the empty studio when the compare comes up to Paul and he starts talking to the judges

"Judge one what do you think of Paul's act."

"How long have you been doing this act Paul?" Paul answers him by telling him only a few weeks. Well the judge is taken back by this and said.

"A few weeks God you're going to be brilliant in a few years, I'm telling you up there with the greats, just keep it up Paul and entertain them like you are now a true professional."

Paul thanks him and it was the same with all the judges. Paul comes off waving at the judges and audience.

The first to great him is Carol she stands there and claps him and plants a big kiss on him saying.

"You're through you have no problem."

"Thanks sweetheart just give me a moment." Paul takes of his leather jacket and he is sweating profusely, he plonks down on a chair with hands on his head, then looks up to Carol and tells her.

"You go out there and give it all your best I'm right there with you."

Then the compare tells the so called audience, "Please welcome on stage Carol York. Carol looks at Paul and tells him.

"I love you." She goes running on to the stage and stands talking to him when he asks her what she was going to sing, well when she tells him that she is going to sing the song by Whitney Huston I will always love you.

Paul suddenly sits up in his chair and is looking straight at Carol. She sings it perfectly and always looking at Paul has she preformed. Paul is in a trance just listing to her. She bows

Why Me

and the compare comes back on stage and just like the other contestants asks the judges their views on Carols singing.

Just like Paul all her views are top marks from the Judges. She comes off and stands with Paul when they are all asked to come back onto the stage.

They start to give there verdict and the compare asks the Judges to give them their first artist through to the final, and the first one out is Carol York. She goes running onto the front of the stage and bows and blows kisses to the Judges. Then comes the second and you guest it Paul Young's name is chosen, he comes onto the front stage and straight up to Carol and they are in a full embrace and kissing.

The day is done and it was back to the Hotel with you know Miss Frances, back in the Hotel at reception Miss Frances is with the one's that were eliminated when Paul and Carol go by she sees them and said.

"Paul Carol congratulations on reaching the final, and with all my heart I hope you go a long way." Paul stops in his tracks and goes over to her and tells her

"I've enjoyed the little banter we have had, and thank you." He leans forward and plants a kiss fully on her lips, well if you could have seen her bright red and telling the others that she truly thinks they will do well.

That night Carol and Paul dine at the hotel, then relax in the Hotels bar and sit reflecting on the day's event. At about 10.30 it was off to bed and they stop outside Carols room and Paul is kissing her good night and that he would see her in the morning for tomorrow it was back home. Carol puts her finger on Paul's lips and he stops talking.

"I'm more relaxed now it is all over, would you like to come in and sleep with me tonight."

Paul turns the door handle and they go into the room with Paul kissing her, he kicks the door shout with the back off is shoe and he starts to unzip her dress walking forward towards the bed Carol the same is undoing the buttons on Paul's shirt and before long they are in-between the sheets and making passionate love.

They are making love for well over an hour and a half, they both lay back and Carol asks Paul.

"You will still won't to see me after we are back home Paul."

"What, you try and stop me you're the one for me. I've never felt like this before towards anyone, and if I make it or not, I will wont you by my side."

"I to have the same strong feeling for you."

"I've got your phone number, how about you come over a week today and you could stop at my house and meet my Mum and Dad."

All sorted and they both drift of into deep sleep both contented in each others arm. The next morning it was up and breakfast before they catch the 10.30am train back to Leicester and Nottingham. They are on the train and Carol is snuggled up to Paul, it seemed to fly by when the sign comes up in the carriage that they were pulling into Leicester, Carol is up and Paul goes to the door with her and gives her a last kiss he is telling her that he will ring her. They wave and the train starts to pull out off the station.

Chapter 6

Back home Paul comes in and his Mum and Dad are sitting on the settee when Paul comes into the room and plonks himself down on the chair; his Mum and Dad look at him and then each other. Paul sat there with that desponded look.

"Never mind son I bet you did your best." Is Mum feeling sorry for him, and then his Dad tells him.

"Never mind son there is always the printing firm." Paul looks at them both and suddenly smiles at them.

"Not bloody likely I am in the final and so is my girl friend." Well Paul's mum is jumping up and down and Paul's Dad is up and shaking his hand.

Then his Mum stops dead in her tracks and looks straight at Paul.

"Your girl friend is also in the final."

"Yes my girl friend we met down there at the show and if you don't mind I've invited her up next weekend and asked her to stop at my home so she can meet you."

"But we have not got a spear room for her." Then Paul's Dad nudges Mum and whispers well Paul has a bed. Well Mum looks at Dad and yes I think she clocked on.

"Well Paul if that's your wish so be it I will be delighted to meet her.

We all know what sort of joker Paul is and he tells his Mum.

"Thanks for that Mum and I'm sure her hump and buck teeth and glass eye will not put you off her." Mum sees the funny side of it and tells him.

"To get away with it." That night Paul gets ready and is off to Conrads to meet all is mates and to tell him how he got on.

Bob the landlord comes over and he is delighted at the good news of reaching the final and telling Paul that he has already set his recorder to record the programmes for with him serving and running the pub will not have time to watch it. Everyone is telling Paul that they could not wait to start watching the final. Then Paul asks Bob that if he liked he could do a little turn next week and if his new girl friend agreed she to could give a little turn, well Bobs eyes light up at the prospect of having two of the BBC Talent show on and tells Paul right on and I will pay you alright for it. All Bob is doing is just seeing the poster that he will run up, and asks Paul what is her name for the poster. Paul tells him that her name is Carol York.

The time is 9pm and Bob comes over to Paul and asks him if he would like to give a little turn.

"Yes if you would like me to, I'm up for it." Bob is straight up and onto stage.

"Ladies and Gentlemen, lets have a warm welcome, for straight off the telly how own Mr Paul Young."

Paul is up and onto the stage.

"Hello and its good to be back, don't forget to set your recorders for the final you won't be disappointed with the new BBC Talent show. They are whistling and cheering Paul and then he starts.

"Did you here about the three vicars talking about the problem with bats in the belfries, the first one said I catch them drive them miles away and release them. But after a few

Why Me

days they are back. The second Vicar said I fire a shotgun into the air and it scares them away but after a few days they are back. The there'd Vicar tells them I catch them one by one baptise them, and I never see them in church again.

"What did they pay the gipsy in when he won the lottery? Traveller's cheques."

"What's brown smells and giggles, tickled onion?"

"What bird is always out of breath? A puffin?"

"Where do toads put their coats? Croak room."

"I've got a one man dog. A one man dog. Yes it only bites me."

Hamish the Jewish tramp is walking down the road when, Coeing pulls over in his Rolls Royce.

"What happened Hamish?"

"Fell on hard times you haven't got £5. For a bed have you." Coeing said. "Bring it round in the morning and I will have a look at it."

"A man turned up for work 4 hours late, his Boss demanded a proper answer to why he was late. The man said I just broke down on the way to work. The boss said did you manage to repair your car. No said the man it was my dog it had just died, not my car and I just broke down in tears."

"What do you call a Manchester City supporter with a bottle of champagne?"

"A waiter. Bum-bum."

"Irish man being mugged by four skinheads, one was going through his pockets and only finds forty pence, the skinhead said is this all you have. The Irish man tells him. I thought you were after the fifty quid I've got in my Willie's."

"Well that's it from me hope you will be in the Conrads next week for you will have me plus if I can get her the only one who also is through to the final of the BBC Young Talent Show. Miss Carol York." Well they are all clapping and stamping their glasses on the table. Paul comes off and is straight to the bar for a drink.

"Thanks for that Paul here is something for your trouble." Bob passes him an envelope and pulls him a pint on the house. Paul goes and sits with his mates and to be sure the talk is all about Paul and the trip to London.

Paul is there till 11.30pm; he suddenly looks at his watch and makes his excuses to leave, for he promised Carol that he would phone her. Outside Conrads Paul starts to walk home and he phones Carol. She answers the call and Paul straight away apologises for the late call and tells her that he was on stage at Conrads.

"You're really truly hooked on this comedy lark Paul."

"I no baby but I've spoke to my Mum and she will be delighted to put you up and meet you next Saturday. And I hope you don't mind I've told Bob the Landlord that you will give a little turn next Saturday."

"That's OK Paul I will think of something appropriate for this so Called Conrads, miss you Paul, I must go for you have phoned me and I'm in bed."

"Sorry about that love I miss you to, love you and I will phone you where and when I will me you from the station." With this he hanks up and heads for home.

The week seemed to drag and mid week Paul sees the poster up inside and outside of Conrads that Bob had put up. Welcoming this Saturday his to top guest off the BBC telly programme.

Saturday soon comes round and Paul is standing on platform one waiting for the train from Leicester to arrive. Dead on time the train comes in and people start to embark off the train Paul is looking all around and then the train pulls away. The people start to thin and still no Carol then at the far end of the platform Paul sees Carol standing with her overnight bag. Paul goes running up to her and shouting out her name, well Carol sees Paul and she her self goes rushing towards Paul, they fling their arms round each other and are in a full embrace. It's if they had not seen each other for years the way they were kissing.

They jump into a taxi and it was off to Paul's home, on arrival Paul shouts for his Mum and she comes out of the kitchen and sees Carol.

"My you are a lovely girl Paul has told me all about you." Paul's Mum goes and kisses her on the cheek and tells her that it was lovely to meet her.

"Thanks for that, I'm sorry Paul has not tolled me your name." then Paul butts in.

"Sorry Carol this is my Mum Pat, Mum this is Carol."

"You don't say Son, Carol if you would like to you can call me Mum or Pat." Mum smiling at Carol. Then down the stairs comes Paul's Dad, he sees Carol and comes over to her.

"Hello Carol I'm Paul's Dad Jim, please to meet you." He kisses her on the cheeks.

"Thank you Jim and it's a pleasure to meet you."

"Away with Jim if you would like to you can call me Dad." Then Paul tells them that he will just show Carol her room so she can put her things away. Paul shows her to his room and he closes the door behind them.

"This is it baby my domain on that computer there I've sat and learned all my jokes and thinks for my act."

"You have a large bedroom Paul she is looking round when Paul puts his arms round her and starts to kiss her and they fall onto the bed and are kissing for about 5 minutes when Paul tries it on.

"No not in the day time your Mum could come up at anytime, you will have to wait I'm not going to suddenly disappear."

"Sorry love but this feeling it's if I want you by my side all the time."

"What do you think I feel like being in Leicester and you're here in Nottingham, things will work out lets just have a little patient."

"You're right but love is truly a cruel thing in someway."

They go back down and sit with Paul's Mum and Dad; they tell them that they are both going to do a little turn at Conrads that night. Well Mum looks straight at Dad and tells him.

"Your taking me out tonight there is no way that I will miss Carol sing and Paul is comedy thing, so you had better start to get ready."

"Get ready but it is only 1-0-clock."

"Well you will have to start by ironing your shirt and press that tatty suit of yours." Well Dad at what Mum had tolled him, just sits there with mouth wide open.

"Don't worry you will look fine by the time I have finished." Mum with that cheeky look, and looking at Carol.

That night Paul Carol and Mum and Dad catch a taxi, but just before they came out they are watching the start to the new BBC Young Talent show. And Mum and Dad are memorised at seeing Carol and Paul being introduced at the beginning of the show. Before they leave Mum makes sure that they are recording the programme for you can bet a bottom dollar she will be watching it when she gets back.

Why Me

They arrive at 8.30pm and Bob had reserved the front seat for Paul and his guest, Paul introduces Carol to Bob. Well Bob in a way seemed to bow when he shakes her hand. The time was approaching 9pm and that was the end of the programme on the telly, and they started to drift into Conrads and into the concert hall.

Paul noticed that people were looking at them and pointing, well the truth is known he had the feeling that they had been watching the telly before they came out. He turns to Carol and points this out

"Have you noticed that people are looking at us?" Paul looking at the crowed, and where he had seen them.

"Yes I suppose its one of those feeling of being famous, just think it will be like if one of us ends up winning the competition."

And before Paul could answer Bob the Landlord is up and on the mike.

"Good evening Ladies and Gentlemen, yes you have it those who have just watched the first show on the BBC you will have noticed we have here at Conrads two of the contestant. Yes two and the first to give you a little starter we have how own Paul Young and after we have all the way from Leicester Carol York, so put your hands together for Paul Young.

Bob leaves the stage and Paul stands up and onto the stage.

"Good evenings Ladies and Gentlemen are we alright." holding the mike out towards the audience, and all reply by clapping and cheering.

"What a week I've had down London recording and I bet some of you tonight have watched the first round, and you have seen the wonderful Carol York." Well they are all clapping when he mentioned Carol name.

"Well she is here tonight and I will not take up to much of the time because I truly believe you are going to really be taken back by her wonderful voice thank you." They are all clapping and cheering and shouting out Carol's name, Carol stands up and gives a wave to the audience.

"Right I had better make a start or I will be out of time."

"A man and a giraffe walk into a pub and order 2 pints, they sit drinking till closing time and stand and start to make their way out, very tipsy. Just before they get to the door, the giraffe collapse in a drunken stupor with legs all over the place. Then the Landlord said "Ho you can not leave that lying there," the man replied. "It's not a lion it's a giraffe."

"What's Dracula's favourite coffee, a decoffin-ated?"

"What do you call a Manchester City supporter with a bottle of champagne, a waiter?"

"Man goes to a house and knocks on the door, a man answers and the tramp said. "Have you a bit of cake, the man said, "Why?"

"It's my Birthday, I'm an old soldier."

"Have you been to the front," Asked the man.

"Yes said the tramp but there was no answer."

"Did you here about the pianist who kept banging is head on the keys, he was playing by hear."

"Why did the punk cross the road?" "Answer he was stapled to the chicken."

"A man puts an ad in the local lonely hearts club, asking for a wife and within a week he had 100 replies all from men saying you can have mine."

"Two men were hiking in the mountains when one of them suddenly stops and takes of his hiking boots and puts on trainers. The second man asked. "Why have you done that?" The first man answers, I thought I heard a bear."

"You can not out run a bear even with trainer's on."

The first man grinned and said. "I don't need to outrun the bear only you."

"Cannibal went on holiday and came back with one leg missing, is friend asked. "Did you have an accident on holiday? "No said the cannibal, went self-catering."

"That's all from me folks I'm sure you are all waiting for your next guest, so its see you later love you all and thank you." Paul goes off the stage with an overwhelming applause and cheering. He sits next to Carol and they are chatting for 10 minutes and Paul noticed that the concert room by know was starting to get rather full. He terns to Carol and he tells her that the.

"Next attraction must be you." Carol turns and looks and sees that one or two have spotted her and are pointing and smiling at her.

"God look at them they must think I'm a star." Paul reassures her by telling her.

Why Me

"You are love and I think the late comers have just seen you on the telly."

Then Bob is on the stage and telling all of the audience that I bet some of you have seen the next guest on the telly tonight, so please give a Conrads big welcome to the one and only Carol York from Leicester."

Carol takes the mike of Bob and tells them all that they are wonderful for the welcome you have just given me and I would like to start by singing one of my favourite artist number by the one and only.

"Witney Huston I will always love you." She stands and looks at Paul wile waiting for the music to start.

She is singing it to perfection and Paul is mesmerised by her, Paul's Mum turns to Dad and is saying that she is very good. But even Dad is just glued looking at Carol perform on stage. She carries on giving them a little classic and also rock, they love it when she gives a little bit of Lulu, and rock-an-roll. She is fully at it song after song and before you know it she had song for well over an hour when she finally gave her last song

"Thank you ladies and Gentlemen I would like to finish with a song, Dance with my Father again. By Luther Vandross." She starts singing and looking at Paul's Dad and Mum, she seems to memorise the audience with her voice. Paul's Dad sits there and Mum looks at him and she can see that he had come emotional that the words she is singing. He sits there and the tears are running down his cheeks. After the song she bows and tells the audience that she had loved being at Conrads and wish them all her love and a safe journey home. Well if you could heard the applause and clapping and cheering that seemed to last forever, she comes and sits next to Paul with the sound of the audience still applauding her.

"You were fantastic sweetheart just listen to them, and don't think you are coming here again and out doing me." Paul planting a kiss on Carol.

She sits there and thanks them. Well Mum turns to Dad and asked him.

"Did you like that dear."

"Not bad." Answer Dad.

"Not bad you had better wipe those tears off your face." Mum smiling at him.

Then to top it up Bob the Landlord comes to their table and he is straight to Carol.

Why Me

"Anytime you would like to do a gig here just phone me I will pay you top dollar.

"Thanks for that Bob I will consort with my boyfriend and ask his permission. You know don't won't to upset him." well Paul answers.

"I do the jokes around here." With a big smile and he kisses her on the cheek.

They sit there and the last orders bell rings out, Paul goes and refreshes all their drinks. And at 12.30 am. The taxi is waiting outside for them.

Chapter 7

They are back home and they go into the living room, Mum and Dad can not stop praising Carol on her performance that night at Conrads and even Mum told her.

"My Paul's got his hands full to beat you love."

"Thanks for that Mum and I will see you tomorrow."

"You certainly will love, come on Dad let's get to bed and leave these two alone." Mum and Dad retire and Paul and Carol and are on their own, Paul asks Carol if she would like a drink.

"Have you a drink of white wine before we retire."

"Coming up sweetheart." He goes and fetches the wine, and he has a can of larger. They sit there on the settee and are reminiscing on the night at Conrads.

"You are good Paul I just don't know how you can remember all those jokes."

"It just comes to me It's if I'm just reeling them of a piece of paper that I have just read."

"What about me, did you like the songs that I did." looking at Paul for a little reassurance.

"You have no problem if you keep the audience looking and memorized at your singing and voice, I think I stand no chance."

"Thanks for that Paul." She kisses Paul on the lips and tells him that she is ready for bed.

They start to go up stairs and Paul turns off every thing has he went, they are in Paul's room and they start to undress and get into bed they lay there and have arms rapped around each other. They are talking sweet nothings in each others ear and telling how much they love each other. And before you know it they were both fast asleep, it was properly all the excitement on the night and exhaustion.

The next morning Paul wakes about 6.30am and turns and puts his arms around Carol, with this she turns and is facing Paul they start to kiss and after about 10 minutes they are having full sex, all the time they are telling each other how much they love each other.

After they lay there and look out of the window, when Carol said to Paul.

"I wish we were one, I'm going to miss you so, when I go back to Leicester." Paul sits up looks turns so he is looking straight at Carol with his arm still round her and tells her.

"If I win this contest what I'm going to do with the money is look for a place for me and you." Carol pulls him to her and plants a kiss on him and Paul can feel the tears on his face. He pulls away and asks her what was wrong.

"Nothing Paul I'm so happy that's all."

"Silly girl lets stop in bed till you have to go."

"Oh yes I can just see your Mum Sunday just saying to your Dad the little ones must be tiered." Carol gently tapping Paul and smiling.

That Sunday Paul shows her around Nottingham till it was time for the return to go home. At the station Paul is waving to Carol as the train pulls out of the station he is telling her by lifting one hand to his ear that he will phone her.

Before you know it the day had come for the return to London for the big day, Paul had phoned Carol and told her to meet him on

Why Me

the first carriage of the train. They sit holding and snuggling up to each other all the way to London. At the Hotel who do you think is there to greet them, yes no other then Miss Frances. What a difference this time it was a kiss on the check from Miss Frances and Paul returned the compliment and tells her it was lovely to meet her again.

They are shown into a special room set aside for the contestants and not long and all six are there and are sitting chatting to each other over a cuppa when Miss Frances comes into the room and starts the meeting off telling them all the preparation for the final. They are told that that morning at 11am, they will go to the studio to meet the host off the show and the time scale for the show. They are told that they will have a make up artist to assist them with their make up.

Miss Frances had noticed that Paul and Carol seemed to be closer together then last time, she asks the question when they were on their own before they drop their case off.

"You seem to be more closer then last time."

"Yes said Carol Paul is my boyfriend."

That's nice did you meet at the first auditions."

"Yes I suppose you could call it love at first sight." Carol looking at Paul and holding is hand. Miss Frances turns to Paul and she tells him.

"What ever the out come, you two are on a winner."

"Thanks for that Miss." They turn and head towards their rooms. They are on the same floor and they both go into one of the rooms' and Carol asks Paul.

"Do you thing we should give one of the rooms up."

"Suppose it would stop any tongs wagging." The day seemed to fly by and after the rehearsals at the studio they are in the bar at the Hotel and all the talk is about the contest tomorrow, they are joined by the others and it seemed to be well relaxed and informal. At about 8.30 pm they go into the Hotels restaurant and have dinner, Paul buys a bottle of champagne and Carol asks what the occasion was it for.

"Well have it now you never know we might not be in the mood tomorrow night." Carol eyebrows cringe at Paul. They retire at 10.00pm for an early start tomorrow with them having to be there at 9.pm for final rehearsals.

Why Me

8.30 am. The coach is here for them, they board and Paul tells Carol this was better than the mini bus. They sit on seats with table and start to look at the programme for the day; the first morning is to meet the crew and host then lunch, and the afternoon all about the time table and were to stand on stage with the final count down at 7.50.pm.

They are told their places of appearance Carol is fourth and Paul last, Paul turns to Carol and asks.

"Are you happy with the placing, you know being forth."

"I would have gone on first to get it over with."

"Yes you are right I mean I will have to sit it out till last."

Chapter 8

The programme starts dead on time and the first three go on Carol is standing waiting to go on when Paul comes over to her and puts his hand round her waist and is about to kiss her when she pulls back from Paul.

"Not now Paul not with this entire make up on, God I'm nerves."

"Come on now you go out there and give it to them if you do feel nerves just look at me and I will stick my tong out." Carol smiles at Paul and the same time the host calls out her name.

"Let's give a big hand for Carol York from Leicester."

Carol comes running onto the stage with the host hand stretched out looking at Carol and at the same time exiting to the left. She stands and the music starts this time it is a live orchestra and Carol smiles and starts her song. She had surprised everyone for she had not said what she was going to sing, it was a love song written by her only the orchestra and the producer knew. She sings it to perfection and when it came to a part that said I love you, she turned and looks straight at Paul.

Paul stood there and he can not believe his ears for the tune and the lyrics are very catchy, the truth is known he has tears in his eyes, she finishes and you should have heard the applause.

She bows and exits and is straight into Paul's arms and she is totally exhausted. She kisses Paul and as she did his name is called out. Paul stops kissing Carol but unknown to him he had lip stick all over his lips and powder on his face.

The compare finishes calling out Paul's name and he sees all the lipstick on Paul he pulls out a tissue and wipes the lipstick off Paul.

"Sorry about that boy she was good, I had to giver one a kiss." The audience laugh and Paul starts. All the time he is walking up and down and bringing the audience into some of the act right here we go.

"What happens when one jelly fish met another, he looks at the children in the audience and said they produce jelly babies?

"What do you get if you cross a chicken with a load of cement, he puts his hand to his ear and the children shout; don't know. You get a bricklayer. Well the children are laughing out load and so are their parents.

"What do you call a duck that trains to be a Doctor, same again waiting for the children, A quack."

"Why did the egg go to the jungle, it was an egg-ploer"

"What have you got when you have a taxman buried up to his neck in sand? Not enough sand."

"What do you call a Woman playing snooker with a pint on her head? Beatrix Potter."

Right kiddies, that's playschool over with now for Mum and Dad.

"Two cowboys were stranded in the desert and had not eaten for three days then one said. "Look over there that sure looks like a bacon tree."

"No Clint." The other said. "That sure ain't no bacon tree you're just seeing a mirage, on the account of we've been out here so long."

Why Me

"Well Jack I'm sure going to investigate anyhow." Said Clint, and he picked up is rifle and headed off. Hours later he crawled back dusty and bleeding with several arrows stuck in him.

"I should have listened to you Jack, you sure were right it weren't a bacon tree at all. It was a red Indian ham bush."

"Two cannibals in the jungle are feeling hungry; suddenly they spot a hunter strolling through the undergrowth. And they decide he'd make a tasty dinner for the two of hem. "We will eat half each." One tells the other, so they grab him and start eating. After a few minutes one cannibal said to the other. "How are you doing." His pal replied. "I'm having a ball." The other said.

"Stop eating so fast."

"One worker feet stunk so his mate tells him to change is socks everyday, after a week he said. "It's no good." "Why," said his mate. "I can't get my shoes on."

"How too confuse an Irish man put a shovel and a fork up against the wall and ask him to take is pick.

"Two men were relaxing in a nudist camp, one ask the other have you read Marx. They other replied. "Yes it must be these wicker chairs."

The audience are loving Paul's act and are in stitches, when Paul in is ear piece the producer telling him that is time is up and to finish.

"Well that's all for now folks I hope you enjoyed the fun we've had and don't forget kids to be in bed before the 10.o.clock horses Bye for now."

They are clapping and whistling and it takes the compare a few minutes to calm them down. He brings them all back on one at a time and they are taking their bows when he tells viewer the number to ring for the first contestant. One by one they come on till Carol comes and you should have heard the clapping and cheering. He tells the viewers Carol's number to ring and last comes Paul well the same load clapping and cheering just like Carol. He tells them the number for Paul to vote for.

After 15 minutes on showing clips of all the acts they had on that night came the results of the phone in. the compare starts, Carol and Paul are standing in the wings hand in hand then the compare starts.

Why Me

"Ladies and Gentlemen in 3rd place please put you hands together for Jimmy Fletcher." He comes out bows and waves to the audience, and then it came to second place.

In second place Susan Blanchard, she comes out and the same. Paul and Carol look at each other and they say at the same time "it's you." They have the feeling that one of them is going to be disappointed and they give each other a kiss just when the compare looks at the paper work looks up and looks straight at Carol and Paul.

"I don't believe this please give a big hand for Carol York." Well Carol jumps up in the air kisses Paul and go's running on Paul gives the biggest wolf whistle you have ever heard a clap, and turns to go and sit down. When the compare tells the audience.

"Also put you hands together for Paul Young."

Well Paul suddenly turns and he can not understand he go's slowly back onto the stage he had something up is sleeve but this seemed right he goes straight up to Carol and stands and holds her hand. Just when the compare was telling the audience that they had both pulled in the same score on phone votes, and it was up to the judges to find a winner.

Paul turns to Carol and goes down on one knee pulling out off is pocket a box which he opens and holding it in both hands and pointing it at carol asks her.

"Carol will you marry me for I truly love you so much." Well the tears are flooding down Carols face and she replies.

"Yes Yes I will." Well the whole audience are clapping and cheering and the four judges are just sitting there and can not believe what had happened. The compare had hands in is face and he to was crying.

Paul stands and they are in a full embrace and kissing, the compare looks at the two of them and asks the judges to give their verdict on the winner. One of the judges who is a little camp stands and he to had hands in is face tells the compare.

"How can we judge a winner when we are looking straight at two winners? God they are one they are both winners the viewers have gave us the winners both of them." The whole audience are cheering and chanting both, both are winners.

The Compare with hanky in hand asks the judges.

"Is this you verdict."

Well all four are shouting.

"Both winners."

The compare announces that the winner of the Young Talent Compatison is Carol York and Paul Young. The audience go wild Paul and Carol stand there hand in hand and are blowing kisses to the audience and the judges. After about five minutes they are standing back stage when Paul suddenly tells Carol.

"Bloody hell I've just realised."

"What's that?" Carol asks.

"The programme is live your Mum and Dad and mine will have heard me propose to you."

"Ho yes I had better phone them." Carol looking in her bag to find her mobile. And at the same time Paul is doing the same they both stand there on their mobiles and they seemed to be getting the same answer from their Parents congratulating them on winning and Paul's proposal. They leave the studio and are back in the Hotel when Miss Frances approaches.

"Carol and Paul I've a message from the production Manager asking if you could go back to the studio just before you go home tomorrow."

They both tell Miss Frances that there is no problem, and what time in the morning.

"I know its Sunday but would 9.am be ok."

"Fine we will be in the reception at 9.am." Paul telling her. That night Paul and Carol have a quiet drink in the Hotels bar and all the talk is about that evening's event and Paul's proposal. The time is approaching 10.30pm and they decide to turn in for they are very tiered with what had happened that night, back in their room they undress and slip into bed they are kissing and cuddling and before they knew it they had both dropped off to sleep. 8.am and the phone rings, Paul answer and the voice on the other end tells them that this was their early morning call. Paul thanks them and turns to Carol and plants a loving kiss on her shoulder she wakes from her slumber turns to Paul and they are kissing. Carol tells him.

"I can not remember going to sleep, the last think I can remember was giving you a kiss then I fell asleep."

"Don't worry love me to I was the same kissing then I had gone." Carol sees the time and tells Paul that they had better shake a leg for we

Why Me

have this meeting at 9am. They shower dress and head for reception at 8.50am, there to meet them is Miss Frances who takes them to a waiting Taxi and escorts them to the Studio.

9.15am and they are shown to the Production Managers office they go in and he stands with hand stretched out and tells them.

"Good morning Carol and Paul my name is James Wright and congratulations on the win last night, the reason I've asked you to attend today is for me to present you with these cheques for you performance for last night you might notice that there is a little extra for the forth coming wedding from the BBC. And secondly to help you with your future. You must know that you are about to be bombarded with all sorts of offers, that is why I would like to sign you up and become your agent.

I 'am one of the top superstar agent and have a dedicated staff who will look after all you're needs in the future, if you decide to sign I can guarantee you work and the chance to exceed over a million pound earnings each in your first year."

Well Paul and Carol just can not believe what they are hearing; Paul tells James could we have a cuppa over this and decide.

"No problem two cuppas coming up." He stand and leaves the room, the first thing Paul is opening the envelope with the cheque in and he sees the amount for £18.000.00.

"God they have given me eighteen thousand pounds." Carol opens her envelope and she tells Paul.

"Me to I've the same amount, that's £36.000.00 we have between us."

Then Paul asks Carol what about this offer to sign up with him, Carol tells Paul.

"If he works for the BBC and produces programmes for the BBC he must be big, but it's freighting at what he said that before we have done a years work we will be millionaires."

"Are we going to do it then." Asks Paul.

"Yes let's take the plunge." Just when Carol had said yes, James comes in holding the two cups of tea, sits back in his chair and asks the question.

"Well have you made your minds up?" Paul tells him.

"We have but I've one question."

"Fire away what is it." James asks.

"If possible could we work together for we are just about to set out on a new path way of marriage?"

"And we would like to stay together if we can, work on the same bill." Carol telling James.

"No problem." Pulling paper work out of his draw he passes them to Carol and Paul to sign. He tells them that for the next to weeks they have time to relax.

"You will be left alone for two weeks and I will start to put together a time table of work over the next 6 months, and will call you with the details in the second week." He tells them that they have done the right thing and he wishes them all the luck in the future, and shakes their hand.

Meeting over and it was back to the Hotel, they are catching the 2.30pm train Home and Carol asks Paul.

"Paul there is one thing I do not won't to do."

"What's that sweetheart?" Paul asking Carol.

"I do not won't to get off at Leicester and say goodbye." Paul thinks for a moment and asks her would you like to come and stay with me." Carol tells him.

"It would not be fair on my Mum and Dad, how about we have only two weeks lets spend lets say 3 nights with your Mum and Dad, then 4 nights at my home."

"OK let's do it that way." Paul kissing Carol, she is straight on the phone and tells her Mum what they were going to do. Her Mum tells Carol.

"You are a grown woman its fine by me." All sorted and it was decided that they stop at Carols house first; Paul is on his mobile telling his Mum, the arrangement that they had decided. Paul's Mum tells Paul the same answer what ever he decided they are with him.

The train pulls into Leicester station and they disembark they are walking towards the exit when someone recognized them from the show.

"Look its Paul Young and Carol York off the telly." Well everybody on the platform were looking and pointing at them. They smiled waved and carried on walking towards the exit with everyone stopping and looking at them. One or two were clapping and telling

Why Me

them well done. They leave and jump into the first Taxi.

"Blimey did you see that lot boy hope we are not going to get this with everything we do." Paul looking out of the cab and seeing them just looking into the cab when they pulled away.

They pull up outside Carol's house and Paul seemed to be a little nerves.

"Come on now Paul my Mum and Dad won't bite." Paul just smiles back at Carol. They go in and the first impression Paul gets is the size of Carol's house.

"What is your Dad's job an MP, with a big house like this?"

"You will meet him in a minute and no, he is not an MP, just a Director of a building firm." They go into the lounge and sitting there is Carols Mum and Dad. Carol tells them.

"Mum Dad this is my fiancé Paul, you seen him on the box last night."

Then Carols Dad stud up looked at Paul and said.

"So you're the bloke who going to marry my Daughter." Paul sees the size of Carols Dad and tells him.

"Yes Sir and to put things right could I have you're Daughters hand in Marriage."

"Bloody to true come here Son." Carols Dad hands wide for Paul to come and have a hug. Carol stands looks at her Dad and said.

"Dad pack it in, he's not one of your work mates you tease with." Paul just smile at Carol. The formalities over with, Paul and Carol go up to Carols room.

"I did not know you live in a great big house like this, your Mum and Dad will not mind about us being in the same room."

"No they are broad minded, anyway you're my boyfriend."

They sort out their things and come back down and into the lounge, Carols Dad asks Paul if he would like a drink and at the same time asking him to tell them what it was like at the BBC.

"It was tiring and we won over £36.000.00 pounds, on the night and we have been signed up with one of the top agents." Well

Carols Dad just sat there and trying to take it in.

"You're telling me that you have that sort of money, for just that one show."

"Yes and we have been told that over the next year we are guaranteed over a million pounds each in wages." Well Carols Dad nearly choked at what Paul had told him, he sat there and seemed to look at him and his Daughter in a different light. Then Carols Mum asked.

"What happens next?" Carol tells her Mum.

"We have this week off and after that sometime in a week's time they will contact us to tell us what happens next." Well Carols Mum and Dad just sit there trying to take it all in.

Over the week they stop at Carol's house then back to Paul's house. In the second week they receive a letter from their agent James Wright.

Chapter 9

Paul opens the letter and can not believe what he is reading, stands there and with mouth open just looks at Carol, she asks.

"What's wrong Paul?" All Paul did is pass the letter to Carol with out saying a word; she looks at it and the same she just looks back at Paul and can not believe it. All this time Paul's Mum and Dad are watching and the same think all Carol did was pass it to Paul's Mum. You guest the same she just stood there gob smacked at what she had read and once again just passed it to Dad. He looks at it and out load said.

"Hello Paul and Carol hope you are well and please find attached a programme of contracts that I have arranged. In three weeks time we have set up a 3 month contract at one of the top Hotels in Las Vegas for you and Paul to perform, the price you will receive is £125.000.00 each. Also a singing contract for Carol to cut a single song, plus one album to be cut on your return from Los Vegas.

Why Me

If everything is satisfactory please let me know on the phone number provide. Yours James Wright."

They just flop back onto the settee trying to take in what they had just read. Dad's straight into the kitchen and brings on a tray two cans of larger and two glasses of wine for the girls, he comes in and tells them.

"This calls for a drink here you are help yourselves."

The day goes by and Paul and Carol Are in bed when Paul suddenly sits up and tell's Carol.

"Let's get married in Los Vegas and take you're Mum and Dad and mine with us, it will be magic for all of us."

"OK Paul let's do It." turning and facing Paul, putting her arms round him and kissing him. Over the weeks they book the holiday for the four of them and the wedding that is going too beheld at the Little White Chapel in Vegas. Things are moving fast for Paul and Carol they seem to be in a world of fantasy, they have only 2 weeks to book everything and they did not forget to phone James Wright to tell him that they will accept the contract he tells them that they have two first tickets to Vegas, and the first thing they do is get onto the airline to book four more First class tickets for their Mum and Dad.

They have booked the Little Chapel of the West in Los Vegas; they go over and over again everything that they need. Comes the day to go to Vegas and Paul had hired a mini bus to pick them up and on to Leicester to pick up Carol's Mum and Dad. They arrive at Heathrow and they had butterflies, Carol asks Paul if he liked flying he tells her.

"Yes and No I like the take off and landing's but do not like the long bit in the middle."

The flight time is 11 hours and they land at 6.pm Vegas time. On the approach they see the strip with the stratosphere tower at the bottom of the strip; the runway seemed to run alongside the strip. They book into their Hotel which is the Imperial Palace, the receptionist when she sees the name and what room they were in gets on the phone and Paul wonders what she was doing and before long the Manage is at the desk and greeting them.

"Good evening MrYoung, and Miss York I'm the Manager and would like to at 10.00am tomorrow show you around and take you to the theatre were you are working And To give you all the details, if that is alright by yourselves."

"Fine at reception here then."

"That will be fine and I hope you have a pleasant stay at the Imperial Palace." All sorted and it was of to their room to refresh them self's up after the long haul flight. In their room the first thing they notice is the Queen Size bed and they even had a Jacuzzi.

"Boy, Carol we are going to feel like Royalty here." Carol comes over to Paul and she asks for a hug, he obliges and they are kissing and fall on to the bed, after about ten minutes they are fast on, they are asleep for an hour when there is a knock on the door. Paul goes to the door and there is Carols Dad standing there and asks Paul if they were coming down for a drink, Paul tells them that they will be there in ten minutes.

They go and join their Parents and it was a cosy Family chat with bar snacks for supper, Paul's Dad asks them.

"When do you start performing you act?"

"In three days time we are going to get married on Tuesday and start on the Wednesday."

"No honeymoon." Carols Mum asking. Carol tells her.

"When we have done here Paul is taking me to Hawaii for four days before we fly home." They are no late that night for they are all feeling the affect of the long flight and the time difference, and it is only 10pm when they retire.

The trouble is the time difference for they are up at 4am wide awake for back home it is 12.00 dinner time. At 10am they meet the Manager and he shows them their dressing room and a time scale of the show that they are in on Wednesday, Paul notices that he is on first and Carol at 10pm. All sorted and it was round the pool, the Sun was beating down and it is over 80f.

The day of the wedding Carol stops with her Mum so she could get ready in her white wedding gown for her wedding. It is at the Little Church of the West. The Church it's self is a lovely setting.

Why Me

Carols Dad is there to give her away, it's a wonderful occasion and there

Were even people gathered outside the Church to watch them come? It's if the word had got out that celebrities were getting married.

After the wedding it was back to the Imperial Palace for the reception for Paul and Carol were on stage the following night. The wedding and the day is an occasion that will live in their memories for the rest of their lives.

The night goes on and at 11.30pm Paul and Carol start to give their leave for they are on stage the next day. Everyone is wishing them all the luck in the future. They go up to their room and Paul stops outside their room and picks her up and tells her.

"This will after to do, I will pick you up in every house we require through our life. I love you so much Mrs Young." Carol smiles at Paul and he carries her into the room and puts her gently onto the bed.

The next morning they are up and are sitting in their room and both are rehearsing for the night ahead for they are going to perform on one of the biggest stages that they have ever seen. Paul looks at Carol and just comes out with.

"What other couples have done this the day after they are married, I mean rehearsing and all this stuff, I think I should be looking at you like this." Paul lifts his eyebrows in a suggestive way. Carol just tells him.

"You will after to wait till we are on how honeymoon." Then just smiles back at him. Come the night time Paul and Carols parents are sitting in the theatre waiting for them to come on. The first to come on is Paul.

He comes running onto the stage and starts.

"Boy look at the size of this place, are you all enjoying the entertainment." They all cheer and whistle at Paul.

"Have we any Americans in tonight." Well they all applaud and whistle.

"Anybody from England." Same again applaud and whistles.

"Ok if you are sitting next to an American just explain and visa versa, what's with this just going to put some gas in my car, gas its petrol.

And just going to put something in the trunk, trunk that's a suitcase, but they mean put it in the boot. And there is something wrong under the hood, hood that's the bonnet. Come on now lets get it right. We English love a fagot, the Americans think we are talking about a puff, shirt lifter, not something to eat, no don't even go there. Well here we go."

"Irish Pat gets a job with a big firm. The boss said to him your first task is to sweep the floor, and gives him a brush. Hold on said Pat I'm a University Gradate. OK said the boss I will show you how."

"You know when you're getting old, when you feel like the morning after. But there was no night before."

"Doctors have fount a cure for seasickness. GO BY PLANE."

"Young Lad, "Mum can I be good for 50 pence, Mum said. "No be good for nothing like your Dad." They are really into Paul's jokes they are laughing and some are holding their stomachs, clapping and cheering.

"You have heard nothing yet let's speed it up."

"Police arrested two kids one was drinking Battery acid and the other eating fireworks. They charged one and let the other on off."

"How do you find a man in a nudist camp? It's not hard."

"Woman." "Do you sell Viagra?" "Yes we do said the chemist". "Can you get it over the counter?" "I could if I take two."

"Herd about the new sushi bar that caters exclusively for lawyers. It's called SO SUMI."

"A man says to his Doctor, I can't stop singing green grass of home. The Doctor replies you've got Tom Jones syndrome. The man asks is it common. The Doctor assures him, well it's not unusual."

Why Me

"An idle Husband I've fount this great job huge salary company car and 10 weeks paid holiday. The wife says that great dear. Husband I thought you would like it you start Monday."

"The mother in-law has a new job, test pilot in a broomstick factory."

"A Zulu was driving a Ford Sierra and drinking a can of tango. When he was pulled over by a policeman the officer radioed base and said. Zulu Sierra Tango you are not going to believe this."

"Did you hear about the unemployed exorcist, his house was repossed?"

"Did you here about the flasher who was thinking of retiring, he said he would stick it out for one more year."

"Why has no woman gone to the moon, answer it doesn't need cleaning yet?"

"Why do woman have smaller feet then Men. So they can get nearer the sink."

"Two portly Gentlemen were standing in a pub when one said your round. The other said so are you fat basterd." Well Paul had done well on his first night in Vegas; he gives his goodbyes and leaves the stage with tremendous applause.

He comes off and stands just back sage when Carol comes up to him and tells him that you were fantastic, she tells him.

"I stood in the wings and looking at the audience and they were doubling up in stitches with some of the jokes. I do not know were you get them from, you seem to be in control all the time."

"Thanks baby I'm all in just look at me." Carol stands there and can see all the sweat running off Paul. Then it was Carols turn and she goes on and the difference, one minute the audience are in stitches the next just memorised by Carols voice.

She sings for over 40 minutes and comes off and Paul is there to greet her.

"Well done sweetheart they loved you." Paul and Carol go walking off and back to their dressing rooms.

That night they are in bed and are saying to each other that when they have finished their contract at the Hotel, the honeymoon looks very inviting. They kiss and cuddle and before long the both of them are fast asleep.

The next night it was the same but this time Carol was on first for they told Paul that they would like him to do the last performance at 10.30 till late so if he would like to change his material he could for at that time of evening there should only be adults so he could put a little slut into his performance. The time comes for Paul to go on and Carol kisses Paul, and tells him good luck and double them up with laughter. Paul smiles at Carol and goes running on.

"Good evening Ladies and Gentlemen is there any children in." Paul putting his hand to his ear and looking round and there was no answer from the audience.

"Thank fuck for that, they are alright the little ones but come on they should be round the pool during the day and we should all be entitled to throw the little angels in the pool."

"Boy it was bloody boiling round the pool today the temperature at 1pm was 115f. You could have thrown your potatoes in the pool and had mash potatoes in minutes. Anyway never mind about my day lets get cracking.

ARE YOU READY." Paul razing his voice, they all shout back. "YES."

"You have a very contagious disease, said the Doctor we have to put you in solitary confinement and put you on a special diet, of pancakes and pizza. The patient asks. Will that cure me? No said the Doctor it's the only fucking thing we can slip under the door."

"We have had a complaint said the policeman, about your dog chasing an old aged pensioner on his bike. Wasn't my dog said the man, he has not got a bike."

"Husband if I die will you remarry, yes said his wife. And sleep in the same bed, yes he would be my husband. And would you give him my golf clubs. No he's fucking left handed."

"Woman had decided to divorce her husband, why said her lawyer on what grounds. He only uses bad four letter language. Like what said the lawyer. Fucking cook wash dust and iron."

"Wife to husband, when you die where do you won't to be buried. Fucking on top of you said the husband."

"Polar Bear walks into a bar and asks for Vodka, and then there is a silence for 5 minutes, and Coke. Why the big pause said the barman. Dun no I've always had them."

"What's the fastest thing in the river? A motor pike."

Chapter 10

Paul is just going to start another joke when a man in the front row gets up and starts to go, Paul follows him and when Paul got to the end of the stage asks the man.

"where the fuck are you going." The man tells him.

"Just nipping to the toilet." Then Paul stands for a few seconds and when he is near the exit Paul shouts.

"Make haste will you don't have a tom-tit." Well the audience are looking at the man and you can imagine how embarrassed he was for he knew that at one stage he had to go back to his seat.

"Patient, I keep seeing spots in front of my eyes. Optician have you seen a Doctor. Patient tells him. No just spots."

"A man had been drinking all-night and driving everybody mad with his bragging, he tells them that he can imitate any bird you mention. The barman said how about a fucking homing Pigeon."

Just when he had finished he caught sight of the man returning from going to the toilet once again he follows him till he reached is seat, smiles at him and I think he knew what was coming next.

"You alright now I'm not going to embarrass you." Paul smiling at him, then he tells him.

"After having a good shit, must be very uncomfortable." Well they are all laughing at the man; I don't think anyone else will try to go after that.

"Did you here about Tom Thumb, Snow White, and Quasimodo, went to Blackpool for the day and went and seen a clairvoyant. Tom Thumb said I will go in and see if I'm still the smallest. He came out and told them he is. Then Snow White went in and asked if she was still the beautiful girl in the World, she came out and said she is. Then Quasimodo tells them I will go in and see if I'm still the ugliest. He came out with a face tripping him and said who the fuck is Mike Jagger." asked Quasi.

"Englishman Scotsman and an Irishman were in a Japanese Prison Camp when they were about to be flogged when a Jap asked the

Englishman what he wonted on his back. He replied, nothing. Then it was the Scotsman turn and same again what would he like. A little salt so it stings. Then it came to the Irishman and the same question. The Irishman said I would like the Scotsman on my back.

"My mates Dog s an engineer, Paul stands there and someone on the front row said "Don't be daft." Paul leans forward and said. He was you know, say bath time to him and he makes a bold for the front door." Well the laughter from the audience and clapping, and they are shouting for more.

"What's a cannibal's favourite pie? Steak and Sidney."

"Did you here about the Vicar who was on a Prison visit asked an inmate, you say you are here because of your beliefs. Why's that. The prisoner answers, because I believed the security guard was at the other end of the fucking building."

"A boy broke his leg playing football when the Doctor had finished plastering his leg. He asked will I beadle to play the violin after the plaster comes off. OF cause you will, replied the Medic. That's good I could not play it before."

Why Me

"A burglar broke into Scotland Yard and stole all the toilet seats, the police said that the detectives had nothing to go on." Well Paul is looking at the guy who went to the toilet and the audience were in tears. The guy just grins and puts his hands in whatever position.

"Did you here about the man walking by a farmer milking his cows by hand and the man ask the farmer what time it was? The farmer lifts the left tit up and then the right and tells him it's 9.30am. The man that night is in the pub and tells his mate about the farmer and telling him the time by milking his cow. Rubbish said the man, well he bets him £50 quid he could. The next day they both go and the man asked the farmer what time it was, well the farmer lifts the left tit then the right and tells them that if was 10am. There you go you who me £50 quid. Well the other man asks the farmer how he did it.

The farmer tells him that when I lift the left tit then the right I can see the village clock."

"A man who through bleach over is local priest was arrested for bleach of the priest." Well Paul himself his buckled up and saying to himself pack it in. this also triggered the audience with them seeing Paul prancing and doubled up laughing made them do it the same, they were holding their stomachs and a lot of them had handkerchiefs out and wiping tears from there eyes. Paul told them.

"Hold on to your seats there is more to come." He turns and looks at the side of the stage and Carol is standing there and is just clapping at Paul, he smiles looks back at the audience and tells them.

Well here we go again hang on to your seats."

"A guy walks into a shoe shop with to left feet and asked for a pair of flip flops."

"Quiz's show, a man was asked question on cricket. Who are England's best all rounder, he answers Ian Botham, who is England's captain, Alex Stuart, who's been hit in the face the most with balls. He answers Michael Barrymore."

"Doctor what should I do about my yellow teeth, Doctor wear a yellow tie." Then he gets the message to wind it up for he had run out off time.

"OK folks I'm afraid that that's it for tonight, but remember if you would like to book for another night's fun and laughter you can for I never tell the same joke twice. And by the way the guy on the front row who went on the toilet get you self a drink for you family, just tell the barman that Paul Young told you, for

Why Me

being a good sport, well that's it folks and in a traditional goodnight from Nottingham, SEE YOU ME DUCKS." Paul goes running off and waving at the audience and the reception he got was deafening. Standing in the wings waiting for him was Carol they go and sit in their changing room and Carol gives Paul a long tender kiss.

The time by now was approaching 1am. And they go for a drink in one of the bars and the reception from the customers was clapping at seeing them they order their drinks but I must admit the public gave them their own space and did not but in on them.

Both of them are really going down well even to the extent that a T.V company come to the last night of their 3 month contract to film the show for broadcast around the U.S.of America. Carol goes on first and sings her songs and Paul stands watching her, her voice is so enchanting that you are there with her on every note. When she had finished she comes of to Paul. Listen to them Carol they love you, go on give them one more this is your last night in Vegas.

She is back on to stage and thanks them all from the bottom of her heart, and just be for she goes she tells them that tomorrow she is off with her New Husband Paul Young to Hawaii, she out stretches her arm to Paul to come and join her he goes running on and plants a kiss on her they stand and the audience are clapping and whistling she tells them.

"Thanks a lot and hear to entertain you is My Husband Paul Young." She goes of stage backwards with her arm stretched out pointing to Paul.

Chapter 11

THE LAST SHOW IN LOS VEGAS

"Thank you good evening hope you are enjoying your stay in Vegas, did you her about this large muscular guy meets this Woman at a bar, they go back to his place. As they're kissing he starts to undress. After taking his shirt off he flexes his biceps and says. See that baby that's 1,000ib of Dynamite, the man then drops his trousers and says referring to his bulging thighs. That's another 1,000ib of Dynamite. Finally he drops his boxer shorts, after a glance the Woman runs screaming to the front door. The man asks why she is in such a hurry, she replied. With 2,000ib of Dynamite and such a short fuse, I'm frightened you're about to go off."

"What's the definition of a geriatric? A German who scores three goals in a game of football."

"A Man parked on yellow lines. A traffic warden told him to move his car. The man replied, why the sign says Fine for parking here."

"My uncle's hobby was collecting watches and clocks. When he died it took me six weeks to wind up his estate."

"Steve, why don't you like girls, said Bill. They're biased. Steve what do you mean, Bill it's always biased this, and bias this."

"How many drama writers does it take to change a light bulb? Two, one to put it in. The other to give it a surprising twist at the end."

"What do you call a Scottish cloakroom attendant? Angus McCoatup."

"What did the Judge say to the skunk? Odour in the court, odour in the court."

"Two TV aerials meet up on the roof one day; they fell in love and eventually got married. The service was rubbish but the reception was brilliant."

"Did you here about the Vet who told a Woman I'm going to have to put you dog down Madam. Owner, Oh my God why's that? The vet said, because he's fucking heavy."

"Why are Owl's clever than chickens? Because you never see a Kentucky fried Owl."

"Why did the archaeologist start to weep? Because he realised that his career was in ruins."

"A Consultant was doing his rounds in a Hospital, when he turned round and said nurse. Why is that man crawling along the floor? Ignore him, he's off his trolley, said the nurse."

"Woman to her friend. The good news is my husband likes Fashion. The bad news is he's a cross-dresser. The terrible news is he looks better than me." Paul is doing another fine act with everybody laughing their heads of when Paul tells them hang on to your seats you have heard nothing yet."

"A man, going out for a night with the boys promises his wife he'll be back before midnight, but doesn't get back home until hours later.

As he walks through the door the cuckoo clock in the hall cuckoos three times, realising it will wake his wife he cuckoos another nine times. He's proud of himself for having such a quick-witted solution even when smashed. The next morning his wife asks him what time he got in, midnight he tells her. She seems to accept his answer, whew got away with that he thinks. She tells him they need a new cuckoo clock. When he asked why she explains. Well last night it cuckooed three times then said, Oh damn, after four more cuckoos it coughed, cuckooed three times then giggled, cuckooed twice, then farted."

"What did the electrician's wife say when he came home late. Wire you insulate."

"A red Indian drank 50 cups of tea before going to bed. He was found next morning drowned in his tea-pee."

"A Taxi passenger taps the driver on the shoulder to talk to him, the cabbie driver screams, loses control, hits a Bus climbs a wall and does a flip before coming to rest upside down. Once they climb out of the wreck, the punter apologises profusely, the cabbie says it's not your fault this is my first day, and for the past 20 years I've been driving a Hearse."

"Did you here about the bus crash and forty football fans were killed. They all go to heaven and stand outside the pearly gates. St Peter comes along and asks, what they won't, they all shout out to come in. So St Peter goes to see God, God said what's up Peter. We have forty football fans at the gates. God said, we don't won't that many, only let the holly ones in. So Peter goes away. Twenty minutes later

Why Me

he returns. God said. Have they gone, Peter said. No but the gates have."

"I went into a shop asked the assistant if she had anything for stains on a tablecloth. She gave me a beetroot."

"A man walks down the street and enters a clock and watch shop. While looking round he notices a gorgeous sales assistant. He immediately walks over to where the woman is standing, unzips his fly and slaps his Willy down on the counter. What are you doing Sir, she asks, this is a clock shop. I know it is he replies. And I'd be grateful if you'd put two hands and a face on it."

"A butcher is in is shop when a Yob comes in and said. Gizza sausage rolls fat man, the butcher said. That's no way to ask for something. The butcher gives the Yob his apron and hat, saying you stand behind the counter and I'll show you what to do. So they swop places, the butcher says to the Yob, good morning butcher are you well. The Yob replies yes thank you what would you like. Butcher a sausage roll please. Yob FUCK of FATTY you wouldn't serve me."

"An elderly couple were stopped for speeding along the motorway. You were doing 90, the officer told the man behind the wheel. Rubbish said the driver no way was it 90. It was 60 and you know it. His wife piped up, oh ignore him officer, he's always argumentative when he's had a skinful."

"What's the difference between men and pigs? Pigs don't turn into men when they get drunk."

"Two little lads were talking in the playground, the first asks, do you know how old our Teacher is.? The other lad says, no but to find out we should look inside her knickers. Why's that? Asks his mate. Well in mine it says 4-6 years."

"A police officer runs up to the Chief Inspector at the scene of a bank robbery. They got away Sir He gasps. But I told you to put an officer on all the exits! Yells the angry Chief Inspector. The officer replied, but they left by one of the entrances."

"A policeman stopped a man and asked. Where were you between four and eleven? He replied Primary School."

"A Teacher asked a little boy what his Dad did for a living. The Lad replied that he wasn't sure, but that he thought his Father might be a collector of medieval musical instruments. Really, said the Teacher what makes you think that? The boy replied. It's the Police they keep coming round and asking him what he done with the lute."

"Woman says to her friend, My Husband was in the garden picking beans for lunch today and fell over and died. Her friend replies, goodness! That's just terrible. What did you do? The woman replies no problem I opened a tin of beans."

"What runs round a field but never moves? A fence. Bum-bum, do you won't more. Paul lifting his arms in the air. The whole audience are whistling cheering and clapping and shouting for more.

"OK Let goes for another quickie get ready and be on your toes."

"Doctor to his patient I can't diagnose the cause of your bad breath. I think it must be the drink. The patient, OK I'll come back when you're sober."

"A man was walking down the street with a chocolate bar on his hat. A policeman spotted him and cried out. There's a bounty on your head."

"Did you hear about the Pensioner who streaked through the main Marquee at the Chelsea flower show? He won first price for best-dried arrangement."

"Two drunks come staggering out of the Local Zoo, their clothes in tatters and covered in blood, one said to the other. That's the last time I try Lion dancing."

"What do you call an 80-year old man who has just made love twice in one night? An ambulance."

"Donald my poor Canary has just died of flu David, I didn't know that Canaries got flu, Donald, they don't he flew into a wall."

"What do you call a crazy blackbird? A raven lunatic."

"Who is the patron saint of bad-tempered footballers? St off."

"What do you call a Planet, which is populated by video recorders and cassettes? Planet of the Tapes."

"An Englishman Scotsman and an Irishman were given a test to cross a desert but they could only take one thing with them. The Englishman said I will take an umbrella with me. Why's that, to keep the Sun of me, and at night I can you'se it to catch the due init. The Scotchman said he would take a barrel of water with him so he could have a drink. The Irishman when asked said. I will take a car door with me. Why's that. So when it gets hot I can wind the window down."

"The actors Sylvester Stallone, Bruce Wills and Arnold Schwarzenegger decide to make their image a bit more high-brow by making a film about classical composers, sly says I'll play Beethoven. Bruce says, I'll do Mozart. Arnie says, I'll be Bach."

"Did you hear about the Irish wood worm? It was fount dead in a brick."

"What do you do when your washing machine breaks down? You slap the bitch."

"Notice posted in a golf club, would members please refrain from washing their dirty balls in the sink. The Stewards wife is quite willing to wipe them with a damp cloth."

"Why don't you say anything to someone who's stealing your gates? He might take a fence."

"Did you hear about the Welsh athlete, Dai Young, who covered 1.500 meters in 20 seconds? He fell down a mineshaft."

"What did the man who was sacked from his job on the dodgems do.? He took his Boss to court for funfair dismissal."

"Don't knock the Irish they invented the toilet seat? But the English put a hole init."

"Old farmer Ted pulled up his cart with a jerk, full of manure. Know he is up to his neck in his work."

"Chap walks into a barber's shop and asks, how much for a hair cut? The barber says £6.50 Sir. Man replies, how much for a shave? The barber says, that'll be 50p Sir. The man smiles and then answers, well shave my head."

"A man on honeymoon tells his wife, I must confess I'm a golfing nut I play Wednesday, Saturday, Sunday and Bank Holidays. It comes before everything. His Wife says I must confess, I'm a Hooker. He replies, don't worry, just grip the club and stand close to the tee."

"Girl, Daddy, can you make a noise like a frog, Please Daddy, well I suppose so, but why do you want me to do that. Girl, because I heard Mum saying she can't wait for you to croak."

The sweat is pumping out f Paul and he is not feeling alright, he slumps to his knees and is telling the audience.

"Well Ladies and Gentleman this is it I've done my time with you, it's over. I Love you

Why Me

all goodnight and God bless." The whole audience are standing and just clapping at the performance that they had just witness. In the wings Carol had seen Paul collapse and comes on to stage and they all are clapping and cheering for both oft them. She bends and asks Paul if he was alright.

"Fine sweetheart, just drained." He stands holding on to Carol and the applause is deafening. For two people so young and to have this sort of ovation is unthinkable. They both exit the stage waving at the audience and go back to their dressing room, once inside with the door shut, Carol once again asks Paul I he was ok.

"Yes sweetheart lets just go and have a relaxing holiday in Hawaii."

They retire to their room and are sitting on the balcony of their Hotel room with a class of champagne on the house when Carol looks at Paul and reaching out and holding his hand said.

"How can something like this happen to us, I mean we are both coming up to twenty sitting in a Hotel room in Los Vegas married and have money in the bank when back home, other people of how age have nothing."

John Bolstridge

"I don't know what to say or coment, we have followed how dream and achieved it, is it fate or destiny. I just don't know."

They sit there looking at the starry night sky and are fully content. The truth is known they are both looking forward to the relaxing trip to Hawaii, in the morning.

Chapter 12

THE HONYMOON AND THEN BACK HOME

The next morning it was all the goodbyes and management telling them that they would be back for they had been a great success. All the formalities out of the way and it is off to Los Vegas International Airport.

They travel Business class and they both feel like Royalty, all the fuss that they were receiving from the flight crew wishing them all the best in the future. In away it's if they knew who they were, and we all know how celebrities are treated.

They arrive early afternoon and it was a hot and sunny day, they unpack and head for the pool for some sunbathing and relaxing refreshment.

They stop round the pool till about 6pm, and then they decide to go back to their apartment for a rest before the evening. By 8pm they have showered and ready for the evenings entertainment at the Hotel restaurant and at the front there was a stage were all the acts preformed for the guest entertainment.

After they had eaten and having a few well deserved beverages, well when you have been performing at a top Hotel in Vegas, this was a welcome break.

Then suddenly something they were not expecting, onto the stage came the evening's entertainment Compare and really set Carol and Paul back.

"Good evening Ladies and Gentlemen would you all put your hands together for two night we have two top Young entertainers from the U.K. Carol York, and Paul Young, or should I say Mr&Mrs Young."

Well the whole room are looking at them and they are all clapping, and then came another bomb shell.

"If I ask them nice would you like to here and see them perform." The compare arms stretched out pointing to where they were sitting; the audience are clapping even harder. Paul tells Carol go on love give them one song, she sighs and tells Paul.

"Well only one and one only." She stands and bows to everyone and makes her way to the stage. She goes up to the band and is whispering if they could play Whitney Huston song I will always Love you. The band nod and they start the intro; carol goes and stands in place and all the time looking at Paul belts out the song. Well Paul is totally enthralled in her singing it's, if this song and with Carol singing it seemed to hold him in a magic spell.

She finishes the song and taking the encore and applause; she lifts the mike and tells the audience now it's my Husbands turn. Paul stand and goes running down to the font and waving, up onto the stage takes the mike of Carol gives her a kiss and she starts to walk off.

"Good evening Ladies and Gentlemen, what about that song then I has got a cracking woman there." Paul looking at Carol she shouts you be careful no funny business we are on honeymoon don't forget. She grins at Paul with that look that said it all, behave or no supper that night. The audience start to laugh at what Carol said to Paul.

"A I'm the funny one, well give them and inch and they." Paul is about to say, when Carol points her finger at him, the audience laugh and Paul sheepishly.

"Sorry my sweetheart, anyway let's get cracking."

What do you call a hairdresser attacked by Japanese in World War 2. Pearl Barber."

"Why doesn't Cinderella play Golf? Because she keeps running away from the ball."

"Why did the chicken cross the road? So he could see his flat mate."

"The boys had arranged a fishing trip, but Fred hadn't turned up. He finally arrived late and his pals asked him where you have been. Sorry lads but it was a toss up whether I came fishing or stayed at home with the wife. That shouldn't have kept you. One of his friends said. It took 27 tosses, said Fred."

"A successful man is one who makes more money than his wife can spend for him."

"Why did the orange make an appointment with the Doctor? He wasn't peeling well."

"Blimey, it's raining cats and dogs out there, said Bill. Looking out of the kitchen window. I know said his Mum entering the room. I've just stepped in a poodle."

"How do police manage to chase criminals underwater? In a squid car."

Why Me

"What's the difference between Match of the Day and a toilet seat? A Man never misses Match of the Day."

"Tom said to Fred, when I got home last night there was a packet of Persil on top of the telly. I asked why. She had Persil on the T.V. she said it was because there was no aerial."

"What is you job, asked the Prosecuting Council in Court. I'm a Locksmith, replied the defendant. So could you tell the Court what you were doing in the Jewellers shop at 2am when the Police arrived? Asked the Prosecutor. I was making a bolt for the door, the man answered."

"What's an ig? An Eskimo's home without a loo.

"A Woman asked her Husband to take more interest in their son. What do you mean? He asked, well take him to the football, talk to him and get to know him. He needs a Father figure. Later the man walked up to the boy and said. Your Mother says we should get to know each other better. I'm your Father what's your name."

"A horse and a chicken are best friends and live on a farm, one day they're playing when the horse gets stuck in a ditch. The chicken goes to get help. Finding the farm empty, he borrows the farmer's BMW. And drives to the ditch. He ties a rope to the bumper, reverses and pulls the horse out. A few weeks later the chicken has the misfortune to fall into a mud pit. He cries out to the horse to save him. The horse trots over, straddles the pit and tells the chicken to grab his Willy, the chicken reluctantly does this and the horse walks backwards, lifting his friend to safty.the moral of this story is. When you're hung like a horse, you don't need a BMW to pick up a chick."

"What do you call a Scottish Chef.? Dinner Ken."

"What do you call a Woman in the distance? Dot."

What did the electrician's Wife say to him when he came home after midnight? Why are you insulate?"

"Two old men met in the pouring rain. One said, it's great weather for duck's. the other replied. Yes foul."

"What do you call a cowboy who left is glasses in the saloon? Squint Eastwood.

"How do you describe the mood of a pig in a truck on its way to the bacon factory? Disgruntled."

Why Me

"Man in a pet shop, Do you have any cats going cheap? Shop assistant, no all our cats go meow." Paul is up to his elements and just doe's not know when to stop, well Carol suddenly shout's to Paul to wind it up.

He looks at her and it was if he had come out of a dream he looks at the audience and tells them.

"Well it looks like her in doors wants me it is my honeymoon, well one last joke."

"One morning a wife asked her husband, if he wanted any breakfast. No he replied, the Viagra I took has ruined my appetite. Several hours later the woman asks, so do you feel like some lunch? No it's still not worn off, came the answer. Later the woman tried again, you must want some now. No still not hungry. Well for fucks sake will you for heavens sake, let me out of bed, she said I'm absolutely famished." Well Paul tells them that that was it.

"I've got to get back to my lovely wife thanks for listing and I hope we meet up again in the future, good night and God bless." Paul bows and the clapping and cheering from all that were in the restaurant was defining.

They have a few more drinks and at 11.pm they leave with all the occupants in the restaurant applauding them as they left. Their

John Bolstridge

Hotel is on the sea front and they go down to the waters edge and are strolling along a moon lit beach. The sea is calm and a gentle ripple can be heard, they walk arm in arm with Carols head leaning on Paul's shoulder.

"I love you so much Paul, will we ever be on our own or will we be forever in the lime light."

"Come on now we are on our own now look at the setting, we will always find a place and time to be on how own." They both face each other and are kissing in one off the beautiful places in the World, with the moon beams bouncing of them.

The 4 day's goes by and they are left alone to finish their honeymoon bar the odd autograph hunters. It is time for the journey home and they sit in the dispatcher lounge of Hawaii International. The plane takes off and they are both looking at the island of Hawaii and the volcano from their window, it's a long and tiring journey home and they arrive and head for their new home.

They see Carols Parents first and tell them about there honeymoon and having to work in the Hotel they stopped at. And then it was off to Paul's Parents and the same they were telling them all about their stay in Hawaii.

Why Me

They are stopping over at Paul's parents and at the night time they go to Conrads to see Paul's friends and Bob the Landlord who gave Paul is start to stardom. Well if you could have seen them all they were all over Paul and Carol, well its not every day that you have celebrities in you local watering hole. Bob pulls them a drink and straight away tells Paul that they were on the house, thanks for that Bob would you like me to give the boys a turn.

Well Bob eye's light up at what Paul had told him and Bob tells him give him half an hour and he will introduced him.

Chapter 13

THE HOME COMING

After about half an hour Bob like he always did puts his thumb up to Paul and goes on to stage, Paul had noticed from the time they had come in the concert room was stating to swell. The truth is known Bob had done a few phone calls.

Bob on the stage taps on the mike and asks them to be quiet for a moment, for he had something to say.

"You all know Paul and we have met his wife Carol, they won the BBC Young Talent of the Year contest and have just finished a 3 mouth tour of Los Vegas. To warm you up this winter evening Paul is going to give us a little session so please put your hands together for the one and only Paul Young. Bob hands the mike to Paul with one almighty cheering and clapping from the audience.

"Good evening." Paul looking round to a packed house there was not a seat to be had anywhere.

"Where the bloody hell has you all come from, is there someone on famous tonight after me." Well one or two shout out yes your wife Carol York.

"OK then just one joke from me and we will have her on." No shout the audience give us a good session.

"Only kidding but it will be up to my wife if she is not tired with all the house work and cooking and cleaning while I sat on the settee hard at it looking at the football results."

"A man walks into a swanky seafood restaurant where customers choose live food from a tank in the dinning area, which is killed and cooked in the kitchen. Gervaise the Head waiter comes over and the customer spots a green furry squid and orders that, this saddens Gervaise as the squid is a mild manned creature that had lived in the tank for years and has become a bit of a pet. But because the customer is always right he catches it and takes it into the kitchen. There he lays the floppy creature onto the chopping board where it lies limp and forlorn. He lifts his cleaver, but doesn't have heart to kill it and breaks down in tears.

Hans the German washer-up hears the sobbing comes to help, he takes the cleaver from Gervaise lifts it above his head but then realises that he can't kill the creature either. Which goes to prove?

That Hans that does dishes can be soft as Gervaise with mild green furry limp squid."

"What do you put on a pig's face if he is suffering from pimples? Oinkment."

"What happens when pigs fly? The price of bacon goes up."

"Why was the computer in so much pain? It had slipped a disc."

"How do you know when a computer is annoyed? It has a chip on its shoulder."

"What is rhubarb? Celery with high blood pressure."

"A man who got a job as a fork lifter in a warehouse drove into a brick wall his Boss surveying the damage said; right this will cost £500 pounds. I'll be stopping £5 pounds a month off your wages to pay for it. The driver sighed, what a relief I've finally got job security."

Why Me

"A man with five earrings in each ear, a nose stud. Eyebrow ring and lip stud. A walk into a pub and the barman says. I can't serve you Sir you're too pierced."

"My wife had plastic surgery last week the bank removed her credit card."

"What's the difference between a trumpet and an onion? No one cries when you chop up a trumpet."

"Have you heard about the new burglar-proof houses? They're called Surelock Homes."

"A nudist camp is a place where the peeling's mutual."

"What do monsters eat for breakfast? Dreaded wheat."

"What do you call male teabag? A Hebrew."

"Woman My husband drove me to drink, Pal, really? Women yep don't' know how to thank him."

"George Michael went to spend a penny and came back with two coppers."

"A man and a Woman walk into a pub with a Lion, all three go up to the bar and the man says to the barman. Three pints of bitter,

John Bolstridge

please and I'd like a ham sandwich and my wife would like a cheese roll. The barman say's isn't the Lion hungry? The man replies, do you think we'd be standing here with it if it was?"

"Hear about the pregnant bed bug? She's having a baby in the spring."

"A tourist in a museum was looking at a dinosaur skeleton. The curator walked up to her and said. It's 23 million and 18 years old, you know. Impressed by his knowledge the woman asks the curator how he could be so precise. The curator replied. Well it was 23 million years old when I started working here-and that was 18 years ago."

"A solider goes to the front line in World War one. There a hard line sergeant asks him. Have you come to die? No said the man I came yester-die."

"Man in the butchers shop got the sack for putting his cock in the bacon slice her. The Manager also sacked the woman bacon slice her.

"Every Friday night a man goes into the same pub orders three pints of beer and sits at the same table while he drinks from each in turn. When all three are finished he leaves. After a few weeks the curious Landlord asks why. The

Why Me

man replies. Its simple my two brothers and I used to meet every week for a pint. But now that they both live abroad I like to keep up the tradition. One Friday he goes in and only orders two pints. The Landlord is shocked and asks him timidly. Has some thing happened to one of your brothers? Oh no. the man said. They're fine, but I've stopped drinking."

"Napoleon is sitting on his horse demonstrating the professionalism of his army in front of all the crowned heads of Europe. As he shouts, left turn right turn. The men give an immaculate display of formation marching. After a while, Napoleon shouts halt! All the men snap to attention all except for one man who marches right through the ranks and up to Napoleon. What are you doing you horrible little man.? Asks Napoleon. Oh sorry says the Squady I thought you said Walt."

"A man is walking past a graveyard dead at night, when he hears strange music coming from the graveyard. So he reports it to the Police. An Officer arrives and the man says. Can you hear that strange music? The Officer walks amongst the graves and suddenly said. It's OK it's coming from this grave it's only Bach decomposing."

"A Bride-to-be asks her Doctor to recommend a form of birth control. He says; orange juice.

Puzzled she asks. Before or after? He replies. Instead of."

"First Woman; so tell me, Susan what about your Husband? Does he exercise? Second Woman: Yes Sandra, He's very dedicated. Last week he was out four night running."

"The Funeral Director solemnly asks a grieving Widow what inscription she would like to have engraved on to her Husband's head stone. She replied. Fred is dead. He said. But you are allowed to have three more words engraved at no extra charge. She replied. OK then Fred is dead, Volvo for sale."

"Two sausages are in a pan and one said to the other. It's hot in here. The other says. Fancy that, a talking sausage."

"On the morning after returning from honeymoon, a man cooked his Wife breakfast in bed. Have you noticed what I've done he said. Oh yes, she said. Good, he replied, that's how I won't my breakfast cooked every morning."

"Did you hear about the Dentist who married the manicurist? Within a month, they were fighting tooth and nail."

"A couple brought a water bed-but then they drifted apart."

Why Me

"A man phones his Doctor and says. I feel like a game show contestant. The Doctor replies, then come on down."

"A man took his dog to the Vet and asked him to cut off its tail. Why do you won't me to do that? Asked the Vet. The man replied. The mother-in-law is coming to visit us tomorrow and I don't want anything to make her feel welcome."

"What do you call a bra lying on the floor? A booby trap."

"What do you call a hare with its paw stuck in a beehive? A honey rabbit."

"What did the Mexican push his wife of a cliff? Tequila."

"A man went into a pet shop and asked to buy a wasp. We don't sell wasps Sir. Said the shopkeeper. Well said the man, you've got one in the window."

"Why do barbers make god drivers? Because they know all the short cuts."

"First Woman do you file your nails? Second Woman no after I've cut them I throw them away."

John Bolstridge

"I beg your pardon, sad the man to a Woman as he returned to his cinema seat. Did I step on your toe on the way out? Yes you did. Replied the Lady, crossly. Good said the man. I'm in the right row."

"If crocodile skin makes a pair of shoes, what do you get from a banana? Slippers."

"A man goes to the chiropist and says to the girl assistant. What are you doing after work? She says. I've got to do my Husbands dinner. The man says. Tell him you're working late. She replies. Tell him your self he's doing your feet."

"A bloke goes into a pub and orders three glasses of whisky. As soon as the barman puts them down in front of him he drinks each in one gulp. I shouldn't be drinking all this, he said. Why's that. Asks the barman. Because I've only got 50p on me." The whole place is in tears at Paul's jokes when Carol shouts to Paul.

"Paul no more you've been at it for an hour." He looks at her and he nods back to her. Then he tells everyone.

"Well that's it for me for know I hope you enjoyed the jokes and we both hope to see you again so from my lovely wife Carol and my self God bless and we love you all." Well everyone is one there feet and cheering clapping and whistling for Carol and Paul. He stands and looking up at the bright stage lights, he can not believe what has happened in the few months from his first appearance at Conrads, for he had gone from here to the BBC and on two Los Vegas.

The future looks bright for Carol and Paul, it just shows you stick to your dream and if Lady Luck shines down on you, then anything can come true.

THE END.

FOR THE LOVE OF BRANDY

For the Love of Brandy.

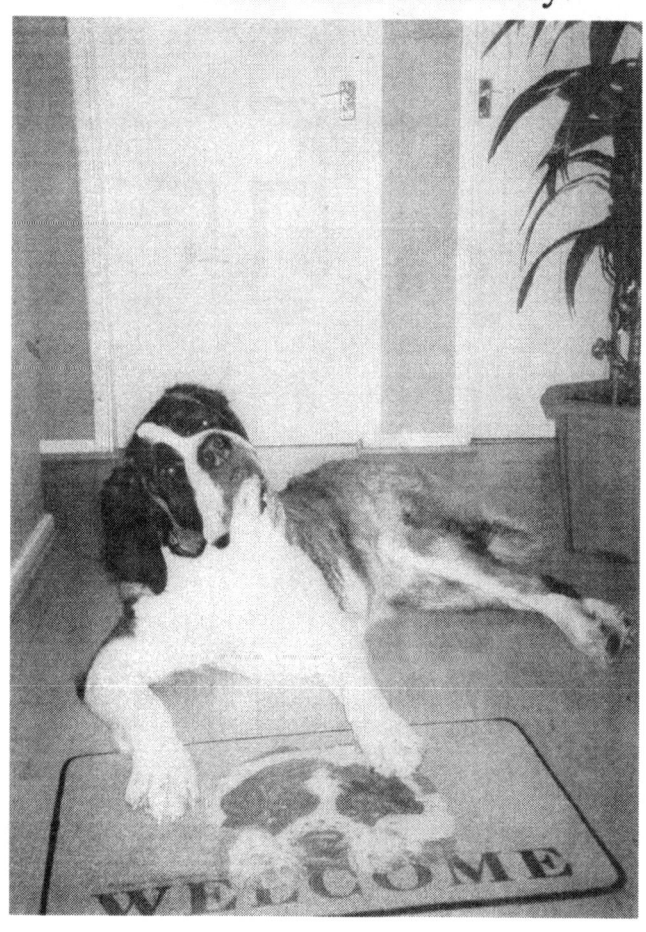

Chapter 1

This story is about the life of Brandy Snaps a St Bernard and the love from one man, who from the first time he set eye's on her the bond between a man and dog, is overwhelming. We pick up the story of John Bolstridge the Father of Mandy, who is married to Lyndon and they live in a small Lincoln village called Washingbrough.

Mandy's Father lives in Nottingham, over 54 miles away.

One evening Lyndon sitting in the spare bedroom on his computer, and surfing the net. He comes across a site advertising St Bernard dogs, and starts to read all about them. He's so intrigued by the stories of St Bernard's that over dinner he mentions the site to Mandy.

"This evening love I came across a site all about St Bernard's, did you know that 2.500 years ago the St Bernard in the alps at the Great Saint Bernard Pass used to guide and protect the monks of the monastery of Great

Saint Bernard Pass. And later started to rescue travellers within the Pass. The dogs at the time were not the St Bernard's of today, no what the Monks did was cross breed the dog they had with Newfoundland dogs. Thus the St Bernard was born, and did you know that with crossing them you had two types. The long hair and short hair.

"What's brought all this on?" Mandy putting down her knife and fork and looking straight and Lyndon.

"Well with us living here, we have room and there are fields all around us."

"Don't tell me you're thinking of getting a great big thing like that." Mandy sees the look in Lyndon's face.

"You are aren't you?" All Lyndon did is sit there and smile back at her.

"Well if we did get one, you will have to build a kennel for it."

"You're telling me you would like one."

"Well if it will stop you pestering me for one." Lyndon comes over to Mandy and plants a kiss on her forehead.

Why Me

"I'll go on line and see where the nearest dog breeder is to us. Lyndon off and back into the bedroom to see what he can find on the net, leaving Mandy to finish her dinner on her own.

Lyndon is on the internet, when he comes across the site of Ken and Sylvia's St Bernard's breeders. Located in Farnborough only a few miles from them. He calls Mandy to come and have a look at this. Mandy comes into the bedroom and she asks.

"What's up?"

"Come and have a look at this web site, Ken and Sylvia's Kennels, they are selling new pups at only £300 pounds. That's cheap for a St Bernard." Mandy sits next to Lyndon and they sit reading all about the dog and the up bringing of them.

"Let's go and see them tomorrow night." Lyndon starting to get excited at the thought of owning a St Bernard.

"Well give them a ring first and tell them that you are interested in purchasing a St Bernard."

Lyndon on the phone and talking to Ken the owner of the Kennels and he gives Lyndon directions to get to the Kennels, Lyndon thanks him and tells Ken that he will see him at 6pm tomorrow. The following evening Lyndon waits for Mandy outside Marks&Spencers where she worked in Lincoln. She sees Lyndon's car and walks over to him. She sits down in the car looks at Lyndon and tells him.

"Well let's get it over with."

"Come on Mandy it's a puppy we are going to purchase, not visit the dentist."

"Drive on I'm only kidding." They set off for the Kennels and Mandy directs Lyndon with the rout given to them by Ken, they pull up outside a disused village school and Mandy tells Lyndon. That this was the place.

They park up and gingerly walk up the narrow path that leads to a side door, and they knock, a few bolds click and standing there is Ken.

"Don't tell me you are Lyndon Yates the one who is interested in purchasing a St Bernard."

"That's right Sir and this is my wife Mandy." Introductions over Ken invites them in, the first thing they notice in the room that Ken was leading them through was. All the large bags of of dog feed the smell were one of; well Ken did have over 17 St Bernard's. That slept in the school over night, even outside there was a large dog kennel that looked like it would

Why Me

be more at home in a Zoo, the cage not the dogs.

Ken leads them through the room and into a large opened plan room which served as a sitting room come kitchen, and when you looked up you could see an open plan bedroom on a floor that you could see from below. Lyndon asked Ken.

"What did this used to be before you converted it?"

"This used to be the school assemble room, I brought the school 10 years ago and converted this part and sold the rest off."

In from the back door comes Sylvia with 4 large St Bernard's following her, Ken asks her to come and see Mandy and Lyndon. Who have come to see about buying a St Bernard? Sylvia starts to walk towards them and the four St Bernard go trotting over to Mandy and Lyndon. Well two of the St Bernard's are long hair males and two smooth hair, well both Mandy and Lyndon get a Royal St Bernard's welcome. One of the males jumps up onto its hind legs and looks Lyndon straight in the face, well before Ken could tell the dog to get down it gives Lyndon one of the biggest kisses he had ever had.

"Major down," Ken shouting at the dog, well the dog goes back onto all fours and Lyndon stands there with drool dripping of his nose ears and everywhere. Mandy stands laughing at him when one of the dogs starts to shake its head and drool goes flying all over Mandy. Well it was Lyndon's turn to stand there laughing.

"Sorry about that but it will be one of the things you will have to live with when you own a St Bernard."

They sit down and Sylvia goes to make a cuppa, after a few minutes and they are all sat, even the St Bernard's just lying there looking at Mandy and Lyndon. Ken starts asking them why they wanted a St Bernard, Lyndon tells Ken.

"Well I've been thinking of getting a dog but I can not stop thinking about is owning and loving a St Bernard." Ken nods his head at what Lyndon had said and starts to tell them.

"My dogs are only £300 pounds, the Kennel club don't like me selling them so cheap, the average price is well over £400 plus. But I only sell my dogs to people who agree to come and bring their dog back once a month for the first year, so I can see that the dog is being feed and looked after in the right way."

"I don't mind that, but why once a month?" Lyndon asking Ken.

"St Bernard's in the first year are not to be exercised to vigorous, there bones are weak and to much exercise could deform them, and there is one thing that I must stress. Don't let you dog play with others." Then Mandy asks.

"Why this was so important."

"Well St Bernard's don't know that they are large dogs and lets say you are on the park and there was a collie running lose, well a St Bernard would love to run and play with the collie. It would not think about its own bones just the other dog." Then Ken tells them that Major's mate Bella is expecting in two weeks." Just then there is scratching at the back door, Sylvia goes and opens the door and in comes Bella a smooth coat St Bernard.

"Here comes Mum now." Bella coming over to Ken then looks at Mandy and Lyndon sitting there; she gives off a load bark at them. Ken tells her to be quiet. Bella goes over to Mandy and Lyndon but this time they are both ready for her and make sure she does not give them a kiss. But they still get droll over their hands, Sylvia smiles at them and gives them a towel to wipe their hands on. This is when Ken asks the question.

"What sort of dog would they like Male or Bitch."

"Male St Bernard, long hair." Lyndon stroking Bella.

"Well if she has two males one will be yours, but if she only had the one Male then I'm afraid the first one s spoken for, would you still consider a Bitch."

"Yes." Came the answer from Lyndon. They sit talking for hours about the dogs Ken even told them about St Bernard's having web paws this was to help them in deep snow from stopping them dropping to deep in the snow so that they could not walk, they were just like us humans if we walk in deep snow we use snow shoes that look like tennis rackets on your feet.

Chapter 2

Then Mandy looks at her watch and tells Lyndon that they had better go for it's well past 10.30pm, they stand and Ken and Sylvia show them to the door. Lyndon and Mandy are just getting into their car when Ken shouts that he will phone them when Bella is ready to give birth. Lyndon starts the car and they wave goodbye to Ken and Sylvia. Just down the road on their way back home Mandy turns to Lyndon and said.

"God the smell did you notice it." Mandy blowing a sigh of relieve.

"Notice it what do you think with having 17 of them in there at night." All the way back home all the talk is about St Bernard's and the two weeks wait they have.

Over the next few days Lyndon is busy digging a 14ft by 8 ft patch in the garden ready for concrete to be delivered for the dog kennel, and run for their new arrival in the near future. The base down and Lyndon erects the wooden hut and run with wire mesh and felt roof, it takes him all day and by the time Mandy arrived home from work the job is complete. Mandy comes walking down the path and notices the new dog kennel.

"My you've made a good job there Lyndon." Mandy walks inside the run and into the 8ft by 5ft hut; she opens the door and tells Lyndon.

"It's lovely, shell we move in here and let the dog have the bungalow."

"It's taken me a few days to complete, let's hope the dog likes it."

They stand admiring Lyndon's handy work, when the phone rings Mandy tells Lyndon that she will go and answer it. Inside she picks up the phone and on the other end is Mandy's Dad.

"Hello sweetheart, everything ok at home."

"H'l Dad yes, I've just finished work and I'm ready for a bath, you're not going to believe this Dad but Lyndon and I have ordered a dog. And any day now we will know what sort, a Male dog or Bitch."

"That's nice what sort, poodle cocker." Mandy's Dad had a golden cocker spaniel male called Rocky.

"Well I hope you are sitting, a St Bernard."

"What you mean one of those dogs that are like a Pony."

"Not that big Dad, Lyndon's heart is well and truly looking forward to its arrival."

"Yes and lets hope he takes it for long walks", well Mandy explains all about walks and the bone structure of the St Bernard's and all the information that Ken had told them.

"Well in the end it's your decision." They make small talk and after 10 minutes Mandy tells her Dad that she was going to get a bath.

That night Mandy and Lyndon are settled down watching the box when the phone rings.

"Who's this at this time of night?" Lyndon getting up of the sofa, he picks up the phone and asked who is calling.

"Hello Lyndon Ken here just phoning to tell you that Bella had gone into labour early, so if you would like to be here for the birth you had better get your skates on."

"Ok on my way." Lyndon slams down the phone and shouts to Mandy, as he runs into the bedroom to get dressed; Mandy comes into the bedroom asking what all the fuss is about.

"It's Bella she's Gone into labour don't stand there get dressed."

Well both of them are hurriedly getting dressed, anyone would think that someone was giving birth, both dressed and it was straight to the car. Lyndon goes rushing off with wheels skidding and a screech of tyres. About a mile down the road and Mandy asks Lyndon to slow down, we will be on time, ten minutes and they are there with them both rushing up the path leading to the school, they knock on the door and Sylvia answers.

"Come on in you're just in time, they go into the kitchen and Bella is lying there and Ken is just helping Bella and he is pulling the first pup out. He wipes it and shows it Bella then puts it in a small basket under a heated light, he turns to Lyndon and tells him that it was a male a few minutes later and another one is born. Ken wipes it and once again he shows it Bella, who licks the pup's face, Girl Ken informing them.

"They are so small and cute." Mandy amazed at what she is witnessing. After about an hour all the pups are born, in all Bella had 6 Bitches and one Male. Lyndon looks at Mandy and tells her that it looks like a Bitch for them.

Mandy tells Lyndon that they will still love her; they both look at the litter and one St Bernard lies there and cocks its little head to one side.

"That's the one there Lyndon do you see her." Mandy trying to point at the one she had seen.

"Do you mean the one with its head on one side looking at us?" Lyndon also looking at the little pup and pointing.

"Yes she's so little and fluffy, just look at her it's if she wants us to take her home." Mandy just can-not take her eyes of her.

"That will be in six weeks my dear." Ken putting the pups onto their mother's nipples.

"Six weeks, that's a long time." Mandy looking at Ken.

"It will soon elapse, and then you can take her home."

"But how will you know witch one is how's." Mandy looking a little concerned.

"Don't worry, if that one there is the one you want so be it I will not forget."

Lyndon and Mandy stay till well past 9am, and then they decide to go, telling Ken if it was alright to come up every other day. Ken tells them they are welcome at any time. On the way home they stop of at their local the time being only 9.20am they know that the landlord will serve them their local is the Ferry Boat, and Lyndon goes to the bar and orders a pint, he turns to Mandy and asks her what she would like.

"Make mine a Brandy after all that, wait a minute Brandy that's it."

"That's what." Lyndon paying for the drink and passing it to Mandy.

"Brandy that's the name we will call her, Brandy snaps." Lyndon burst out laughing.

"That's what you get at the fair, Brandy snaps."

"Well I think it is a good name."

"OK Brandy it is we will have to start to get something's together, like Ken said in six weeks will soon pass."

Over the next few weeks Lyndon and Mandy go to the kennels and watch Brandy get stronger and bigger, she still hold's her head on one side every time you speak to her. One night Mandy sits there holding Brandy when the dog suddenly sits still on Mandy's knee

Why Me

and puts her head on to one side, Mandy sits smiling at Brandy when all of sudden she feels a warm feeling on her legs. She looks down and Brandy is urinating on her, she picks Brandy up with her still peeing and gives out a small scream. Lyndon and Ken sit there laughing at her.

"Well she likes you." Lyndon trying to contain himself.

The time has come for Brandy to leave the kennels and Lyndon and Mandy go up to the old school house after work to pick Brandy up, at home they have everything you can imagine for the dog. Basket food plenty of it, the time is 7pm and the weather is warm for mid June. The Sun has been beating down all day and the temperature is well into the eighties, they knock on the old school house door and are holding hands.

It was if they were waiting to take home their first born, both were excited at the thought of taking Brandy home.

Ken shows them through and all the pups come running up to them, Brandy pushes her way through and jumps up Lyndon's leg. At six week she is quit a large puppy Brandy looks like a big fluff of wool, Lyndon stands making a fuss of all the dogs. All the time Ken is stressing all the time on points of feeding pups and things to watch out for, he truly is a St Bernard breeder and wants all the best for all of his dogs.

Lyndon picks Brandy up and they say their goodbyes to Ken and Sylvia, they put Brandy in the back of the car with Mandy and they pull away with Ken and Sylvia waving to them. This is the start of bringing up Brandy Snaps. In the back of the car Brandy sits looking round at her new environment and the sound of the car engine is something that she was not use to and sits shivering. Mandy can feel Brandy's shivers and picks her up to comfort her at the same time telling Lyndon.

"God she's shivering Lyndon." Brandy cocks her head onto one side if to tell Mandy to help her, she strokes her and all the time trying to give her comfort that everything will be alright.

They are soon home and Mandy carries Brandy into the bungalow; the first thing Brandy did is wee on the hallway carpet. Well Lyndon straight away starts to tell her.

"Brandy you could have done that outside" All Brandy did is sniff all-round the hallway and then she flops down in the corner of the hall and starts to whimper. Mandy starting to get worried at seeing her.

Why Me

"What's wrong with her?"

"Ken told me that she will go through this sort of thing; don't forget she is away from her Family and Mother. For the first six weeks of her life she had been eating and sleeping with her brother and sisters."

Mandy goes to pick her up and enters the lounge, all the time talking to Brandy.

They settle down to watch TV Brandy is fast asleep on Mandy's knee when she suddenly realises.

"I've just thought Monday and Tuesday are alright as I work half a day, but Wednesday is my full day in work. What are we going to do with Brandy?

"What about asking your Dad, it's his day off work."

"Yes but Nottingham to Lincoln is over 50 miles, 100 round trip." Mandy stroking Brandy.

"Well give your Dad a call he might doggy sit for us while you are at work." Mandy tells Lyndon that she will phone him tomorrow when she is on her break.

That night they turn in just after 10.30pm, Brandy is on the bed at the bottom. It was only about 30 minutes that they had been in bed when they here Brandy whimpering, at the door, Mandy pokes Lyndon in the back and tells him that Brandy must wont to go outside. Well Lyndon mutters gets up and goes and stands at the door just with his underpants on, Brandy goes outside turns and stands there with her head on one side and looks at Lyndon.

"Go on you daft dog do your business standing like that." Brandy no more than settles down on the path and closes her eyes and starts to fall a sleep. Well Lyndon can not believe it looking at Brandy fast asleep while it's his turn to start shivering. He picks her up slams the door behind him saying out load.

"This daft dog thinks I'm going to stand at the door while it sleeps." He puts Brandy onto the bed and climes back into bed and snuggle up to Mandy. Then Mandy tells Lyndon.

"Lyndon can you remember when we first seen Brandy lying on her Mums front leg."

"Yes WHY."

"It's this feeling that I have, don't thing me silly but have we done the right thing."

"What are you on about right thing?"

"It must be the Mother instinct that woman must have you know with us seeing her with her Mum and brothers and Sisters, and then we come along and take her away from her environment."

"You are silly if everyone felt like that then no dog would leave it's Mum and us humans would not have them and where would that leave the dog breed, almost extinct.

Mark my word Brandy will soon lose that feeling she had with her bothers sisters and her mum, don't forget that she is a dog and not a human."

"You're right love but."

"She looked so content do you think she will be ok on her own." Before Lyndon could answer Brandy comes and jumps onto Lyndon's head and starts to bite at his scalp.

"Get off me you daft dog its bed time not play time." Lyndon trying to lay her down at the bottom of the bed, but Brandy grabs

Why Me

hold of his arm and with all four paws starts to nibble at his arm.

"Mandy please sort this dog out." By now Lyndon is out of bed and stands there with Brandy still hanging on to his arm, well Mandy turns the light on and bursts out laughing at Lyndon standing there looking pathetic.

"Come her Brandy, we don't want to go upsetting your Dad to much, she wraps the blanket round Brandy and snuggles down with her on the pillow. Not long after and all three are fast asleep.

The next morning Mandy is getting Lyndon's breakfast the time is 7.30am, and Brandy is outside playing on the grass.

Chapter 3

"What time are you having your lunch Lyndon, I leave for work at 12 and Brandy will be on her own."

"I'll come home and see her at 2pm, so she will be on her own for only a couple of hours."

"Lyndon kisses Mandy and Brandy goodbye and he reminds Mandy to call her Dad about Wednesday, Mandy sits in the garden with Brandy watching her play with her toys. Mandy thinking to herself looks at the size of her legs and paws, at 6 weeks she looks like a little pony on stilts.

Then Mandy is brought back from her deep thought by the phone ringing, she stands and tells Brandy to be good while she answers the phone. Well Mandy starts to walk into the house and Brandy follows her and sits next to her while she answered the phone.

"Hello Mandy here."

"H'I sweetheart it's you Dad how are you and what's more how's my little baby."

I'm fine and Brandy's fine to, I'm clad you phoned because I want to ask you a favour."

"Fire away what it is." Dad waiting for the question.

"Well on Wednesday that is you day off work, and Lyndon and I were wondering if you would come and doggy sit for us. It's the only day that Brandy will be left on her own and." Before Mandy could finish her Dad butted in and told her.

"You bet I'll catch the 8.45am train, then the bus and will be there by 9.50am."

"You've soon worked that out."

"Well you're Mum and I was discussing it and it will make a break for me to get out and into the country side for the day, Wednesday it is then."

"I'll ring you from work to make sure everything is alright."

"No problem sweetheart."

Over the phone Mandy tells her Dad all about St Bernard's and not to walk them to much in the first Year, Mandy's Dad was surprised at what she is telling him about what they eat and the do's and don'ts.

Wednesday morning soon comes around; John Mandy's Dad is up at 7am by 8 am he is on his way to the station for the 8.45am to Lincoln. He stands on the platform and it is a warm and sunny day he is thinking all the time what a nice day for walking the dog, dead on time the train pulls into platform 5 and John boards the 45 minute journey to Lincoln.

The train thunders on with the sound of the wheels hitting the joints and points making a clickerty clack, so much which John starts to nod.

He opens his eyes looks at the field and closes them again; he's soon fast a sleep then suddenly over the telecom comes the words.

""Next stop Lincoln all change this train terminates here." John jumps up wiping his eyes.

"That was quick." he looks at his watch and the time is approaching 9.25am, he is saying to himself that Mandy told him to go to the bus station just outside the station and catch the number 5 to Washingbrough.

John catches the 9.30am and by 9.45am he is walking up to Mandy's bungalow, he looks under the pot where Mandy had left the key. He opens the door and there sitting in the hallway is Brandy who stands and starts to wag her tail at seeing John.

"My you're a beauty Brandy cocks her head to one side, and still stands there looking at John. Then she suddenly bounds forward and although she is only about a foot high at nearly seven weeks she has quiet a push on her when she hits your legs.

John picks her up and Brandy whimpering and kissing John at the same time he is stroking her and giving her the love that any pup deserved. The truth is known this is when man and dog bond for life; it's if there was a little magic or something between them both. For John was not the top dog in the pack but Brandy loved his company.

He's sitting on the sofa with Brandy on his knee when the phone rings, John answers.

"H'I Dad how's my baby then."

"She's fine my she's a lovely dog." John looking at Brandy as he talked to Mandy. Brandy sits in the comical way that makes you smile, head cocked to one side and sitting with her hind legs sticking out front.

Then all of a sudden Brandy dashes out of the lounge and John can here her barking outside, he shouts out her name and Mandy asks what was going on. Then Brandy comes in and stands there completely soaked.

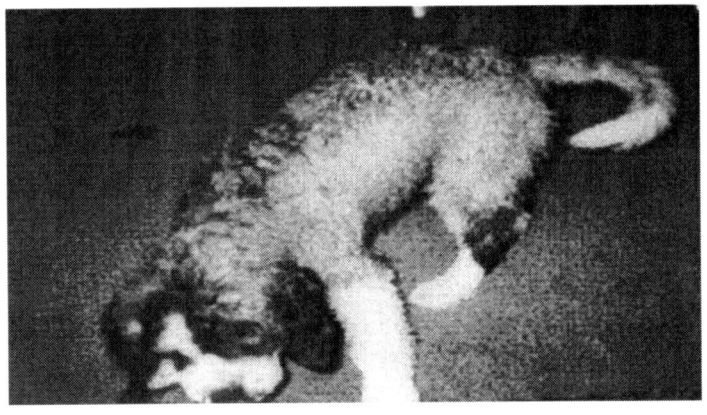

"What happened Dad, Mandy sounding concerned?"

"Just a second." John puts the phone down and goes to have a look; he comes out of the back door and sees the postman standing at the gate.

"Is this you dog?" the postman asked.

"No it's my Daughters, why what happened."

"Well this great big thing came bounding towards me and with out thinking I turned and knocked the water barrel over, I'm afraid it

Why Me

went over the dog." this brought John to tears and laughter at seeing the postman standing behind the gate and Brandy standing there looking sorry for herself. After John had calmed down a little he apologised to the postman, telling him that Brandy was only seven weeks old and that she was only a puppy.

Well the postman himself felt silly at knocking over the barrel and he to start to apologise.

"I'm sorry to; you see it was my postbag that caught the barrel." Then John suddenly remembers that Mandy was on the phone, he tells the postman that he had to go and tells the postman not to worry it was a good laugh. He said goodbye to the postman and goes back into the bungalow to the phone, were Mandy is still waiting on the end of the line.

"What's happened Dad." John explains to Mandy about the water barrel and poor old Brandy getting a good soaking, in the end even Mandy laughed and sees the funny side of it and starts to laugh herself.

John comes of the phone and gives Brandy a good wipe down, all the time talking to her. He settles down with Brandy next to him on the sofa, Brandy jumps down and brings John one of her cuddle toys. It's a big bunny rabbit Brandy offers John it and when John had hold of one end Brandy starts a tug the other end with her teeth firmly gripping the rabbit. John gently starts to pull back saying to Brandy.

"Its mine." Well before long Brandy is growling and pulling harder and John starts to pull harder to, then all of a sudden the rabbit's ear rips off. Well Brandy stands there spitting out cotton wool, and John is telling her what will she do when her Mum gets back home and sees the rabbit earless. John puts the rabbit in the dustbin and gets Brandy's lead, stands in the hallway and shouts Brandy to come they were going for a walk. Brandy comes running up to John and jumps up onto John's legs.

"Brandy steady, one of these day's you will knock someone over. Lead on and it is off for a short walk round the block, John would love to take her into the fields. But he had been warned about walking her to far, Brandy walks along side John and everybody passing comment on how beautiful she looked. John feels proud at walking her and getting all the attention. Going by some workmen digging up the road John over hears one of the workmen telling another.

"Look at the size of those pups paws." John looks down and he is thinking to himself.

"Yes and to think what size she will be in another Year." The Sun shining down makes

Why Me

John feel that the trip today was well worth it, little did he know but this is the start of every Wednesday. His day off would be the beginning of his weekly trip to see Brandy.

Walk over and John sits waiting for the clock to reach 2.30pm, for this is the time to catch the bus back to Lincoln bus station and the train back to Nottingham. He looks one more time at the clock and it is time to go, he stands and goes into the hallway were Brandy is lying he crouches down and starts talking to Brandy.

"Well it's time you're Grandpa was off you be a good girl, your Mum will be home soon."

John stands at the door and looks back at Brandy who sits there with her head cocked to one side looking at John. Well John shuts the door and starts to walk up the path and the feeling he gets at leaving her, starts to overwhelm him so much that standing at the bus stop all he can think of is Brandy sitting there watching him leave.

The bus pulls up and John still stands there in a daze.

"Lincoln mate." The voice of the bus driver brings him back to reality, and he boards the bus and all the ways back to Lincoln all he can think of is Brandy.

It's the same on the train he sits there swaying to the clickerty clack of the bogies and soon he is fast asleep, and no guessing what he was dreaming about you've got it Brandy.

You would not think that just on visit could have such an affect on one person and a dog, but the bond that started that day will last for a life time with memories. John over the years had well over 5 dogs but never a feeling like this, sometimes you can have the same feeling for an animal just like another human.

I personally have know one man who lived on my road when his dog died it affected his so much that within 6 weeks he had died himself, it is said he died of a broken heart.

Anyway let's get back to the story about Brandy, with the Lincoln to Nottingham train; just outside Nottingham the conductor announces that the next stop will be Nottingham.

This brings John out of his sleep and he stands wiping the sleep out of his eyes.

One the platform at the station John's Wife had finished work and had come to me him of the train; John steps off the train and sees Margaret.

"Hi love she's a smash, you'll have to go and see her."

"Who how Daughter." Margaret teasing John a little.

"The St Bernard." John cannot stop talking about her, all the way to the pub for a little refreshment its Brandy this and Brandy that.

"What about our Daughter is she alright." Margaret asks.

"She's fine." they sit there over a drink, and John is on about is next Wednesday his day off. Well Margaret tells John that next Wednesday she to is off work, so we can go together to Lincoln to see Mandy. John is about to say what about Brandy, when Margaret plants a kiss on his lips and tells him.

"And your new baby Brandy." John smiles and he goes to order another drink.

The following Wednesday both Margaret and John are up early and are off to Lincoln, they are both talking about what they will do when they get there. John is telling Margaret that he can show her a lovely walk through a wood that leads to some fields.

"One minute young man the only thing that I will be looking at is shops in Lincoln with

Mandy, it's her day off so its girl's morning shopping hope you wallet is full." Margaret looking at John with a big grin on her face for she knows that when it comes down to his Daughter he knows that is wallet just goes into melt down.

"So you are not walking out with Brandy."

"I think she will not mind me not being here." Margaret telling John, in a small way I think John was looking forward to the walk with Margaret. But we all know that girls are more interested than doggie sitting. They arrive at Mandy's and they go down the path and from the back garden Brandy comes barking at John and Margaret, well when John tells her to shut it she stops barking cocks her head to one side and starts to wag her tail. Well Margaret is laughing at seeing her do this, and then Brandy goes straight by John and jumps up Margaret.

"My your every bit like your Grandpa told me your beautiful."

Brandy is getting a lot of fuss and loving from Margaret and John, Mandy comes from the kitchen to welcome her Mum and Dad. They chat for an hour when Margaret and Mandy tell John that they were off to Lincoln and they will see him in a couple of hours, well John can see Mandy smiling at her Dad when

John gives of a sigh and pulls out his wallet and gives Mandy £20 pounds telling her.

"Get yourself something nice in Lincoln."

"Thanks Dad you enjoy your walk with Brandy." Margaret and Mandy say there goodbyes and go to catch the bus.

John sits talking to Brandy for a few minutes and tells Brandy to fetch her lead for it's walky times. They go for their walk and the day seemed to fly by till it is time to say goodbye to Mandy and Brandy, for there journey back to Nottingham.

Chapter 4

The weeks turn into months and John with out fail every Wednesday is on the train and off to see Brandy, the walks get longer and the bond between John and Brandy becomes stronger. On walks John plays with Brandy letting her jump up and grab the lead and they both stand having a tug of war, with people stopping and watching them making fools of them self's.

One walk John really likes is the walk through a wooded public path, if it's raining he can shelter in the thick dense trees. When the Sun is shinning it's a shaded place nice and cool. There is just something about the place with Brandy off the lead and John walking ahead to make sure that there is no other dogs coming, the smells of the wood and flickering light of the Sun through the trees. Really makes this place one of the places that you can unwind. All the time John is talking to Brandy and she stops sometimes and you guess sits looking at John talking and cocks her head.

One day John had just come back from one of the walks, had just entered Mandy Bungalow when the phone rings.

"Hello John here how can I help?"

It's me Dad, how's Brandy."

"She's fine; we've just come back from our walk."

"Well that's why I'm phoning for; Lyndon wanted me to tell you to walk her on the lead. For this weekend we've entered her into the young puppy award, at Farnborough with her being 11 months old."

"Core wish I could be there." Then John is thinking that if they wonted him to walk her on the lead, well what she will be like when Lyndon has her on the lead. God if she tries to play with him like I do in the arena God help him. Then Mandy brings her Dad out of is thinking mode and tells him.

"I'll video it for you." Mandy telling her Dad that she will ring him after the show on Sunday night."

By now Brandy is starting to grow even John with the tug of war he plays with her are starting to get one sided with Brandy all most pulling him of the sofa.

Sunday morning comes and Mandy and Lyndon are up early and grooming Brandy, Lyndon with the hose in the driveway is showering Brandy and rubbing in shampoo over an hour they are brushing and grooming to make her look at her best. All done and they both stand back and look at her, well Brandy just what she is good at just cocks her head to one side and sits there looking at them.

"Well we can't do anymore." Lyndon turning to Mandy who in turn looks at Brandy sitting there with her head cocked, and looking back at them. 9.45am and they are off for the show with Brandy sitting upright in the back seat of the car, every time Lyndon looks in the rear mirror all he can see is Brandy sitting bang in the middle of the seat.

"God Mandy just look at her it's if we are transporting Royalty."

Mandy looks back into the back turns to Lyndon and just laughs.

By 10.50am they are all set with Brandy looking all-round at all the other St Bernard's that are there, she seemed to be well pleased with herself.

They announce the start of the contest and start to call out names.

Why Me

Lyndon is looking all-round the other St Bernard's and tells Mandy.

"Look at all the other dogs they are looking fabulous, do you think we have done the right thing with entering Brandy."

"Yes she is magnificent and what ever happens we will still lover her to bits, I mean just look at her." All Brandy was doing is looking round at all the others and I think she is thinking that she would love to be playing with them.

Then all of a sudden Brandy's name is called out Lyndon stands and with Brandy on the lead, turns round looks at Mandy and said.

"Wish me look." He starts to run into the ring with Brandy along side of him, Lyndon is looking all round at all the other St Bernard's in the ring.

One by one they are called and told to trot across the ring with their dog at the side of them. Brandy is the forth to go and her name is called out.

"Brandy Snaps next please." Lyndon starts to trot with Brandy at his side when suddenly Brandy stops dead and grabs the lead, well poor old Lyndon is suddenly pulled to a halt with a jerk and before you know it Brandy is pulling on the lead. With Lyndon trying to get her back under control, Brandy loves it growling and pulling even harder.

She thinks it's a game of tug of war just like she is use to-do with John.

"Bloody John I'll kill him" Lyndon muttering under his breath to himself, well the audience love it, laughing even loader when Brandy pulls Lyndon even harder nearly knocking him of his feet. At on point you have Brandy with the lead in her mouth and Lyndon nearly on his knees trying to get her to stop. Well the audience are clapping and charring it's if they are watching a wrestling match, not a dog show.

Lyndon finally gets Brandy back under his control goes and stands with the other St Bernard's, they are all looked at one by one by the Judges. They come to Brandy and start to talk to Lyndon, well Brandy sits looking at the judges and they look back at Brandy and just like her she sits there and cocks her head to one side, this brought a big smile form all the Judges. They are finally told that they can leave the arena, and they go walking back to there seats. Well Mandy can see Lyndon's face is thunder, before you say anything you were very good out there.

Well this stops Lyndon from saying anything, he looks down at Brandy sitting there and smiles at her, well Brandy jumps up and puts her front legs on Lyndon's shoulders and gives him a sloppy kiss and face wash.

"It's you're Dads fault I mean how are we suppose to keep her under control when your Dad is letting he do whatever she likes, on the walks with Brandy."

"Come on now Lyndon Dad comes up every Wednesday and looks after Brandy; he was not to know that we were going to enter into competitions."

I know love, I'm sorry but out there I felt such a plonker with her."

"No you did not, you looked champion with her." Mandy leans forward and kisses Lyndon, well tried to for Brandy joins in and kisses them both.

They are sitting and rubbing Brandy when over the speakers they announce the results of the Young Puppy Awards, for the under one year olds.

In reverse order in 3rd place General Tom." The audience clap the owner of the dog comes running into the ring to receive their Rosette. Then when they had left he announces the next winner.

"In second place the adorable and the most full and fun of life the dog Brandy Snaps." There is a pause and Lyndon sits there just stroking Brandy not realising they had called Brandy out. Well Mandy pushes Lyndon.

"Go on its Brandy get out there." Mandy pushing Lyndon out of his seat, he jumps up and tells Brandy.

"Come on it's us." Lyndon trotting out into the ring with Brandy thinking that it is play time again. Starts to jump up into the air to grab the lead, she get it between her teeth comes back down to earth and puts her large front legs forward crouches and. Well Lyndon his pulled straight over and lays there in front of Brandy and she is pulling him backwards.

Well there is uproar in the audience people are crying with laughter even the Judges at seeing such a funny site. Lyndon manages to get control patting himself down heads towards the Judges.

"You've one fine and lively puppy there son you must get a lot of pleasure out of her."

"Thank You Sir we certainly do and I must profusely ask for forgiveness for my dog's behaviour." The Judge pins the Rosetta onto Brandy's collar.

"Nonsense its Puppies like Brandy that brings a little fun into the puppy competition, and don't forget Youngman you used to be young at art yourself, the puppy does not know that it is in a show. So go and tell yourself that she is truly a winner, bless her." The Judge smiling at Brandy and is about to rub her head when without warning she jumps up him and gives him a sloppy kiss that he will remember for a long time. He stands there wiping the droll of his face and laughing.

Lyndon goes back to where Mandy is sitting and this time Brandy seemed to know that she is the centre of attraction, for all the way back to where Mandy is she is trotting next to Lyndon's side. Lyndon is thinking to himself that this was the way she suppose to do it not make a fool of him.

Mandy is videoing Brandy and Lyndon coming towards her.

"Bravo Brandy." Mandy putting the camcorder to one side and stroking Brandy. Well Brandy sits there with the rosette attached to her collar and you would think she had won Cruffs.

"Look at her you didn't get us on video when she pulled me down did you." Well Mandy just looks at Lyndon for a few moments and bursts out laughing.

"I certainly did, boy wait till Dad sees it I don't know what he will make of it." Well Lyndon sits there looking at Brandy and the way she looked back was a look that tolled him that everything was alright.

Then the winner of the Young Pup of the Year is called to come and be presented with the winner's rosette. Lyndon at the same time is asking Mandy if she was ready to go home. The judge in the centre of the ring after the presentations he announces.

"Ladies and Gentlemen can I have your attention for a few moments, we have a special prize for the most adorable St Bernard. Will you all put your hands together for Brandy Snaps?"

"Not again." Into the ring comes Brandy with Lyndon bringing up the rear, with his arms out stretched barely holding onto the lead. This brought more cheerers from the audience at Brandy's antics, she went straight up to the Judge who is holding onto the rosette and sat there waiting to be presented with it. She sits there with her head on one side and her

Why Me

tong hanging dangling out, and with drool all-around her mouth.

"OK Brandy let me put this rosette on, and no kissing." The Judge leans forward and pins the rosette onto Brandy, well Brandy no more than shakes her head and the Judge is covered in drool. Lyndon is about to apologise when the Judge holds out his hand and tells Lyndon.

"Please say nothing." The Judge wiping the drool of his face, and at the same time smiling at Brandy.

Lyndon comes back to Mandy and they start to head back to the car with Mandy trying to stop herself from bursting into tears.

Back at the car Lyndon and Mandy are sitting in the front and Brandy sitting upright in the back with the two rosettes on her collar.

"I don't believe it, look at her sitting there it's if she planed it all."

Looking in the rear view mirror at Brandy, sitting panting away."

"Wait till Dad finds out he will be so proud." Mandy turning and patting Brandy.

That evening Mandy is straight on the phone to her Dad to tell him all about Brandy and the two rosettes she won that afternoon. John is proud as punch and shouts for Margaret to come to the phone, well Margaret comes rushing from the kitchen at hearing John shout for her.

"What's happened?" Margaret stands there looking at John with a worried look on her face. John puts the phone onto his chest and tells Margaret he had the biggest grin on his face.

"It's Brandy she had won two rosettes that afternoon, in the Young Pup of the Year contest."

"Is that all it was you daft bat, for a moment I thought something was wrong with Mandy."

Margaret turning and walking back to the kitchen, and murmuring to her self.

That night you can imagine what poor old Margaret is going to get is Brandy this and Brandy that, well by the time it was bedtime Margaret must have had John repeat himself time after time.

The next morning John is on his way to work and the same even the bus driver had the there'd degree about Brandy, and the same at work.

There is one thing about this is he is considering getting another car to keep down the expense of travelling from Nottingham to Lincoln, he had to scrap his last one on you know M.O.T.failer.At work all John talked about is the two rosettes that Brandy had won, so much even his work mates keep telling him that he as told them about Brandy.

The next Wednesday John is up early and off to the train station, in stead of the 8.45am train he catches the 8.15am, in the carriage he sits down waiting for the train to pull away when a lady with a collie comes and sits on the facing seat. Well John straight away strikes up a conversation with her.

"Good morning that's a fine looking dog you have there." John leaning forward and stroking the dog.

"Yes she's called Emmer; she's my friend and companion." Then John starts to tell her all about Brandy and the show at the weekend, by the time he had finished the train pulling into Newark station.

"Must go this is my station it's been nice talking to you." John smiles at her and she disembarks with her collie close by her side.

John Bolstridge

John sits there and all the way to Lincoln John is thinking of Brandy, field after field goes by and John looks at all the wild live rabbits playing in the fields. And pheasants rummaging amongst the crops and before he knows it the train is pulling into Lincoln station, the first thing John did is head for the butches shop just outside the bus station.

John enters the butches shop, and the butcher asked how he could help him. Reply's John.

"Could I have the biggest bag of scratching that you do please?"

"The biggest it depends what you mean." Well the Butcher wished he just got the biggest bag he did, for all John did is start to tell him all about Brandy and the competition that she had won and the fact that she loved Scratchings. He is going on about Brandy for ten minutes the butcher gets an ear bashing, and then John looks at his watch and tells him that he had to go. Well the butcher gives John a weak smile and wishes him well.

John goes out of the shop and he can see that the Washingborough bus is in the bus station, he goes marching off at a brisk pace with the bag of Scratchings for Brandy. Back at the butchers shop the butcher looks round to his assistant and tells him.

"Why do I all ways get them." Is an assistant just shrugs his shoulders and smiles.

The bus leaves the station and starts to head for Washingborough with the Lincoln Cathedral standing out on the hill, ten minutes later and the bus pulls up outside Mandy's home. The thing about country buses they drop you off in the estate were you would like to get off, not designated bus stops. John thanks the driver and heads down the drive to the gate, he stands at the door and he as this overwhelming feeling. It's hard to explain but as he turned the key he could hear Brandy sniffing at the door and whimpering, no sooner had he opened the door and Brandy was straight up to him jumping up and already she was taller than John.

"Steady on Brandy you'll have me over." Brandy back on her all fours sniffs at the bag that John had.

"Alright they are yours." John starts to open the bag and feeds Brandy the contents, in minutes Brandy had devoured the whole bag. She stands there and gives the biggest burp you have ever heard.

"Good grief that was load, come on then let's get off to the fields for how're long walk." John slips the chain collar around Brandy's neck.

John Bolstridge

Off they go with John leading and Brandy for once is walking by John's side and all the time looking at John, the truth be known I think Lyndon had been a little stricter with her. Before long and they are walking across the fields with Brandy off the lead and running free, John looks at her and starts to talk to himself.

"Never mind what anyone says this has got to be the stress release and place to be on ones day off." He walks along looking at the trees and scenery around him, with a big deep of breath he gives of the biggest sigh.

Down the field he walks with Brandy a few strides in front of him. On the way back along the pavement towards the shops there is a tight blind corner; Brandy by now is starting to get a little hot for the drool round her mouth is starting to build up. They approach the corner and just when they are about to go round a Gentleman comes round and stops dead in front of Brandy, well Brandy just jumps up the Gentleman who out stretches one of his hands at being confronted by such a large dog.

Well by the time John had Brandy under his control and before he could apologise to the Gentleman, the man had drool all over his hand and trousers. All that the man did was smile at John and start to shake the drool of his hand and trousers.

Chapter 5

Well John at seeing the mess the Gentleman starts to walk hurriedly away from John and Brandy, He was feeling a little embarrassed well Brandy just shakes her head and the rest of the drool goes flying into the air.

Back at Mandy's John sits on the sofa and all he can think of is the man he met coming round the corner, he sits there and the grin on his face tells it all.

Then the phone rings and John comes out of his daze, he jumps up and answers the phone.

"H'l Dad what have you been up to."

"Don't ask you would not believe it."

"Why what's happened." Mandy feeling a little concerned.

"It happened when we were walking back home you know at the shops with the blind bend, this Gentleman walked right into Brandy. Then all hell broke lose for Brandy jumped up him and before you could do anything, he had a bath not with water but Brandy's drool that went all over him." well all John could her is Mandy laughing her head off on the other end of the phone.

"Come on now sweetheart, it was not funny at the time."

"No it's just the thought of seeing Brandy jumping up him, he must have thought his life was over." Then she bursts out laughing again.

"Must go Dad, look after you're self and I will see you soon love you and give my love to Mum." John puts the phone down and looks at Brandy sitting there, with her tong hanging out. The look on Brandy's face is the look that she is laughing at what she heard over the phone.

"Come on let's go and sit in the garden for awhile." Brandy close by John's side, on the way out to the back garden, John sits stroking Brandy's coat and talking to her.

"Boy do I miss you when I go home Brandy." Brandy pushes Johns hand out of the way and plants a kiss on his face, well if you could call it a kiss. John wiping the drool of his face, he looks at his watch and it is approaching 2.30pm And John this is the time that he had to start to get ready for the journey back home. This time of day is the time he dreads for the look on Brandy face and the thought of leaving her on her own.

He leaves through the front door and Brandy sits in the hallway watching him, he stands waiting for the bus and the feeling in his stomach is a sickly feeling.

He sits on the bus and it goes by Mandy's place he turns and can see the front door and he can imagine Brandy just laying there and sighing.

Thursday evening John is sitting at home with Margaret when the phone rings, Margaret answers the phone, and it is Mandy. Margaret tells John and they both are pressed up to the phone, Mandy says hello and both John and Margaret say hello back to her.

"H'l Mum hope you had a good day at work the reason I'm phoning is to ask you if you would like to come and stay this Friday night, Lyndon is working all day Saturday. You and I could go shopping while Dad takes Brandy for a walk."

"Stop for the weekend I'll have to ask your Dad." Before Margaret had time John butts in.

"Yes I'll hire a car for the weekend, with there being no trains on Sunday morning."

Margaret tells Mandy that there was no need for her to ask her Dad, we will be there at about 7pm after you Dad finish his early afternoon work.

John sorts out the hiring of a car over the internet and it is all booked for him to pick up Friday morning.

John finishes work Friday afternoon and goes home to pick up Margaret, all loaded and it is off to Lincoln. On the way John tells Margaret that they ought to in vest in a car.

"Well with you going on train every week to look after Brandy, if you won't to get a car fine by Me." telling John.

John looks at Margaret and smiles; you can just see John now he is thinking of this car and that car. Will it be a Rover or Jaguar, no don't think she would let me get on of those. The one thing about John once he has the go ahead it's if it's got to be yesterday that he should have one you can bet your bottom dollar that he will be looking at cars and on the net for one.

They pull up at Mandy's at 7.45pm, John with overnight bags and Margaret go down the path and ring the bell, well through the glass top of the door John can see the shape of Brandy and she did not bark but you could here her sniffing around the bottom of the door.

They hear Mandy from inside telling them that the door was open.

"Should I open it?" Margaret looking at John, he tells her.

"Go on then we are bound to get it." Margaret opens the door well Brandy is straight out and jumping up John, the force of her makes John drop the overnight bags well Margaret stands there laughing at John but not for long.

Brandy turns her attention to Margaret jumping up her and trying to kiss her, now it is Johns turn to stand and laugh at Margaret. Mandy comes out and straight away she tells Brandy.

"Get down Brandy." Then Margaret gets her under control and Mandy looks at them both.

"Hi Mum and Dad did you have good journey down."

Yes fine sweetheart." John answering Mandy, just then Brandy jumps up to him and gives him the biggest drool of a kiss.

"BRANDY DOWN." Mandy raising her voce to Brandy.

"It's alright she's just glad to see us." John reassuring Mandy, Then John suggests.

"Lets all go down the pub and take Brandy with us; it's a lovely evening we can sit outside with Brandy."

All set and Brandy on the lead with one guess who is holding the lead, yes her buddy John. Mandy and Margaret walk together and make small talk, just like Mum and Daughter do. The walk is about 10 minutes to get to the pub, John walking with Brandy and they seemed to be making small talk. Well John at lease. Mandy looks at her Dad with Brandy then turns to her Mum.

"Don't take this the wrong way Mum but Lyndon and please not a word to Dad promise."

What is it out with it; you know it will be safe with me." Mandy's Mum telling her.

"Well its Brandy Lyndon comes home at night from work and how can I put it, well he sees Dad with Brandy and the way she reacts with him and it's not the same with Lyndon."

"Don't be daft your Dad only sees Brandy once a week."

"Yes I know but you know that dogs live in packs in days gone by, Lyndon says that John is top dog to her." They reach the pub just when Margaret is about to answer Mandy.

"You two are top Dogs to Brandy." John hears what Margaret had said, he holds out the lead for Mandy to hold while he goes inside to get the drinks.

"What are you on about top dog." Just be for he goes for the drinks.

"Nothing dear, just get the drinks I will have a white wine.

"White wine, I'm not Roth child you know." John looking at Margaret.

"Just get them in and bring Mandy one." John goes into the pub moaning to himself.

They sit in the pubs garden under an old large apple tree, with fruit in abundance on the tree. There are loads of little apples on the grass that had been discarded by the tree, John comes out and puts the drinks on the table.

"Thank you love, now go and get your sweetheart a drink of water. John stands there gob smacked and is about to say something, when Margaret chirps up.

"Look at her she's sweating look at her tong, it's nearly on the grass." John takes a drink of his beer, then turns to go back for Brandy's water.

After about ten minutes they are sitting having a drink when Lyndon comes into the garden, John sees Lyndon and asks.

"How did you know we were here?"

"Mandy phoned me and said you would be here, so I've come straight from work."

John goes to the bar to fetch Lyndon a drink and on the way back into the garden he sees Lyndon throwing apples down the garden and Brandy chasing after them.

"She's not eating them is she?" John looking a little concerned at seeing Brandy chasing them and grabbing the apple in her mouth and trying to bit down on it.

"Don't worry she only bites them and spits them out." Lyndon picking another apple up of the grass and throwing it down the garden, with Brandy in hot pursuit.

Why Me

The night sky is black with stars twinkling, and the moon low on the arisen.

"Do you know this is a lovely setting to be at, after a long day at the office and to unwind?" John sighs and takes a sip of his pint.

"What are you on about Dad?" Mandy asking her Dad.

"You know living out here in a little village, instead of the City with people rushing here and there. Motorist getting up tight just because they are a minute late, getting to the next set of traffic lights." Then another heave a sigh from John.

"Drink up Mum let's get back before Dad gets us all depressed."

"What do you mean?" Asks John.

"Nothing Dad you walk Brandy home while we go to the chippy to get our supper. John clips the lead onto Brandy and tells her to come; Mandy Lyndon and Margaret sit in the car and watch John start to walk up the road with Brandy.

Margaret sitting in the back tells Lyndon and Mandy.

"He's totally devoted to that dog, I mean just look at both of them."

John is patting her on the back lifting the lead and Brandy is jumping up into the air trying to grab the end of it, then Lyndon speaks out.

"Look at them no wonder at the dog show she would not walk properly." Lyndon shaking his head when they were pulling out of the car park.

Back home they all settle down to their chip supper, they are all having it in the lounge watching T.V. Brandy sits watching John eat his supper, John looks at the rest watching the box, then when they are not looking slips Brandy some chips and the odd bit of fish.

Well Brandy sits there and from her mouth comes the biggest stream of drool; well we have all experienced it. You know when you see strawberries and ice cream we all start watering at the mouth, well a St Bernard s like someone had turned on the tap. Well Mandy suddenly turns away from the TV and looks at Brandy with all the drool flooding onto the carpet.

"Dad look at her stop feeding her." Mandy jumps up and grabs Brandy by the collar and tells her.

Why Me

"Come on young lady you're out of here till we finish." Just when Mandy sits back down, John stands and tells her.

"Finished I'll go and put my plate in the sink." John leaves the lounge and Mandy turns to her Mum and tells her.

"I bet Dad is outside with Brandy." And sure enough John is sitting in the garden keeping Brandy company.

At about 10pm Margaret comes out to John and asks him.

"Are you stopping out all-night or what."?

"No coming now, just look at all the stars out there." John looking up into the night sky, with Brandy looking straight and it is if she is wondering what he is looking at.

"Come on then love lets say goodnight to Mandy and Lyndon before we turn in." Margaret out stretches her arm for John to hold her hand on the way back in.

They go into the lounge to tell Mandy and Lyndon that they are going to turn in, they go to their bedroom and start to get undressed with Brandy looking on. John is first into the bathroom followed by Margaret; John comes back into the bedroom and gets into bed. He leans forward to where Brandy is laying on the floor and kisses her goodnight, he flops back onto his pillow and after about two minutes Brandy jumps up onto the bed and lays fully stretched out on the bed next to John with her head on the pillow where Margaret is suppose to be. After 10 minutes Margaret comes out of the bathroom and goes into the bedroom and sees the site that greets her.

"Margaret looks at her.

"where am I supposed to get." John murmurs turns and sees Brandy looking back at him; well Brandy gives a big sigh.

"Come on sweetheart down." Well if you could have seen Margaret's face at hearing what John had said to Brandy, muttering to herself when she gets into bed? She no more gives a big shove to remove Brandy from the bed, snuggles up to John and they are soon fast asleep with Brandy down on the bedroom floor.

A about 2am Brandy jumps back onto the bed and tries to get into the bed with John, one of her large paws hits John in the face and pushes one of his eye balls. Well John jumps up at the pain he had in his eye and gives out a screech.

Why Me

"What's the matter?" Margaret waking and putting the light on.

"It's Brandy she just pushed one of my eyes, the pain God when she put her paw onto my eye all I could see was a bright light." Margaret looks at his eye and reassures John that it was alright, commotion over and they try and get back to sleep with John lying there opening and shutting his eye that Brandy had inured. Brandy herself flopped onto the bed and rests her head on John's body and gives off a big sigh. The rest of the night is uneventful and at 8am John wakes with the feeling of Brandy's tong lapping up and down his face.

Chapter 6

This wakes John up with her licking him.

"Brandy stop it." John trying to wipe the drool of his face. Brandy caries on till John submits.

"Alright then I'm getting up." John slips on his jogging bottoms and goes to let Brandy out, he opens the door and Brandy steps out into the early morning Sun with John stretching and yarning. He looks down and Brandy just lies facing the door looking at John.

"Well young lady you might be comfy, but I'm ready for a cuppa." John goes into the kitchen to brew a cup of tea, with Brandy walking close to his side and every few steps John makes Brandy keeps touching his hand for reassurance. Not long and they are all up and having breakfast, Mandy asks her Dad what he was doing this morning.

John looks round the table for a moment then answers.

"Well if you are going shopping, I think I will take Brandy down to the common for a run round."

"Fine Dad." Mandy looks at Lyndon and asks.

"What about you are you coming with Mum and I or." Before Mandy finished Lyndon replies.

"Shopping with you." By 10am Mandy Margaret and Lyndon are ready to go into Lincoln shopping. John slips the lead onto Brandy's collar and tells them he will see them later. John gets into the car the car with Brandy sitting up right in the back, he pulls away and down the road to wards Lincoln common. Well everybody stops and looks at John gong down the road with Brandy sitting there proud as punch, it brings one or to giggles from passer-by's and motorist following John's car. Glances at seeing such large dog in the car.

John pulls up at the common and takes Brandy out of the back of the car; they walk to the gate that leads onto the common and go through the gate on to the common. John looks round to see that there is no other dog around and lets Brandy off the lead and she goes bonding off.

She is stopping every now and then to make sure John is following.

The Sun is shining and John starts to daydream, all the time walking forward with Brandy running and playing.

John deep in thought is mind well into what he was thinking his steps getting shorter and shorter, and then all of a sudden John is brought back to reality with the sound of a pony neighing out load.

Well this startles John and he quickly turns and sees Brandy trying to play with a small pony that is grazing on the common.

"Brandy down come away, come here." All that Brandy did is carry on barking at the pony, as if to encourage it to play with her, by now John is starting to look round to see if anyone was looking at them. He tries to come between Brandy and the pony, and then in a load voice he suddenly tells Brandy to sit. Well with hearing John raise his voice she sits in front of him, and then he quickly snaps the lead onto Brandy's collar.

"Good Girl it's not a dog you daft thing." John turns to see the pony go trotting off and every now and then kicking out with her back legs.

"Let's walk on." John letting Brandy off the lead, they walk for about 40 minutes then John tells Brandy that they had better make tracks back.

Why Me

Over two hours John had walked Brandy and by the time they reached the car they were both ready for a drink. John sits Brandy in the back of the car and starts to pull away with Brandy panting in the back.

It's not long and John's windows start to mist up with the hot breath of Brandy.

"Wont be long before we are home." John winding down the cars window to let some fresh air into the car to clear the windows, this gives Brandy the chance to get some fresh air to cool her down.

She leans forward sniffing at the air rushing in and John with out noticing is getting rather a lot of drool down the back of his coat.

Back home at Mandy's the first think John did is give Brandy a deserved drink of water, then with a cup of tea it was time to relax in the garden till the rest of the family get back from shopping.

About an hour passes and Margaret with Mandy and Lyndon pull up and see John fast asleep with Brandy at his feet, and she to be fast on.

"Just look at those two, we have been walking our feet of shopping and they lay back and sunbathe typical." Margaret shouts out to John, who gives of a snort and starts to come out of his sleep.

"Hello love you're back." John trying to focuses on Margaret.

"Back is that all you have been doing while we've been shopping." Well John is dumb fond at what Margaret had said and before he gets a word in they all disappeared into the house.

"Well Brandy I don't know what to say, we've walked our legs off and they have been enjoying themselves shopping." John looks down at Brandy and Brandy gives off a sigh and rests her head on Johns lap.

That afternoon it's time for John and Margaret to start to make their way back home, with all the goodbyes said John and Margaret get into the car for their journey home.

They wave to Mandy and Lyndon who are standing at the gate with Brandy standing on her hind legs and barking at John when he pulls away from Mandy's.

"Look at her." John's voice drops when he looks back in his rear view mirror and sees Mandy and Lyndon waving with Brandy barking, it is if she is trying to tell John not to leave her. They drive off and the look on

Why Me

Johns face tells it all, it's if he had just left the one thing in his life that he loved dearly then Margaret at seeing John and the look on his face suddenly tells him.

"That dog is devoted to you." Margaret telling John, then Margaret in a soft voice tries to tell him something that was on her mind.

"John." She hesitates.

"What's the matter?" John turning to Margaret with the look on his face, that all is not well.

"Well its something Mandy was telling me when we were on our own last night."

"Well what is it." John starting to get a little anxious.

"It's Lyndon he's been offered a new post, but not in Lincoln."

"Don't tell me that they are moving miles away."

"No Mandy said it is Birmingham."

"I don't fancy travelling to Birmingham to see Brandy."

"No they are looking to buy a new house around Colville." All goes quiet you can see on Johns face that he is trying to work out the miles from Nottingham to Colville, after about ten minutes John suddenly turns to Margaret and tells her.

Colville its only 26 miles from Nottingham, better then going 54 miles to Lincoln. Johns face changes for he seemed to be content with the outcome.

"Fingers crossed he gets the post." John rubbing his hands.

A few weeks later and Mandy is ready to move with Lyndon finally ironing out the contract for his new post and expenses for the move.

The place they are moving to is Ellis Town just outside Colville, she had arranged with her Dad to pick Brandy up while they move out.

So Brandy is not around when the removal men come to pick up their possessions. On the day they are moving to Ellis Town, John sets of early from Nottingham to pick Brandy up. It's a lovely day the Sun is beating down and it's a must for the air conditioner, John had rushed out and had not had any breakfast. The outside temperature is well over 80f John is about ten miles outside Lincoln and about

10 minutes from Mandy's and he is sweating profusely.

"Boy am I hot." John feeling a little light headed driving, and it was if he felt like fainting.

"Must be the weather, boy will I be glad when I get there." Not long after and he is pulling up outside Mandy's, he is getting out of the car when Brandy sees him and comes bounding up to the gate and is barking like mad at seeing John, this brings Mandy and Lyndon out. The way Brandy is barking at John it's if he was getting a good telling off for not coming sooner and leaving her so long.

"Hi Dad are you alright."

"Fine sweetheart but I wish it was a little cooler, boy am I clad I've got air-conditioning in my car, you could not put the kettle on could you I'm gagging for a cuppa. Mandy goes to get her Dad a drink while John starts to make a fuss of Brandy, Brandy to makes sure he is felt welcome by jumping up at him and giving him a good drooling.

"Get down Brandy." Mandy shouting at her and bringing her Dad his drink. John sits down and he does not tell Mandy that he feels a little fuzzy and dizzy. After 10 minutes he feels a little better.

"You will be alright with her in the back while you are driving."

Don't you worry she will be fine don't forget she's been with me before, when we went down the common."

"I know that Dad but 54 miles I don't won't her to jump into the front, and start messing about while you are driving."

"Don't you worry about Brandy and me; you just get moved and phone me in a couple of day when you have settled into your new home." Then John wobbles to one side.

"Are sure you are alright Dad."

Stop fussing, I'll make tracks now and don't forget to phone me when you are in your new home." Mandy puts the dogs bowl and a few things in her Dads boot and slams it shut, John starts the car with Brandy sitting up right on the back seat looking like Lord muck.

Hope she behaves herself." Lyndon looking at Mandy and they are waving her Dad and Brandy off.

"Don't you start we have enough to worry about" just then the removal van pulls up.

Chapter 7

Mandy and Lyndon are well and truly wrapped up in the move from Lincoln and soon forget about Brandy and her Dad, meanwhile John and Brandy are reaching the out skirts of Lincoln. And John shakes his head to try and shake of this feeling of he wants to faint, he turns to Brandy who is sitting in the back looking out of the window and watching the World go by and panting.

"It's alright for you sitting there being." and before he could say anymore, Brandy leans forward and licks the back of Johns neck.

"OK, ok that's enough." This brings a smile to Johns face, and at the same time he lifts his left arm and is hand is shaking.

"Soon be home Brandy." John telling her.

John is about 4 miles from Newark the sweat is starting to run down his brow and he is starting to feel a little nausea.

"What's wrong with me." Then just before a lay-by he suddenly cramps up forward over the steering wheel.

"God I'm going to faint I know it." He managers to pull into the lay-by and collapse over the wheel, the car judders to a stand still.

In front in the lay-by is a young coulple with their two young children, who have stopped to let the children rest before they set off again on the rest of their journey. The driver looking in his rear mirror sees John's car judder to a Holt.

"That car that has just pulled in the driver must be tired, he's just flopped forward." His wife looking round and sees Brandy in the back of the car.

"Look at the size of the passenger." This makes her husband turn round.

"That's no passenger it's one of those dogs a St Bernard."

They both get out and start to look at John's car; at the same time Brandy realises that something is wrong. She leans forward and starts to sniff and lick Johns face, the couple see this and they start to smile. At the same time a Police car pulls into the lay-by and pulls up about ten yards behind John's car.

Well Brandy is getting no response from licking and she then jumps into the front passenger seat, with her head she knocks Johns head back onto the seat. She gently sniffs at his nose and it's if she knew that John was not breathing properly, well she whimpers and presses her large head into Johns chest. Then she sniffs at his face again, then repeats the same again.

The couple see this and think that the dog is attacking the driver and call out to the policemen sitting in their car.

"Offices please help look." The man pointing at John's car.

The Officers embark from their car and look at what the man was pointing to, they see Brandy pushing her head into John's chest then her face into his face and repeat the action. The Officers look at each other and one said.

"What the hell is that dog doing to him?"

By now Brandy is getting a little frantic at getting no response from John, so she turns and starts barking at the two Offices standing watching her.

She jumps back into the back and sits there just barking like mad.

This brings a moan from John at hearing the commotion and the two Officers approach John's car. They open the driver's door and they can see that John is not in a fit state, so one of the Officers goes back to his patrol car and phones for an ambulance and paramedic.

The two Offices stop with John till the Paramedic arrives and they start treating him, after they had done test they noticed that John's sugar levels were only 3.5 very low and the paramedic asked John if he was diabetic.

"Yes I'm type 2 diabetic why."

"Well what have you had today to eat." The Paramedic asking John.

Well John knew he was stumped for the answer he gave him he knew he was in for a telling off.

"Nothing you see my Daughter Is moving house and I'm just helping out, by having her dog while she moves."

"You silly Man you know you are suppose to eat little but more often, through out the day. We know that you can not go into a diabetic coma with type two but things like what has happened today with the heat and combining it with Diabetes this is the result. I

Why Me

don't think there is any reason to admit you to Hospital but if you would like to go to be on the safe side I will leave that up to you."

"No thanks I will pull up in Newark and have something to eat before carrying on with my journey, and I profusely ask for forgiveness for my stupidity."

"That's OK and no more going all day with out anything, you take care now." The paramedic leaves John just when one of the Police Offices comes over and gives John a Mars bar that he had in his car, while the Paramedic talked to one of the Offices.

After the Paramedic left the Offices come to reassure John that he could be on his way and they tell him that the St Bernard was one hell of a dog for what she did to help you. They take all Johns details and he gives them the new address of his Daughter who owned the dog and they to wish him good health from now on. And hey leave. John sits for awhile and tries to finish the bar of chocolate that the Officer gave him, I say try for Brandy is drooling all down John's neck watching him eat it. Just like John he lets Brandy help him finish it. He restarts the car puts the air-con on full cool and pulls away feeling a little foolish of what had happened.

Mandy move in with out a hitch and Brandy goes home the next day, then after about 3 weeks one evening he receives a phone call from Mandy.

"Dad I'm very cross with you."

"What have I done wrong?"

"You should know when we were moving home I could see you were not right and you just did nothing, what if something had happened when you were on your way home with Brandy I could have lost both of you,. She starts to cry."

"Sorry sweetheart you know what I'm like I don't like fuss, I'm sorry truly sorry." John had to pause for he is trying to hold back the tears, and then he suddenly asks Mandy.

"How do you know all this anyway, I've not even told your Mum."

"I've had the report come from the Police with a letter from the Animal awards programme, telling me that Brandy had been put forward for award for her attempt to alert others and to try and revive you when you were on conscious." Then more tears from Mandy you could just see her imaging in her mind of her Dad slumped over the wheel of his car.

"It wont happen again you know once bitten twice shy, I will not do anything like that anymore, boy my Brandy a hero bless her."

"Are you going to tell Mum or me?" Just then Margaret comes in and asks who he was talking to.

"Just Mandy just ringing to see how we are." Well John knew he is snookered when Margaret reaches out with her hand for the phone. He passes the phone to Margaret and makes a hasty retreat to the fridge and gets a drink out and goes and sits on the decking outside.

Well from the inside John sitting on the decking enjoying the evening Sunshine suddenly hears Margaret saying.

"WHAT."

John had the feeling that if the ground opened up he would gladly jump init, after about ten minutes Margaret comes out with a glass of wine and sits next to John on the decking. Well she just sits there looking at John, not saying a word till John looks back at her and said.

"What."

"You keep it all to yourself and not said a word all this time, I'm your wife remember."

"I'm sorry love but I felt a little embarrassed with the whole thing what with Mandy moving and rushing here and there, you know what I mean Police and Paramedics." Margaret leans over and plants a kiss on John and tells him.

"I love you so much and the girl on the other end of the phone to, you can see why she was upset." Then the same reactions just like Johns.

"How Brandy put forward for award, at least we don't have to dickheads in the Family." Margaret turning and smiling at John.

"Very funny very funny." Then they both burst out laughing together.

The last week in September Brandy received a certificate of achievement and Mandy phones her Dad up for a favour.

"Dad Lyndon and I are going to Brighton for a week could you look after Brandy for us."

"No problem just let us know when and bring her down."

"This Saturday if that's alright, you're off work so it is ideal."

"Fine let us know when you are coming and have a nice time down there, love you and give how love to Brandy and Lyndon."

Chapter 8

Weekend comes and Mandy and Lyndon are here at 6.30am for they are setting off early to miss the Saturday people who are going to work.

They say there goodbyes and John and Brandy stand at the gate watching them pull away on there journey to Brighton.

"Come on baby lets get some breakfast before we go on the Park for a walk." Margaret is having a lay in for it to is her weekend off

John lets Brandy out the back for Brandy to investigate her surroundings, Johns garden is perfect for Brandy for it had the decking when you first come out of the kitchen that steps down onto a patio.

Then there is a large area with apple tree, pear tree, and plum tree. That is planted on an area that is covered in Welsh slate, then the bottom with a circle of pebbles with a weeping cherry tree and bark on the sides,

Why Me

finishing of with a garden shed. All round there is a six feet wooden fence so Brandy can not go anywhere and you can relax while she is out there doing her business.

Margaret is up at 8.am and the first to welcome her is Brandy who is trying to jump up her to give her a welcoming kiss or drool.

"No thank you young Lady I'm fine, has Grandpa feed you." Margaret going to her bowl that Mandy had left with a large bag of dried food and large tins of dog food. Brandy after her meal and John with a sausage sandwich and beans. John turns to Brandy and tells her come on girl lets go on Melbourne Park. This is one of the favoured places for dog lovers to take their dogs for the vast area for walking around Aspley Estate.

It consists of a very large area for well over 11 football pitches and a enclosed children's area, but the main part for dog lovers is the walk around the park on the outer circle that is lined with trees around, well over 1 and a quarter miles in total.

John walks Rocky on a regular basses, if you wondering why Rocky is not mentioned is he stops with Margaret's Dad while Brandy come. I don't think they would get on very well with Brandy within Rockies home.

When Mandy lived at home Rocky was her dog but over time Margaret became top dog so when Mandy married she left Rocky with her Mum.

Back to the story. You will see from the photo, you can see al the trees on the outside of the park.

They set of for Melbourne Park John with Brandy on the lead and she is at her best jumping up to John trying to get the lead of him, and the same reaction from people passing at seeing them smiles from them with Brandy's antics.

Why Me

They enter the gate that leads onto the Park, John looks round and with it early Saturday the park is quiet and John lets Brandy of the lead. And they go off walking along the line of trees along the foot path.

Brandy just like a typical Dog is sniffing the ground to see who had been there, she trots off and looking all-round. Suddenly she stops and looks down the field and sees a lone man in the distance. Well at the same time John sees what Brandy is looking at and he to can see the man. Well Brandy goes off bounding along towards the man John is shouting her back, to no avail.

The man looks at what the commotion is with running and barking at him, he just freezes to the spot when Brandy approaches. She stops with a sudden Holt, churning up a large turf of grass. The man just stands glued to the spot with such a large beast just standing there and barking. Brandy does no more than stand on hind legs with her paws on his shoulders. And is barking straight into his face, with her only a few inches from him.

John approaches and he is totally out of breath with the running and shouting to Brandy to get down, she obeys and stands there looking at the man with her head cocked to one side.

"Sorry about this but she is armless, she will not bite." The man just stands there and smiles back at John, with drool dripping of his raincoat and John sees this and does no more than start to pat it off him. John to smiles back at the man, as he is doing it.

The man did no more than turn and start to walk away with John talking to Brandy who seemed to think every think is alright.

They walk off and John starts to talk to Brandy.

"You're daft as a brush, if only you knew you could have given that poor man a heart attack, I mean look at the size of you."

Brandy looking at John and with being on the lead starts to play again.

They spend well over an hour on the park and enjoy the walk through the tree lined pathway and open field.

On the way back home John meets one of his neighbours who asked him.

"Hi John you have not gone and brought a great big thing like that have you." The man is looking at Brandy and at the same time Brandy sniffing at him, while he stroked her head.

"No it's my Daughters I'm just looking after her while she is away on holiday."

Back home John calls out for Margaret who comes from the kitchen to see what John wonted.

"You would not believe what I've just gone through on the Park."

"What's that you came across a box with a million pound init?"

"Don't be daft, it was Brandy." He goes on to tell her all about the incident with the man on the Park, and the look on his face after.

"That's Brandy for you, you know that she's daft as a brush, and she would not hurt a fly bless her."

"Yes but the bloke did not know that, what you would think like seeing a great big think like that bounding towards you barking." John telling Margaret.

"OK forget it whatever you say now will not change a thing what will be has happened, you can not turn the clock back."

That night it was time to turn in, John had only just finished doing the bedroom up, and they had brought a new King size bed. I don't think it was because Brandy is stopping but boy are they going to need it.

Margaret before she gets into bed Tells Brandy to lie at the bottom of the bed were she had put a doggie blanket for her. Brandy did what she was told and did just that but a look and a great big sigh followed, they had been in bed for less than an hour and Margaret is fast on. Brandy goes round to Johns side and just stands there with her face right up into Johns she no more puts her head on the pillow and stands there whimpering, this stirs John who tells her to go and lie down.

Brandy does no more than go to the bottom of the bed and jumps up onto the bed she walks forward on the bed, and plonks down between John and Margaret with her head resting on John's neck. The weight of Brandy seemed to press on John, well she is 13 stone and she starts to drool. John slowly seemed to be moving towards the end of the bed with her weight and before long John is standing on the floor with Brandy right up on his side and she is snoring away.

Roll on when Mandy is back he looks at the clock and it is coming up to midnight and he had only 4 hours to go before he is up and off to work. He goes and gets in the spare bed for a goodnights sleep, well 4 hours.

He's fast on when into the room comes Brandy who is missing him and she sees him fast on she does no more than jumps onto the bed and pushes back the cover and gets in with John flopping down on the pillow and she is snoring in minutes.

The next morning at Four am John is up and he's in the kitchen making himself some serials before he's off to work Brandy had gone outside to do her business and before long John is shouting her in for it was time for the off. Margaret is up and off to work just after seven and tells Brandy to be a good girl till John gets home she shuts the front door with Brandy giving that silly look with her head on one side when Margaret goes.

She meets up with John in the warehouse and John asked how she was when she left, Margaret tells him alright and asked John if he had a goodnights sleep.

"Goodnight sleep I went into the spare room and she followed me and every hour I was up and down stairs to let her out for a wee, and do you know that when she had done her business she no more than lied down on the patio and tries to go to sleep with sucker me standing there watching

Her." Margaret starts to laugh and tells John.

"Well it's you job know you were the one who said you would have her so tuff titis, see you later." She goes off tittering to herself with John standing there gob smacked at the comment. John finishes his shift and at 12 noon leaves for home and he pulls up onto the drive and pulls up straight outside the front window, and the site that greets him is Brandy with front legs on the window shelf and head sticking up on the glass with drool running down it. She is looking straight at John and you could just make out her back moving from side to side, it was obvious that her tail was wagging profusely and the look on her face of joy at seeing John.

John opens the door and Brandy nearly knocks John into next week, he tells her to pack it in for she is well and truly excited. Jon had shut the driveway doors before he opened the door and Brandy goes to do her thing.

After ten minutes they both go in and the sight that greets John anyone would have thought that they had been burgled. For the seats of the entire 3 piece suite are on the floor, and generally amess.

"Brandy I've just finished work and it looks like I've got to start again.

Seats back hover out and a good mop on the laminated floor to wipe the drool of the floor, after a further hour John flops down on his favoured chair with a good earned cuppa and a sandwich.

He gives off a sigh and would you believe it Brandy stood there with lead in her moth and it was if she is telling him, come on then walkies.

Chapter 9

The whole of the week is the same work then walkies and come the Saturday Mandy comes to pick Brandy up, she is in the garden sniffing around when Mandy comes into the decking area and shouts Brandy, well she is like a bullet out of a gun and jumping up Mandy and Lyndon when he to appers from inside the house, they spend an hour with John and Margaret telling them all about the trip to Brighton.

Before they leave Mandy asks her Mum.

"Are you and Dad going to come over for Christmas, it will be nice for us to spend it together in the new house."

"Try and stop us and I think your Dad will like walking Brandy."

John comes in and hears what Margaret had said.

"What's this walking Brandy about?" John looking at Margaret and Mandy.

"Mandy has invited us over for Christmas and I tolled her that you could walk Brandy."

"Is there plenty of fields to walk her." John asking.

"You will be fine and you could walk off all the beer you will drink."

"Funny very funny, what if it's 7 feet deep in snow."

"Well Brandy will love that we will buy her a brandy barrel then you could pretend that you need rescuing and drink the brandy." Mandy and her Mum giggling.

"No thanks don't like brandy." Brandy sitting there with her head on one side. John looks at her and straight away tells her.

"Not you sweetheart." John rubbing her head.

The festive holiday is fast approaching and Mandy and her Mum at the weekends are very busy buying allsorts of gifts and food for the holiday.

The day before Christmas Mandy had one of those very long pork pies with an egg running through it; before she left for work she takes it out of the freezer and puts it on top of her upright fridge freezer to defrost. The fridge freezer stands 5.6 feet tall and she knows that it will be fine till she comes home then she can transfer it to the fridge till Christmas tea time.

Mandy leaves for her last shift before her two day break; Lyndon already at work she tells Brandy that she will see her later. She closes the door and she is off to work. Brandy is lying in the hallway but she had access to all the rooms, she goes into the kitchen and she is sniffing around on the ground then in the air.

She goes over to the fridge and head in the air can smell something she know more than jumps on to her hind legs with her front legs on the fridge top, her head is above the fridge and she sees the pork pie just sitting there waiting for someone or thing to eat it.

Brandy no more than grabs it by her mouth and drops to the floor; you would think she would eat in there and then. O'h no not Brandy she wonted somewhere more comfortable to be, she no more than trot's off to the bedroom and jumps onto the bed, you would think that with it being frozen that she would wait. But not Brandy she starts to lick it to make it softer, and at the same time she is drooling a lot.

She is at it for well over an hour licking and drooling.

Mandy comes home and standing at the door to greet her is Brandy, she smiles at he and tells her that she is a good girl, that's till she goes into the bedroom to change out of her staff uniform.

She enters the bedroom and gives out a scream, for to greet her is the bed all messed up with drool all over porkpie crumbs a lot of crumbs.

Her first words in not a soft voice were.

"Brandy come." Well she comes into the bedroom and Mandy in a stern voice.

"What's all this mess then, you bad girl." All that Brandy did is give one of the biggest burps you have ever heard. Mandy grabs her by the collar and takes her to the back door and throws her out into the cold.

All that Brandy did was settle down for a rest, with a coat that she had I don't think she would feel the cold.

Well Mandy is straight into the bedroom bed striped and vacuum cleaner out and to remake the bed with fresh sheets and cover. Then it is into the kitchen to turn on the washing machine. She looks at her watch and she had only an hour to get things done for her Mum and Dad would be there, for she is going shopping tomorrow with her Mum on Christmas eve for last minutes shopping and things in general, and of course another porkpie if she is not to late.

And well with in an hour her Mum and Dad had arrived, and Mandy was there to great them.

"Hi Mum Dad come on in this is the first time you have seen this house let me show you round." Mandy's Mum and Dad are looking here there and everywhere. Well of course Brandy was following close to John.

"This is lovely you have done yourself pride with buying this house and the location is fine, but where are me and your Dad sleeping." Margaret asking Mandy.

"You're in this room with Dad and hopefully not with you no who." Mandy looking at her Dad, all that her Dad did was smile back and shows Brandy the room. After the tour John asks Mandy the best walk to take Brandy and she tells him about the cut through that leads to fields.

John takes Brandy for her evening walk and exploring the area with her, all the time he is talking to Brandy just as if she was human.

Why Me

The night is cold with the temperature just above freezing but the wind factor made it seem a lot colder. He walks her for about 45 minutes and returns back to the family home and they settle down for the night and watching a little TV.

About 7.30 pm Lyndon returns from work and he to have finished for the Christmas break.

Margaret and Mandy are discussing what they were going to do Christmas Eve shopping, Mandy tells her Mum that they will go into Coleville to finish of their Christmas shopping and of course Dad can look after Brandy.

They are watching the TV when the weather forecast comes on for Christmas eve and the report tells them that there is a small chance in someplace will get a little snow fall of snow, but nothing to Worry about.

Christmas Eve and Mandy and Margaret are off to finish their last bit of Christmas shopping with Lyndon and John staying at home.

Lyndon and John are on there own with Brandy lying on the floor in front of them both. When the conversation turns to St Bernard's.

"Did you know that the St Bernard only lives about 8-9 years at top?" Lyndon looking at John and telling him.

"What you're kidding me." John not believing what Lyndon was telling him.

"Well it's the size of the dog, the bigger they are the young they die."

"Where have you got that from?" starting to look a little concerned John.

"Well before we had Brandy I was on the internet and looking at sites all about St Bernard's and that is where I read it." You could tell that John was racking his brain working out when Brandy was born and he suddenly tells Lyndon.

"That's unfair you mean to tell me that a loving dog like Brandy, her life span has only about 3 years to go."

"Well if we are lucky maybe 4 years" With all the talk about Brandy and talking out load her name made her sits up and just looks at both of them.

Well John sits there rubbing under her chin and she sits there sighing, I think John was hitting the point with Brandy. After about 3 hours Margaret and Mandy come home with arms full of shopping, well John sees then he tells them.

"God the shops are only closed for 2 days, anyone would think that the World is going to end get your stuff in." John looking at all the bags they had, then Margaret tells him.

"Well we hope you've got all your presses in for tomorrow, and don't forget your sweetheart Brandy." Well John just sat there and you could tell that he was thinking, to himself.

"I've brought nothing what the hell is she going on about." Well I think he will tomorrow Christmas Day.

At about 7pm John calls Brandy and tells her to fetch her lead well Brandy is off like a shot and standing at the door where her lead is hanging, John puts the lead on and tells them that he is just going to walk Brandy round the block and back.

They go out and it is a dark and cold night, John looks up at the night sky and tells himself.

"Boy those white clouds look like they have snow in them, he had to cross a small grass area to get back onto Mandy's road and in the distance he could here carol singers singing silent night holly night, when a small snow flake its his nose. He bends down and he is telling Brandy as he looked up and the light of a lamp post and you could see the little snow flakes in the light.

"Look Brandy snow." with the sound of the carol singers and the little snow and singers it was the first time that he had the real feeling of Christmas. Back onto the road and he is walking towards the carol singer who had a little tin fort their collection he puts in a pound and wishes them a Merry Christmas. They wish him the same and he goes back to Mandy's feeling very Christmassy.

He comes into the kitchen and Margaret is just getting her and Mandy a white wine out of the fridge, she sees John with that look on his face and asks.

"What's up you seen Santa on his slay."

"No the first snow of the season and carol singers made the walk magical." He kisses Margaret and he to gets a drink out of the fridge.

The night is a good one they watch old programs and favourite just before they turned in, they watched the Morecombe and Wise show one of the Christmas favourite. They say their good nights and even grown ups tell each other I wonder what Santa will bring me. I think there is a little child within us all.

Margaret and John go to their bedroom and you guessed Brandy follows John, John tells her to lay on the floor but we all know were she will land up, that's right sleeping next to John.

The next morning at 6.30am Mandy comes into her Mum and Dads room and asks them if they are going to get up, John sees Mandy and he asks her.

"What time is it?"

"6.30 come on Dad shake a leg."

"6.30 It's still the middle of the night." John pulling the sheets over him, well trying to for Brandy is still in bed with them.

Chapter 10

"Come on Dad it's Christmas morning." Mandy shaking him and telling Brandy to get down. Mandy's Mum tells her that she will be in the lounge in a short time. Mandy goes into the kitchen and starts to make an early cup of tea.

By 7.00am they are all up and even John, they are having their cuppa when Mandy passes her Mum a box. And wishing her Mum a happy Christmas. She starts to open it with Brandy sitting there hopping for a treat, Margaret opens the box that she had brought her Mum a silver chain necklace and a silver watch.

"Thanks sweetheart they are lovely." Margaret showing John and Lyndon. Then Mandy passes her Dad a box.

"Thanks Mandy I wonder what it is."

"Well open it and you will find out." Margaret telling him.

Why Me

John opens the box and he can not believe it for inside the box, there is a pair of leather gloves scarf and a wool hat.

"Thanks sweetheart, they are lovely and will sure keep me warm with all the bad weather they are predicting for January."

"They are from Lyndon and me." John also thanks Lyndon.

Then Margaret passes Mandy her Christmas present, and at the same time passing Lyndon is present. Mandy goes first and opens her present, well her eyes light up for she had only had a new mobile phone and an MP3 player.

"Mum you should have brought me something cheaper."

"It's from your Dad to, and away with you, you are worth ever penny of it just enjoy and I hope you like the choice of the phone."

"It's fine and thanks Dad." Mandy goes over to her Dad and gives him a kiss then her Mum. Next Mandy give Brandy her present and she just sniffs at it.

"Open it for her; don't forget she does not know what Christmas is about."

"Well she is one of the Family." Mandy bent over and opening it for her and it is one of her favourite a bag of Scratchings.

Then Margaret gives Brandy her present and she is sniffing even harder, when Margaret opened it there in front of Brandy one of her best titbits pig's ears. Margaret gives her one and picks the others up for later. Brandy takes the pig's ear and goes and sits under the tree and is biting away at the pig's ear very content in deed.

Then Margaret sits looking at John and smiling at him, John looks back at her and asks.

"What have I done now?"

"Where is my present then, I'm waiting."

"You had the money for Christmas weeks ago." Yes I know I did but it would have been nice just to have opened a small one on the day.

Margaret looking a bit disgruntled, even Mandy calls her Dad.

John gets up and goes out to his car and comes back with the biggest box you have ever seen. Comes back into the room and plonks it on Margaret's knee.

Why Me

"What's this then?" Margaret looking a little puzzled at John.

"Open it and see, and yes I keep the recipe just in case." Well they both are opening it together Margaret and Mandy, well Margaret's eyes light up when she sees it for John had only gone out and brought her a sheepskin coat. Margaret tries it on and it fitted her like a glove. Well her eyes swell up and she gives John one of the biggest kisses he had ever had and John said after.

"Merry Christmas and I love you."

"You should have not brought me it; it must have cost you an arm and leg. And how the hell did you know my size." Margaret asking John.

"Nothing is too good for you, and the size I asked you're mate on Fashions at work Karen." Then it was Johns turn to stand there and look at Margaret waiting in great expectation for is extra gift.

Margaret passes John a very small wrapped up in Christmas paper packet, he opens it and it is a pair of gloves and a scarf. Margaret is trying to pacify John with it being so small, compared to her gift from John.

"They are lovely sweetheart just what I need to keep my hands warm just lately I've been feeling the cold when I take her out, thanks love.

"Yes but it's not like the present you gave me."

"None of that it's the thought and you know what I said they will come in handy with the weather getting colder and I'm getting older."

Mandy is cooking dinner with Margaret and John tells them that he will go for a drink with Brandy to the pub just up the road and Lyndon tells John that he will come with him.

They arrive at the pub and go in and ask the Landlord if it was OK to bring the dog into the bar, the Landlord tells them so long as it's the bar and not the Best-side. They thank the Landlord and order their drinks and go and sit near the open fire with Brandy who goes down under the table next to John. All the regulars are looking at Brandy and the size of her.

They sit talking and Lyndon suddenly tells John.

"Dad Mandy and I are thinking of starting a family, and what do you thinks about it."

"Who me, come on now Lyndon that's up to you and Mandy you're the ones who have to bring the child up not me." Then John thinks and tells Lyndon.

"That means me a Granddad, Grandpa John." He sits there smiling and then shakes Lyndon's hand.

They seemed to be bonding and enjoying their Christmas lunch drink. They have 3 pints and on the last one Lyndon's phone rings and it is Mandy telling him that dinner will be ready in half an hour, he tells Mandy that they will finish their drink and be on their way back home.

They are walking with Brandy and John asks Lyndon.

"When you lose Brandy will you replace her or wait till you children get older."

"Children is it now, blimey in the pub we where thinking of one and all off a sudden its children."

"No serious would you replace her."

"Look Dad we are starting to go forward in life who knows what will happen, and please don't mention this to Mandy, what we have been talking about."

"Son my lips are sealed." They have truly bonded Lyndon is calling John Dad and John is calling Lyndon Son, it just goes to show that drink in moderation can do you good.

They are back home and the table is set for Christmas lunch, crackers and all. They all sit down and they have a drink before they start dinner. Margaret asks them what the pub was like and John tells her.

"Marvellous you can take dogs into the bar and we sat talking Lyndon my Son."

"Must be good beer if you have come home feeling like that." Margaret starting to make the gravy for the dinner. All done crackers pulled and the jokes inside told, you know all the sad same jokes year after year.

Brandy can smell the turkey and she sits watching them all and the only problem is while you are eating, if you look at Brandy you will see the tap running and all the drool.

John doing is usual thing a little for him and some for Brandy, every time he gives brandy something you can here he gulp and they all can see it Mandy tells her Dad to stop it for Brandy will have her Christmas dinner later.

Why Me

Washing up done and it was retire to the lounge and just like millions of British they sit and listen to the Queens speech, they all have a drink when John said.

"Merry Christmas to us all." he raise is drink and they all clink them and take a drink.

Boxing Day and John and Margaret are going home for John has to be at work the next Day, they all say their goodbyes and they leave. That is one of the problems with working within the retail trade business requirements mean that if it falls wrong then you have to work.

Over the few months everything is just fine, the odd time John ad Brandy at his house witch I must say Brandy really looked forward to stopping with John. Then Easter comes round and John and Margaret are going over just for dinner then back home. The usual John walks Brandy down all her favoured walks and Mandy and her Mum prepare the Easter Sunday Lunch.

They sit down and are enjoying their meal when Mandy tells her Mum and Dad.

"I've something to announce." Well her Dad is tucking into his dinner and also Brandy when Mandy's Mum asked what it was.

"Well to put it bluntly, I'm expecting how first baby in December."

She sits there smiling at her Mum and Dad when her Mum tells her.

"Ho baby you will make a lovely Mum." Then she said.

"My God December you could have a Christmas baby."

""Yes Mum and I don't fancy carrying a lump at that time of year, you know cold Christmas coming and all the other side of Christmas shopping and things."

"You don't go fretting about small things like that we are here for you!" Trying to comfort Mandy is her Mum.

Over the months John is up and doing is usual thing with Brandy and vice verse the odd time Brandy comes down to stay at John's and she loves her walks through Melbourne Park. Come Christmas and they get to gather for the annual Christmas Dinner Mandy is due and all eyes are on her and her every move. She feels like they are ready to bounce at the drop of a pin.

"Will you lot stop worrying about me"?. She sits rubbing her belly and the same they all sit looking at her. Well Mandy as add enough and suddenly screems out and they all jump up, even Brandy is on her feet and looking at Mandy.

"Only kidding I thought I would get my own back, and Brandy come here." Brandy goes to Mandy and she starts to rub Brandy's ears and she is giving off a sound of content, she flops to the floor at Mandy's feet.

"Sweetheart we are only worried about you."

"I know you are but I don't need all this fuss, just enjoy Christmas.

Chapter 11

On the 30th December John and Margaret receive a phone call from Lyndon that Mandy had gone into labour and is in Leicester Hospital.

Mandy gives Birth to a baby Boy on the 31stDecember, her Mum ad Dad go and see her in Hospital, they are well pleased and Margaret just like any other Woman can not wait to hold him in her arms. She picks him up and shows him to John. John smiles and said.

"You know what this means don't you." Margaret looking puzzled asks what.

"He will get two lots of presents at Christmas." Well the way Margaret looked at John, if she had not had her Grandson in her arms, I think John would have had a large clip round the ear.

Brandy is just the same when they brought the Baby home and he is in his carrycot Brandy sniffed at him and lies-down next to him if it was Mothers instinct to look after the young.

A few weeks later Mandy and Lyndon have decided what they are going to name him and Mandy is off to the registry to register is birth. They have named him Jamie Jay, and after Mandy phone's her Mum and Dad to break the news. She also goes on to tell them that they are taking him to Brighton to show one of Lyndon's relations Jamie and would they have Brandy.

It's Mid March and the weather is now on the way to picking up with the temperature well into the 60s f. John had booked a caravan down at the East coast and is looking forward to taking Brandy. They both have 4 days of work and go on the Sunday morning.

John had a Rover two door and John puts Brandy into the back of the car, well if you could have seen her, just sitting there looking all majestic and refine. You would have thought John is carrying Royalty.

Bags in back of the boot and even Margaret made a comment about her.

"Look at her who does she think she is bless her." John turns to have a look, and all Brandy did is given him a good drooling.

"Well I'm going to enjoy this trip, God I hope we don't hit traffic or I'm in for a bath." John turning his head sideways and all he sees is

Brandy panting away looking forward. After about 2 hours with a stop to let the Royalty out of the back to stretch her legs. And they are in the caravan at Golden Sands at Chapel St Leonard's. Margaret unpacks inspects the bed and John asks her if she would like to have a walk up onto the front with Brandy.

"Give me five minutes and I will be ready." All unpacked and they are off to the front with Brandy alongside of them, Brandy has filled out more now from when she was a pup she had long legs and thin body. But now she looks like a proper fully grown St Bernard Dog just like the last photo of her at the end of the story.

They are up on the front and it is very breezy Brandy's nose is sniffing the air; I think she could smell the sea. With it just outside the season the note on the front tells you that they have only 2 weeks left before dogs are not allowed on the beach. John sees this and tells Brandy go on then have a run on the beach, well Brandy is off like a shot running away from John and Margaret and running back to them kicking up sand as she ran. They go walking off towards the sea and when Brandy gets there she is straight in without hesitation.

"Look at her anyone would think that she was a young pup not an old pensioner." John looking at Margaret, and then holding her hand. Margaret asks him.

"What are you going to do when you lose her?" squeezing John's hand.

"Don't let us think down those lines yet, I know that she is getting to the end but just look at her it's so unfair that they don't live to ripe old age."

Not only is it fun for Brandy but John and Margaret are bonding even more, and you could tell that they were both truly in love with each other. They had only been together for a little 30 years. They spend a good hour walking and the walk back along the shops to let Brandy dry off after her frolicking in the sea, I think she really enjoyed her self.

That evening they walk down to the local village pub and they are sitting outside and the temperature had dropped and it was feeling cold when the Landlord approached them and said to them.

"If you would like to come in and sit near the fire in the bar you are welcome, it's not high season yet then we don't allow dogs with us being full. The choice is yours."

"Thank you that is very kind of you, it is rather nippy sitting here."

Margaret acknowledging the Landlords offers. The truth be known it is appropriately to keep them drinking instead of having one and going.

They go and sit next to the fire and Brandy did know more than lays herself in front of the fire, I think it was to warm her coat up after the sea swim, and the frolicking she got up to in the water.

John goes to the bar and there were only a hand full of customers when at the bar one asks John.

"You have a fine looking dog there is she old." the man asked.

"Nearly 8 years old, she is my Daughters, well I say my Daughters if the dog could talk she would say she belongs to all of us for she is Family."

"I had a St Bernard 5 years ago; she was a good one just like yours.

"What happened to her?" John asking.

"She died of old age 9and 11 months old; I think the open fields around us bless her that kept her going."

Why Me

"Sorry about that its one of those things with them, they say bigger the dog shorter the live span." John goes back and gives Margaret her drink.

"Who were you talking to?"

"Just some bloke who said he used to have a St Bernard." They stop for well over an hour and a half and the time is approaching 8.30pm and they decide to go and head for the chip shop to take some supper back to the caravan.

John stands outside the chip shop with Brandy and her nose is smelling all the aromas of the chip shop drifting out, well the drool is flowing and John is saying to himself. I better get her some or I will have chip butty with drool if I don't.

"Margaret get's Brandy a fish." John making sure she had something when they get back.

They settle down TV on and the bread spread and Brandy tucking into her fish for about one and a half seconds and is straight to the table and sits there with a suck sit looking at John and Margaret Tuck into their supper.

Watered and feed it was time to settle down John on one side of the table and Margaret on the other they are bench seats that do turn into beds serving a due purpose table and bed.

They are watching TV and Brandy decides she would like to watch so she jumps up onto Johns side and plonks herself right in front of John so he could not see anything.

"Do you mind young Lady I can not see anything." Well Brandy turns looks at John and does no more than blonk herself across him, with her head on Johns shoulder and John underneath her.

"God get off me Brandy you weigh a ton." She is now 14 stone and you can imagine what that must feel like. She is soon back on the floor and they decide to turn in at 10pm, they are stripped and in bed in the end room which had a double bed init and no other room to walk round.

This is when it play time for you know what, yes Brandy from the end of the bed jumps up and plonks herself in-between Margaret and John with her head resting on John's neck.

"Bloody hell roll on breakfast." Well Brandy sighs and starts to snore right into John ear. After ten minutes then the drool starts to run down John's neck. Well he jumps up saying.

"That's it I'm of into the caravan and make a bed up in there." He slides out the bed the best he can and makes a retreat to the bench and throws some sheets and covers onto the bench.

He climbs in and is off in seconds he must have been tiered for the next thing he knows its daylight and Brandy is standing there licking his face, he looks at his watch and it is 7am.

"OK I'm up and let's go for a walk on the beach, but no swimming." He washes dresses and just before he goes out he tells Margaret that he will not be long, Margaret grunts and John goes.

They take a short cut and are up on the front the Sun is just coming up and walking through the sand dunes they spot rabbits playing on the banks of the dunes.

"I bet you wish you were off you lead girl for you would be straight amongst them." John looking at them and smiling. They walk along the front to the point and John sits on the steps that lead down to the sands and John starts to talk to Brandy.

"You're a hand full Brandy but I would not swop you for the World, what I am going to do when you're gone, there is no way I could replace a one off like you." Brandy sits next to John and puts her head on Johns lap and she closes her eyes. John leans down to her head and kisses her snout saying to her.

"I love you Brandy Snaps in a doggie sense, of course I love Margaret too." John here's someone cough and looks up and there is a couple leaning on the railing above him and they must have eavesdrop to every word John had said, all that they did when John looked at them was.

"Good morning lovely morning for walking the dog."

"Yes fine and John looks down and they had a little Shih-Tzu dog. Well he nearly burst out laughing for if Brandy had seen it she would have a nice tasty snack before breakfast. John gets up and starts to walk back along the beach with Brandy on the lead for there are one or two dogs coming onto the beach. They are back at the caravan and have been gone for well over an hour and a half, they go inside and Margaret looks down at Brandy and asks her.

"Where have you been sweetheart walking the legs of your Grandpa." Rubbing her head and stroking her.

"Wish you would do that to me every time I walked in." well Margaret did no more than ruffle John's hair up and kiss him on the cheek.

"What a good night's sleep I had Brandy was marvellous and no snoring from you." Margaret smiling at John, while she cooked breakfast.

John tells Margaret all about the walk and the couple with the Shih-Tzu dog.

"God Brandy did not go for it."

"No she was more interested in the sand and sea, boy I did not know we have been gone that long, I was up with her at 7am this morning."

Margaret putting his breakfast on the table and telling him.

"Well I think you deserve this then." John looks at the spread in front of him and tells her.

"That will do me fine." He sits and tucks into a full English breakfast with Brandy looking on in exportation for scraps.

After breakfast John asks Margaret what she would like to do, Margaret tells him that

"Why don't they go and have a walk round Inglemells Market, you never know we might pick up a bargain or two."

"Fine by me but let's hope others are not walking round with dogs, you know what Brandy is like when she sees them. I don't wont t go flying off with her pulling me to get to the other dog."

"She will be fine don't fret."

They get ready put Brandy in the back of the car and set off for Inglemells market. They set off and head for the market, it is set within the fair ground off Inglemells and there are hundreds of stalls to walk round you can buy allsorts of things from clothing to house hold goods.

They pull up in the car park and start to head for the market with people that are already there stopping and looking at Brandy. They are really into it when they come to a pet store and Margaret can not believe what she sees for on the store they had a brandy barrel for St Bernard's. She nudges John and points it out to him.

"Look at that sweetheart lets get it for Brandy we could put it on her when Mandy comes to pick her up when we are back home."

Why Me

John sees the Barrel and is eyes light up.

"We will put it on her when we get back to the caravan." They buy the barrel and are both very pleased with the price and perches. They spend about an hour walking round and head back to the car park for there journey back to the caravan.

They are back and the first thing they do is put the barrel round her neck and tell her to sit, well John is taking photo after another and is well pleased with the results of the photos. All that Brandy did was sit there and sigh.

That evening they take her down to the pub where they can take her in and the looks that they were getting John felt like he add one of the best possessions in the World, Brandy just did what she does best and looks the same.

"My you have a handsome dog there does it cost much to feed her." The Gentleman asked.

"No just like any other dog just one meal a day and little titbits." Margaret looking at John, who just shrugs his shoulders for he knew that Margaret was on about all the little slipped nibbles, he gives her.

They both feel pride at having such a lovely dog with all the complements they were getting and they both sit there just looking at the Queen of the show. They really enjoyed their stay with Brandy in the caravan even John with all the bed rumpus and toilet breaks that Bandy needed through the night. They are memories that they will cherish for the rest of their days.

Back home and they are waiting for Mandy to pick Brandy up, John shouts to Margaret who is in the kitchen that Mandy is coming down the path. Well when Mandy comes in and sees Brandy coming towards her with her Brandy Barrel swaying from side to side.

"What have they done to you sweetheart, come to your Mum and give me a kiss."

"Don't you like the Barrel Mandy?" John looking a little concerned at her.

"Don't be daft Dad of cause I like it; I hope you did not pay too much for it."

"You know your Dad it was on a pet store on the Market, and it was a bargain, nothing is too good for how Brandy. And it will come in handy when I take her out this winter, little tot to keep out the cold." Margaret asks.

"Where is the love of my heart Jamie?" He's in the car with Lyndon he's fast on and he's been like it ever since we left Brighton."

Why Me

Well before Mandy had finished Her Mum is halfway up the path heading for their car. She can here him in the back starting to cry and she opens the door and picks Jamie up, and he stops crying straight away.

"Hello Mum, hope you are well."

"Thanks Lyndon very well, we had a lovely time at the coast with Brandy and wait till you see what we brought her." Lyndon suddenly looks and sees Brandy trotting up the garden path on her lead with Mandy, when Lyndon sees her it put a right smile on his face with seeing the barrel move from one side to the other.

Mandy sees her Mum and is just about to say something when Margaret tells her.

"Don't worry he was crying when I looked in the back I'm just looking and getting him off again. And don't forget anytime you need a rest and nights out with Lyndon don't hesitate to bring him down and I will look after him for the night." Margaret kissing Jamie and putting him back into his travelling basket.

"Thanks Mum I will keep you to that. Love you and see you tomorrow."

"Bye baby, Lyndon drive carefully won't you."

"Mum we have just driven all the way back from Brighton." Mandy tutting and waving to her Mum when Lyndon pulls away.

She goes back in and they settle down on the sofa.

"It's times like this when you know you are getting old, I mean Family gone home, your sweetheart gone back." Then John grabs her arm, and tells her.

"Go and throw something on we will go and have a drink that might make you feel better. Old you might be but me, Life is for grabbing it by the tail and wallowing in it not sitting back and let it pass you bye."

"OK Professor Higgins, on my way Sir." Margaret kisses John and goes to put something on to go for a drink.

Chapter 12

Summer time starts at the end of March it's the time of year when the clocks go forward evening are lighter, I don't know what it is but this time of year the feeling of being alive hits home. And I think you feel

Of well being kick in.

Mandy brings Jamie and Brandy down on most weekends for her Mum to have Jamie and of course her Dad to have Brandy, Margaret loves feeding Jamie and she is truly engrossed with his well being, while John is on his favoured Park walking Brandy. Brandy is a lot slower now she is not so boisterous when she was younger, she is coming up to 9 years of age and she is feeling it.

John sits down with her under the trees and sits talking to her. John knows that what he had been told about St Bernard's and the age thing, he knows that time is running out and that time stops for no man or Dogs for that matter.

"You are one of the best companions I have ever had, don't know what is in your head or if you understand a word I'm talking about. But you are one of the best." John notices that Brandy sits there looking at him and this time her head is straight and not cocked to one side. The truth be known I think he had a tear in his eye. He is going to give her a kiss but this time Brandy leans forward and licks Johns face.

They carry on walking taking in the evening sunshine and after a steady long walk start to head home for a well earned rest.

Through the Summer John ether went up to Mandy's to walk Brandy or she came to his house.

When Brandy is down at Johns he sometimes takes her down to his local and every time Brandy had the Barrel on and this brought a lot of attention to her, and she to wallow in the fuss.

The time of Year is approaching November and the clock is put back and the nights are drawing in. John dislikes this time of Year dark nights and cold.

He is sitting in the pub waiting for Margaret to finish work and join him for a drink before they go home, when into the pub comes Mandy and she is crying.

"What is it sweetheart what is wrong?" John looking concerned.

"It's Brandy she went to sleep this morning and she has gone."

"Gone where."

"She died in her sleep."

"She will live forever in our hearts, while we are alive so is Brandy Snaps.

Brandy 9 years and 7 months Died November 5th bonfire night

John Bolstridge

1998-2007

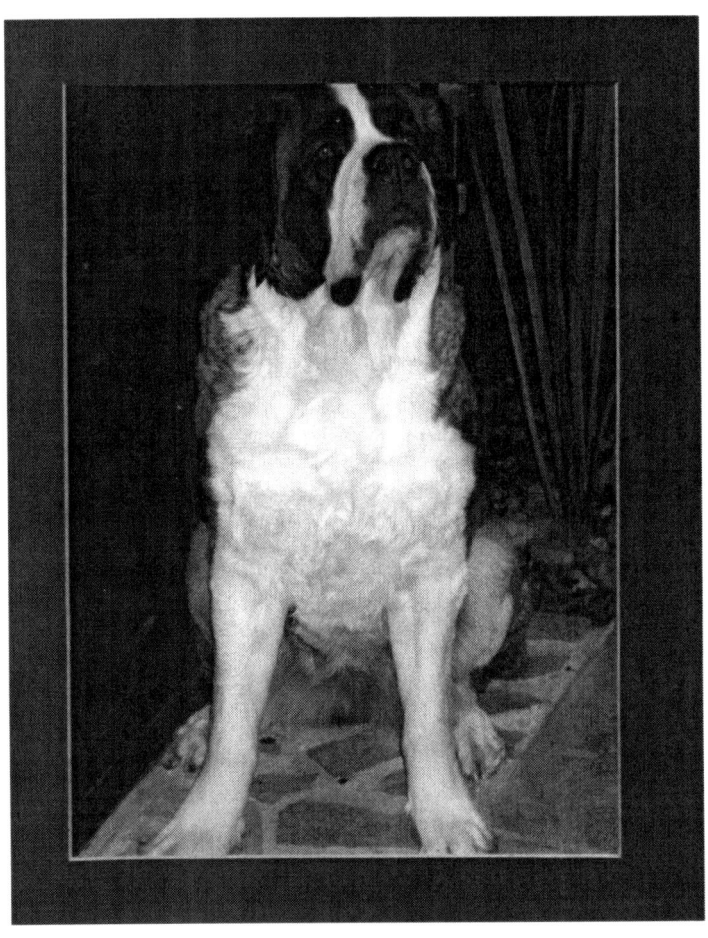

THE END

THE DAY TIME STOPPED

Chapter 1

The year is 2094 middle England, the World after years of wars and violence from terrorists is just starting to go into a time of peace and tranquillity. With people more looking into leisure pursuits then sitting glued to the news waiting to see what poor sole perished under the bombings and assassinations.

We pick up the story with John Grant, a 32 year old special agent with the British FBI created in early 2054. Sitting in their country garden enjoying one of the special moments with his wife Ruth, who is 6 month's pregnant. Who is expecting their first child? The time is 3.30pm mid July, hot and sultry day, put down to the break down of the ozone layers.

"John would you like a drink." Ruth asking John.

"Please love that would be nice." John looking up at the clear blue sky. He looks at Ruth walking back towards the house.

"Boy what I would do to have more time like this." But Ruth stands huffing a little with hands holding her tummy.

"It's alright for you but you don't have to walk with this little bundle all day." Ruth disappearing into the house after about 10 minutes Ruth comes out with the two drinks and starts to walk towards John, and then all of a sudden there is an earth tremor. The Sky for about 10 seconds turns from a clear blue sky to bright red, then back to clear blue sky again. Ruth drops the drinks on the lawn and stands there petrified at what had happened. John seeing Ruth dropping the drinks jumps up and heads straight for Ruth.

"Ruth sweetheart, are you alright." John concerned about Ruth

"What's happening John was that an earthquake." Ruth holding out her arms for John to hold her for a little reassurance.

They stand for a few moments arms locked when John's con-ex communicator rings.

"Hello John here."

"John did you feel the tremor up where you are." On the other end of Johns con-ex communicator is Johns boss Sir Ralph Ward Head of the FBI.

"To true Ruth nearly had the baby."

"Well I would like you to come down to London as soon has possible; we need to look into the cause of the tremor."

"Will do Sir; be with you first thing in the morning." Turning of his con-ex. John looks at Ruth, smiles and tells her that this certainly puts the breaks on is day of rest.

John remakes the drinks and they carry on enjoying the afternoon sunshine, at about 6.00pm they both retire back into the house, John goes upstairs and showers and dresses into more relaxing cloths. The evening is spent sitting arm in arm watching there 3-d monitor, one of their best viewing is of old silent movies. Brought to life with the latest 3-d technology it's about 9.20pm, John laughing at the antics of Laurel and Hardy suddenly turns his head.

And looks to the window and his face suddenly squints, and he his bewildered at what he sees outside,

"Ruth come and have a look," Ruth looks and asks John what was the matter.

"The Sun is still shinning on the lawn." John rising from his chair looking at his watch to make sure that he was looking at the right time, he stands there looking up at the sky.

"It's still bright sunlight; it should be dusk by now."

Ruth joined John and they both stand looking out into the garden. John opens the window and they both step out onto the porch, the temperature is just as it was at about 3.30pm 74 c.

"This can not be right the sun is still high in the sky." John stands there holding Ruth's hand.

"There must be some reason; maybe it's the Northern lights."

"Come off it Ruth not with the Sun this high in the sky," they both just stand there looking at the birds tweeting. Well over an hour as past and John looks at his watch.

"10.20pm and it's if the Sun had not moved, its well over an hour they stand not realizing the time its now 11.20pm. John goes and turns on the news and straight away there on the screen they are showing London and people relaxing in the sunshine, the commentator starts to tell people that they are experiencing some kind of Summer abnormality. After the Earth tremor this afternoon, then they switch to a University Professor who starts by telling them that this is the glasshouse effect coursed by the break down of the ozone layer. That

Why Me

they have been warning people for over 80 years, John laughs at what he his hearing.

"Come and listen to this rubbish Ruth, glasshouse."

"Let's go to bed John, I'm dropping to sleep." Ruth, coming towards him. John holds Ruth's hand and they go off to the bedroom. John finds it hard to drop off, for he keeps looking at the curtains and the bright sunlight reflecting through. He drops off and all of a sudden the alarm rings out, John jumps out of bed and draws the curtains back well the light streaming through makes John squint.

"God, it's still the same." Johns into the shower and dresses for his trip to London. Down stairs he turns the news on just when they are giving out a World report, showing pictures of Australia New Zealand in total darkness and New York just like London in bright sunshine. John goes and gently kisses Ruth telling her that he will be back tonight. Ruth murmurs and John heads for the garage and is two seated sports car that he loves.

(But soon will have to change when the little one arrives.)

The journey to London takes about 1 hour; John turns on the navigation system and the radio. He drives off with the news telling about all-night party's and people Sun bathing around the coasts of Britain, John thinking to himself shakes his head and tells himself crazy people. He arrives and heads towards the FBI entrance he is about to enter when from behind he hears someone call out his name, he turns and running up the steps to the entrance is Tim Bradford. He to be an agent in the same department that John is working in.

"Great this extra sunshine we are having, up this morning and did the lawns before 7am." "Good for you but think of the others around the World who are in total darkness." John striding out a little more telling his college that he will see him later. John goes into his office and on his desk is the message of that mornings meeting, he goes through it when into the room comes Sir Ralph Ward.

"Morning John hopes I'm not intruding."

"No please come in Sir."

"How's Ruth hope she is fine with the heat with her carrying the baby?"

"She's fine Sir, what brings you down here." Sir Ralph walks to the window in John's office and stands there looking at the streets below and the sunshine, with clear blue skies.

Why Me

"The meeting this morning you are aware of this unusual weather we have and what the reason are, but to come to a point it's our comrades abroad what they must be going through." Sir Ralph turns looks at John and tells him he will see him in the meting, with this Sir Ralph leaves Johns office and close the door behind him.

The time is 9.45am the meeting at ten is in the conference room at FBI.

At the meeting there is Scientist on World Global warming, agents from other Embassies in London. The meeting chaired by Sir Ralph everyone is present, John sits down in his chair. Into the room comes Sir Ralph with his secretary who is to take minutes; he sits shuffles the notes in front of him.

"Good morning Gentlemen welcome to this meeting on well I think you all know why we are here, we have to find a solution to the problem facing the World. Who would like to give their opinion of what is happening." There is silence then Professor Clive Watts of Global Scientific Research holds a loft his hand and states.

"What we have is years of neglect by man with emersions and pollution of the atmosphere."

"Rubbish." Comes from the floor. Sir Ralph sees who shouted and asks.

"It's Mr Pollard, if I'm not mistaken please comment."

"Sir we seem to be missing the main thing here."

"Please carry on." Sir John telling him.

"Well Sir Take a look outside." He stands and goes to the window.

"Look at the Sun it has not moved we are not up against ozone layers or terrorist, we are in some kind of void. TIME HAS STOPPED"

This brings roars of laughter from the floor but John sits there Taking It all in, Sir Ralph calls for order.

Then one of the Professors asks.

"If time had stopped, we are still looking at our watches, why the meeting at ten. Time is still ticking on."

"Yes you're watch will tick but look outside its still 3.30pm; it's if nothing happened then tomorrow, it will still be 3.30pm. Then John tells them.

"If what you are saying is true then if we don't find an answer, then all the big country producing wheat for bread. We will run down our food chain with them being in total darkness." They are all looking at each other and murmuring amongst themselves.

Over three hours going round and round in circles then Sir Ralph stands and tells them, that they should all go away and try and come up with an answer.

"This meeting is over good day Gentlemen." Then Sir Ralph looks at John.

"Please sit John, I would like a word in private." The rest stand and start to make their way-out of the meeting, the room empty Sir Ralph stands and starts to walk towards John.

"What do you think we are facing." Sir Ralph pressing the remote controls to open the blinds, and letting in the bright sunlight.

"Sir if I had any idea you would be the first to know."

"Well we had better come up with an answer soon all there will be anticay, after they realise that soon there will be no food to go around."

"Sir I'll try and come up with some answer." They both sit there for another twenty minutes when Sir Ralph stands Shakes Johns hand and tells him to keep him informed.

Chapter 2

Contact

John back in his office looks at his watch and the time is 3 30pm he laughs and tells himself well it's that time again; he looks outside and asks himself. Is it today or yesterday stands and starts to head out of the building for the journey home. He starts to drive through London looking at all of the people enjoying the sunshine, it's onto the motorway and he is enjoying the music. He comes to the turn off and heads down the B road towards home the time is 6.30pm, then all of a sudden there is loud crackling on his music. Something that never happens he tries to adjust the system wondering what is happening, then the windscreen goes bright red and he slams on the breaks. For he can not see anything but the bight red, the car stops and he tries to open the door but it just will not open.

"What the hell is going on?" Then from the back of the car a voice calling him, and not to be afraid.

"What's going on who are you." then there is a voice coming from the front he turns and looks at the windscreen and jerks back in his seat, for coming out of the red light emerges a white face with long white beard and a robe on its head.

"Who the hell are you God?"

"Don't be afraid John; we need your help."

"My help please tell me who you are."

"My name is Zen of Great Thor fourth planet of Unitize" John just sits there for a moment and asks.

"What do you want with me?"

"It's the time zone that you are stranded in we are in the same sort of position, but in another time Zone. We need you to help us undo this.

"What the hell can I do to help?"

"Let me start at the beginning one of our Great inventers developed the time Zone shifter, and was banned by the council from using the device. For on the second time he used it caused over ten thousand deaths on Great Thor, but his greed and lust for more tests used it and went through a time black hole dragging great Thor and the Earth on to an equivalent parallel."

"We need you to find him and send him back that is why we have chosen yourself with your record of finding terrorists. We will let you know more details later." Just before John can ask any questions the red screen disappears and John is looking down the country lane and he just manages to bring the car under control.

"What the hell is going on one minute, standing still the next moving?" John grabbing the wheel and seeing his local coming up pulls into the car park and just sits there trying to gather his thoughts.

"Was that real or was I dreaming." He opens the door and slams it behind him and goes into the bar, the Landlord talking to one of the customers sees John and asks him.

"Pint of Drakes John, how's the weather outside. Any sign of a change."

"No still warm and sunny, tell me Fred did you see the sky go red a few minutes ago."

"Red no, only the other day when it all started, why do you ask,"

"No forget it Fred,"

John picks up the drink and takes a large swallow, Fred shrugs his shoulder and carry's on talking to the customer. John sits for a moment looking out the window, looking at cows in the fields eating and the young calf's playing. He ponders with his thoughts then phones; Sir Ralph up on the phone appears Sir Ralph.

"What have you go for me John?"

"Sir I don't know what to tell you it's what happened on the way home this evening,"

"Well out with it John, I can tell with the look on your face, that something is not right."

"Well Sir on the way home, I just turned of the motorway when suddenly my in car entertainment crackled something that never happens then suddenly." John stops dead and just sits there.

"Well come on man out with it, what happened."

"Well Sir the sky turned red just like it did when time stopped, and then." Again John stopped.

"Yes and what," Sir Ralph trying to push John to tell him.

Why Me

"Sir please I tell you as it happened, all of a sudden there was this voice telling me that someone from another dimension had come into our time and caused time here and their zone to stop in time, we are being pulled into a black hole and the World will end and that they needed me to help them stop him and to restore time to it's proper time."

What Sir Ralph tolled John next really surprised him.

"Well John lets hope this voice gets in touch soon and lets you know what you have to do, you have my full backing John but just make sure you keep me well informer on developments. And come on let's have the John I know, not the face you have on you now."

Well this makes John change his face and he looks at Sir Ralph and thanks him for his support.

Sir Ralph smiles and turns off. John sits looking at the blank screen and then he suddenly thinks of Ruth.

"Better get back home," John stands and heads for the door with everyone saying good night to John, he waves and exits the pub.

He stands next to his car, looks up at the bright Sun and blue skies and he is thinking to himself what the hell I can really do to stop this.

Back at home Ruth greets him as he emerges out of the car, and the first thing Ruth tells John is that he looks tiered. John smiles tell her that he is just tiered from driving from London. They both go back into the house. John changes and they sit talking over dinner when John tells Ruth about the encounter that he had that afternoon. Ruth listens to John explaining and all the time is reassuring John that things will be better soon.

Its if she just wanted to put this to the back of her mind, about 9pm.John stands tells Ruth That he was going to shower before they retire. He goes walking up the stairs rubbing the back of his neck, on the landing he takes off his shirt just as he opens the bathroom door. He enters and closes the door and turns, but what he sees nearly makes his jump out of his skin.

He is looking straight into dense mist; he turns to open the door and it will not open. He out stretches his hand and into the mist, the feeling is cold as the mist rolls round his arm he starts to shout out Ruth's name.

Why Me

"Ruth, Ruth," then from behind him he hares someone call out his name, he swivels round and shouts.

"Who's there?" He stands there and his eyes fixed looking straight into the mist, when out of the mist starts to appear a figure. John steps back as it comes clearer and there standing in front of him is a figure that looks human but the more John stares at it he can tell that it is not human, for when he looks at the face it seems to blend in with the mist.

"Who are you, where am I," John out stretches his hand towards the figure and his hand just goes straight through him, this brings a gasp from John and he steps back.

"Don't be afraid John, I'm Zen, we spoke earlier, and the answer to you second question you are where you are."

"I'm where I am, well this is not like my bathroom." The silence is so hairy John asks what he wanted.

"What I'm about to show you will shock you, this is the man that we require you to send back to us." All of a sudden in front of John comes a figure and John can not believe what he sees, for looking back at him is himself.

"That's me."

"Yes your form, but it's our Great Inventor Deero. First Done of Zen we have the ability to shape change, that's why you are looking at myself in our form. You must find him and send him back to our time zone, or all will be lost as the time zones clash and swallow each other up."

"But I have nothing like this, how the hell do I send him back," John's arms out stretched and looking at the mist.

"On the floor in front of you, see pick it up. This is a time zone interface just hand it him, once he contacts the time zone will deploy and he will be back where we can restrain him and destroy the machine." John bends picks up the device and looks to where Zen was and he is back in the bathroom. He opens the door and shouts Ruth; she comes out of the bedroom and asks what the matter was,

"Did you here anyone in the bathroom."

"What do you mean John? Voice." John stops and tells Ruth not to worry, as he stands looking at the device in his hand, the same size of a small mobile phone.

"What have you got in your hand" Ruth trying to reach out to take the device, John pulls back and tells Ruth to go back into the bedroom,

Ruth sits up in bed and John enters still clutching the device.

"Please John what's wrong."

"What I'm about to tell you, you must tell me your honest opinion." John tells Ruth all about the encounter in the car and again in the bathroom, John is took back with Ruth's reply, for she is totally worried about the thing John is getting into.

"Please John what ever is happening; please think of our baby, I would be nothing with out you." Ruth with tears streaming down her face, John takes one look at her and straight away reaches out and wraps his arms around her and at the same time trying to reassure her.

"Come on now where is my right arm, you know that you and the baby would come first," they just lay back on the bed and just drift into deep sleep with the Sun outside still beaming down.

About an hour they have been asleep when John turns over to face the wall when all of a sudden he is woken and he is lying on the floor with some kind of mist all around him, as he stands out of the mist appears Zen.

"John take this with you, you may need it, Deero can move within a time zone of your dimension so you will be able to follow," John takes the device and before he can say anything Zen reaches out and puts his hand on Johns shoulder and John stands there and it is if Zen was showing him how to use the device, for about a minute Zen holds John then backs off

"You're well informed on how to use the device."

"Yes how do you," and before John can say anything else, he is back in bed sitting up.

"Not again," this wakes Ruth up who turns and sees John sitting there with the device.

"What have you there?" Ruth rubbing her eyes and looking at the device in John's hand?

"Nothing dear, just go back to sleep," they both lay back and John lays there looking at the Sunlight shinning on the bedroom curtains. it only seems like minutes when the alarm goes off and John sits up and turns the alarm off, he's up and goes to the bedroom curtains and to greet him when he pulls them back is bright Sunlight, he stands there for a moment and starts to wonder how the wild life around the area is getting on.

for with it being 6.00am there is no dawn chorus from the birds, they sit in the trees as confused with their environment just like humans, John showers and starts to get ready for his journey to London for work. He kisses Ruth and tells her that he will be back that evening, in the garage he reverses the car out and the thing that takes his eye is the gadget that Zen left him. He picks it up and presses a few buttons as if he knew what he was doing and the next thing he is back in the bedroom looking out of the window.

"Woo," he presses a few more buttons and he is back in his car, he puts the device onto the seat and stars to drive off, looking at the device and telling himself, "boy, that's some toy".

Chapter 3

Down in London the first thing John must do is report to Sir Ralph on last nights events.

He knocks on Sir Ralph's door, and from inside he hears Sir Ralph shout come in, John enters and sits looking at Sir Ralph.

"What have you for me John?"

"Well before I start Sir I would like to show you," John pulls the device out of his pocket and his fingers start to press buttons on the device, and the next thing John is standing behind Sir Ralph as he shouts Come in, John taps Sir Ralph on the shoulder.

"How the hell did you get there," John presses a couple of more buttons and he is back sitting looking at Sir Ralph.

Sir Ralph looks at John if he was starting to go down with something.

"Sir don't worry I will explain."

Why Me

And then Sir Ralph realises that all is not right. John starts to explain all about Zen, and the fugitive Deero, and what will happen if he does not stop him.

John reaches into his pocket and pulls out the other device and tells Sir Ralph what it was for.

Sir Ralph looks at John and tells him that what he had told him and this Deero fellow.

"Well everything is in your hands now John, by the sounds of things you had better makes it sooner than later, at stopping this villain." Sir Ralph starts to look up, but unknown to him. John had pressed a few buttons and he had disappeared.

John was in some kind of vortex, everything is twisting and turning all colours of the rainbow, and then suddenly he reappears out in the country, looking at tall skyscrapers in the distance across the fields.

Then from behind a voice telling him to turn round and not to make any sudden moves, slowly John turns, and standing there is this woman with some kind off weapon in her hand, she asks John.

"What are you up to, and were are you from." John thinks for a moment then just comes out with it.

"I am an F.B.I British agent, from the planet Earth looking for one Deero, to arrest and send back to Zen on Planet Unitize."

"That's O.K. then, my names Merika, Law Hunter," at the same time lowering her sidearm.

"Law hunter, oh yes Bounty hunter, that's what we call them back home, you don't know were we could eat, do you."

"Yes see that tall building over there," Merika pointing her finger across the fields at the tall skyscraper, on the 36 floor, you can get all sorts of meals."

"That's well over 6 miles away, nothing closer," Merika lifting her eyebrow and squinting at what John had said.

"What are you on about, of course you are not from my planet, let me try and pacify you, look over there can you see that, Merika pointing to a sort of archway."

"Yes I see it what about it," John looking more puzzled.

"Well it's a Tran-Tax," Merika just grabbing Johns hand and leading him to the entrance, she swipes a card into it and voice activates it by telling it,

"To the 36th floor tower one, please." She steps forward still holding Johns hand and dragging him forward, there is a flash when she walks forward and Johns hand in Merika seemed to pull him forward. When he is pulled through he appears on a floor that reminded him of a shopping mall.

He stands there trying together his thoughts at the same time saying to himself no way," the first thing he sees is a window goes over to it and he can see in the distance the field were he had been. He turns and looks at Merika, all she does is shake her head and pucker her lips.

Come-on John I thought you wanted to eat. John starts to follow Merika at the same time looking at the arch that he had come from and feeling all parts of his body, to make sure everything was in order.

Inside the shop Merika goes to a hatch, turns and asks John what he would like to eat and drink,

"tea and sandwich, salad no mayo," well it was Merika turn to look at John in a funny face, at what he just said

"What," shrugs her shoulders tell the speaker in the hatch what John ordered and orders her meal.

"One big babe and soft mug." Well if anyone was looking at them they would certainly get some funny looks with them both looking at each other in funny ways. within seconds a try comes down into the hatch with what they ordered, they go and sit at a table next to the window, they start telling each other about themselves, John tells her that he needs to know were he can find out where likely Derro would be.

"Hold on John lets get you sorted with the running of this planet first, I mean what are you going to do about getting about and you're needs if you need to purchase anything."

"Never crossed my mind, it's this Derro he is starting to get at me, you know its back home, I'm in the dark at what might be happening."

"Yes O.K, first thing first," Merika passes John a card out of her pocket,

"This card is valid for all the Tran-Tex, just swipe and speaks into the panel and tell it your destination, when you have the green light move forward, but in no way do you enter if on red,"

"Why what happens if you enter on red."?

"You wouldn't like the outcome, I've seen it once and boy what came out the other end was a complete blob of bone and flesh, all put back in an unrecognised heap."

"What about your currencies for buying things, I mean what about this meal we have in front of us," John looks down at the sandwich that was in front of him and boy it did not look like a salad sandwich,"

"No problem the card you have is also your cash card, on entering your card is read when you order it is put onto the card."

"Merika you know where I come from the Planet Earth, we have one Sun and one Moon, but where is this Plane, what is it called. Other words where the hell am I."

Merika thinks for awhile them tells John,

"Well this will take you back at what I'm going to tell you, you are on the Planet Volgo, we have two Suns and three Moons, we have seen this Planet Earth but it is out of the question to and try and get there for it is well over 12 million light years away, it would need some craft for centuries to travel hence why we decline. So how the hell did you get here?"

John pulls the little gadget out of his pocket and shows her."

"You're kidding me," Merika looking at the little device and screwing up her face."

John them pulls the other device out and shows her how he can shift, sitting next to her one second, then from across the eating place shouting to her, then sitting again next to her.

"You can pack that in," Merika not likening the moves he was making.

"Well that sorted, I think you should be armed, you never know you might need it when you come across some of Derro henchmen, eat up and I will show you." They both finish their meal and Merika makes her way back with John to the Tran-Tex she swipes her card and tells it were she would like to go, grabs Johns hand and walks through the Tran-Tex, reappearing back next to the field from were they came from.

They both go into the field and Merika pulls the little hand device out of her pocket and hands it to John, she shows him how to work it and tells him to firer at the tree across the field, he lifts the device up and fires directly at the tree. There is a beam shooting out of it and it hits the tree in the middle, and the middle part of the tree disappears and for a moment the top half seemed to hover. Then falls back onto the stump, for a few seconds it stands there then goes crashing down to the ground.

John can not believe what he had seen." My God what the hell is in this thing," John looking at the device.

"It's an atomizer, nothing can withstand it, even if you aimed it at the ground you would end up with one of the biggest holes you have ever seen."

"Well you're sorted what you want to do next," Merika asking John.

"Well stopping somewhere tonight then start on the hunt for Derro tomorrow."

"You could come and stop at my place tonight if you would like," Merika putting her propose to John,

John smiling at her.

"Fine by me lead on."

They both go back to the Tran-Tex Merika swipes and tells it," Bottom Grove she swipes and starts to walk this time just telling John to follow, with him not being used to it goes running into it. Well Merika comes out the other end still walking then John appears and crashes straight into her they both land up flat on the floor with John on top of her, she looks at John and tells him in not so many words.

"Well you could wait till we get in doors; it's against the law to do it here."

Well Johns is all apologetic but all Merika does is smile at him.

They rise dust themselves down and go to Merika apartment, once inside Merika tells John that she is going to refresh herself up, she tells John to help himself to anything.

She's in the shower, while John pours a drink while he is doing it he notices a mirror on the wall and he can see Merika in the shower. He can not take is eyes of her slim and fit body; he stands there memorized on her. When she to can see him looking, she no more then invites him to come and wash her back, well John just walks forward and into the bathroom picks up a sponge and with his cloths on starts to soap her back.

Slowly moving the sponge down her back and onto her buttock, Merika turns round and looks at John with a glazed look and starts to pull John into the shower, gently undoing his buttons on his shirt. John is kissing her and squeezing her buttocks, slowly his hand from the back slips his hand onto her virgina from the back, by now John has no cloths on and they are both getting into frenzy.

"Take me to the bed." John picks her up and walks to the bed puts her down and they are both in grossed in full intercourse Merika every time John pushes she screams out with pleasure they are both having climax after climax, and after they both fall flat on their backs with sweat running of them Merika tell John that she will have a quick shower to cool down and he can join her. After they shower they are both on the bed and making small talk on what will happen tomorrow.

Merika asks "what does this Derro look like,"

"You are not going to believe this, but at this moment in time he looks a splitting image of me."

"You're kidding me, just like you."

"Yes till he meets me, then he might shape change." Then John asks.

"Do you know were we might find him,"

"Well that will not be hard, for he advertises in the local and International press, looking for agents for his business involvements in Gold and Silver, and Diamonds."

"Well can you arrange to meet him say to buy goods of him, at where ever he deals from."

"Leave that to me, I'll go and communicate with my hand interconnect device." John intrigued watches her when she goes and sits at a desk and puts her hand on a device and tells it.

"Derro international goods, appointments for agents to buy." The gadget flashes and she tells John that they have a meeting tomorrow at his island plant in Bores Country at 11am.

"You kidding me you put your hand on that and all that info came through into you head, with out pressing any buttons."

"What the hell are you talking about?" Merika looking at John puzzled.

"Just forget it back home we call the device you used the internet."

John goes and sits on Marcia's balcony, the sight that he sees he can not believe for she lived on a lake that looked like an ocean, there were two moons shining off the lake and you could see the ripples of the water flickering in the double Moon light. He sits and

Why Me

starts to think what he had done with making love to Merika and he had a wife back home. But this was the point he could not get his head round, wife back home where is home he is in a different Universe and the Earth is no more than a speck in the distance.

He sits pondering and trying to get an answer but he is still confused, for the feeling he had is the same if you were in a dream. Dreaming about things but no in reality. Then Merika comes with two more glasses of refreshment and sits next to John.

"What are you thinking about." Asks Merika.

"Just back home, what is happening back there is there still hope or will I be to late."

"Come on now lets not get desponded you will pull it off and be the savour of a whole Universe. No, No two Universes." She leans forward and gives John a kiss on the check.

"This meeting where is it and how do we get there."

"Derro holds all the meetings at the plant where he operates the device, if we are lucky we might have a guided tour of the place. And to answer you second question, the place we seek is set on an Island just of the coast, and the mode of transport will be by Hover boat." John asks.

"You telling me we will not be going by the gadget that brought us to your home."

"I'm afraid not you see we have only just made short intercity transfer, they aim to go International within 3 years. They have tried it on animals and you would not believe the results when they arrived at the other end, some of the animals materialised inside out."

Chapter 4

John sits there and is thinking about Ruth back home, it's a strange feeling that he had for it seemed that there was no planet Earth. It's if he is in some kind of dream and will wake up from all this. And even the sexual contact he had with Merika seemed natural and he did not feel he is being unfaithful.

For when this dream ends he will be back to normal, or will I. Then Merika brings him another drink and she had slipped into a very short silk nightie, where she is standing the light went straight through it and did not leave much to the imagination. John puts out his hand and she responds, he puts the drink on the ground and pulls her onto him.

He starts to slip is hand onto her thigh and gently starts to move up to her breast.

He is gently squeezing her breast then moves to her nipples and Merika starts to breathe a little heavier and seemed to stick her chest out.

John is soon kissing her belly and at the same time with his hands still on her breast, starts to kiss her thigh moving towards her virgina area.

Merika starts to move forward and John starts to kiss her clitoris and his tong slips inside her virgina by now Merika is in heaven moaning and groaning at the pure pleasure she is getting. Her juices are flowing.

John had slowly removed his shorts and is fully aroused, Merika puts her hand behind her and down onto Johns penis, she is gently pulling it down and back up. And she can here John moans John starts to make his way back up to her nipples, his tong is flicking her nipples and Merika at the same time slips on to his penis and they are having full sex, under the 2 moons that are just above them.

After about 30 minutes they both move into the bedroom. John is carrying her and slowly puts her down onto the bed, he stands there and in the moon light Merika can see that John had still a full erection, she sits up puts her two hands onto Johns buttocks and starts to slip her mouth onto Johns penis she starts gentle going forward and then slowly backwards with her head.

John stands there and starts to stretch upwards with pleasure, after 10 minutes John turns Merika onto her belly and they are having doggy style sex. They both must have climax more than 3 times and they flop onto the bed fully exhausted.

"That was one of the best fucks I've had, what the hell will I do when you go back to wherever you are from."

"I wish I could stay with you Merika but that will be imposable for if I fail in anyway with the device I will disappear after 3 days."

They wake at 7am and they shower for this is the day that John is going to meet the man he is to detain and send back to Zen of the Planet Unitze.

They have a little to eat and by 7.30am they are ready to depart, John asks Merika.

"Were do we pick up this so called Hoverboat." Merika tells him.

"It will be outside for me at 7.30am." They g to the front door and Johns eyes light up for there is this craft, hovering about two feet of the ground with a gentle hum coming from it.

"How the hell do we get in the thing?" John standing there scratching his head, all Merika did is smile at John and talks to the machine did what she said.

"Open door and start." The machine lowers to ground level and Merika sits at the controls, John enters and sits in the front with Merika.

"What stops anyone from stealing the dam think, if all you have to do is talk to it?" Merika pulling away from her house replies,

"That's imposable to-do for the Hoverboat is voice activated when you order it, then it will only start with my command." Then John is even more curious.

"What makes it hover is it fan driven and if it is why can we not here the blades."

"What the hell are you going on about fans and thinks; this is a Hoverboat works on magnetic pulses from the ground and the boat it will always hover at two feet. Even at Sea the same if you ride a wave on the up, it will always be two feet away from it, you will see this when we get to the Sea. Anyway sit back and enjoy the ride." Merika swinging the Hoverboat to the right and going over a hedge and heading out across wastelands, at well over 80mph. By now John is holding on to the arms of his seat and looking straight ahead, he can not take his eyes off the front and look at Merika.

"Chill out man you're safe with me, I've only tipped one of these over four times." Well

Why Me

these remarks they certainly made John look straight at her and his eyes are well and truly fully open.

"What four times." Well Merika starts laughing her socks off, and tells John.

"I'm only kidding just ease up a little; maybe I will let you have a go when we reach the Sea." They are well into the journey, they have been travelling 2 hours and they have one hour to go, when John asks if they could have a break.

"Will pull over here but don't forget to be careful we are out in the wild country now." Merika slowing down and the Hoverboat comes to a rest. John is first out and the place is dry and hot, there are a few trees and bush, you could say it is like the start to a desert just like back home on Earth. John had walked about 200 yards away from the Hover when in the distance he could see a dust trail and a clacking sound getting louder, he swings round and he nearly had a mishap in his pants.

For coming straight at him, this 14 foot giant long neck bird looking something like an Australian Emu, with this large beak clacking away.

He pulls out his atomiser and points it straight at it, he his about to pull the trigger when Merika spots him pointing at it.

"JOHN DON'T SHOT." Merika shouting at top of her voice,.

"They are Man friendly and will not arm you." John lowers the atomiser and the beast comes skidding to a hold and goes down on its two legs in the sitting position, and all the time it is clicking away with its beak.

With it sitting it brings the animal down to 7 feet and it sits looking at John. Merika comes and starts to stroke its beak and it clacks away even more, well John strokes the back of its neck and the animal just shoots straight up with John hanging on like grim death. The bird is going frantic clicking and nodding its head and at the same time John comes crashing back down to the ground.

Merika is esthetical with laughter and goes to John and tells him the best she can in-between laughing.

"So you're being unfaithful are we with another bird."

"What the hell do you mean and what's up with that daft thing."

"Well you were only rubbing its erotica zone, you have a new mate. I think it's in love with you."

The bird is going crazy, walking away just like a pigeon back home when you are feeding them, their necks bob forward and back, well this bird is doing the same thing. It looks comical for it goes about 100 yard turns and comes walking straight back to where John stood. Circles him and starts walking away again. Merika grabs Johns arm and pulls him back to the Hoverboat and they make a hasty exit away from John's lover.

"God what hell hole of a planet have I come to, I mean bloody 14 foot birds that fall in love with humans what next."

"Don't forget this is my World, what do you think I would be like back on the Earth and all your strange beings. You have a lot to lean about Planet Volgo; you have not seen anything yet."

"Sorry Merika but it's just what happened on the spur of the moment, I mean look at the sky right now two Suns shining bright. I just wish I could see more of it and learn the ways of your Planet but that is imposable." Merika pulls up on the beach just before they are going to cross the water for their meeting with

Derro, and the establishment that transport goods through dimensions.

She steps out of the Hoverboat and a short walk to the waters edge, the Sea is calm and the gentle ripple of the waves hitting the shore. John walks up to her and puts his arm around her.

"You're mad with me I can see this, the way you are standing and the look on your face."

"No John that's were you are wrong, for I know the further we go and it will bring us a little closer to a foreclosure to us. Then you will be back with your wife and baby and a future, but me I will just have memories of the time we spent together."

Merika stands and you could see that she is swelling up inside. John sees her tears and puts his arms around her and starts to comforter her.

"You will always remain in my heart every time I see the moon and the Sun you will be there with me, for what we have no one can take or replace what we feel for each other."

She turns to John and they stand kissing in a full embrace with the sound of the gentle ripple of the waves.

They go walking arm in arm back to the Hoverboat and Merika gives the order for two drinks and out of the front of the Hoverboat comes two drinks.

"What a drinks cabinet, boy that would go down well in my World."

Merika smiles and starts to input messages into the overboat. John starts to walk back to a mound at the top of the beach and suddenly out of the sand appears a plant with a large head and a romantic smell.

John just stands taking in the aroma and leans forward to where he thinks the aroma is coming and suddenly a large jaw appears and is about to clamp down on his head. Merika fires her atomiser and the plant disappears and out pops another. John realises that he is in the wrong place and just stands frozen to the spot. Again Merika fires her atomizer and tells John to start walking backwards. Every step he takes and another one pops up, the same again Merika fires.

"My God help me." John still walking backwards and Merika fires again. He is in the clear and the sweat is pouring off him.

"They were just like the plants back home, a fly trap, how can you bring young ones to the beach with things like that lurking.

"We no where they breed and would not dream of going near them."

They go back to the Hoverboat and John kisses Merika and thanks her for what she had did.

"No problem I've set the controls and let's see how Earthling flies Hoverboat." John's eyes light up for he has the opportunity to fly a Hovercraft on water.

"Come on then baby lets fly away." John in is excitement goes to the other side and gets in rubbing his hands.

"Hover start." The Hover starts and he puts his hand on the control and it starts to skim across the water two feet above the wake.

"Boy this is magical if we only had the technology we would be well away." John is turning left then right and is really getting into this Hover thing.

They are flying for about 45 minutes when in the distance they see the island approaching and all of a sudden a voice comes through asking who they were and what is there destination.

"We are John Grant buyers of the products that Derro is selling by advertising in the mail, we require permission to dock and proceed to the meeting with Derro." There is silence and they come back on and tell them.

Chapter 5

"Proceed and when you see the light at the entrance to the dock just follow the green lights to your docking bay, where you will be met by one of our security staff."

They follow the lights and dock at the bay they are told. They disembark and to great them is one security Staff who immediately salutes John.

Merika in a shallow voice tells John that

"He must think you are Derro."

"Good morning Sir."

"Good morning, please identify yourself to me."

"Sir I'm a new recruit First Officer Year one Wayne Foden, at your command Sir." He salutes John by putting his hand just under his chin and clicking his heels.

Why Me

"Come walk with us Wayne, that's if you don't mind me calling you Wayne."

"Not at all Sir please call me Wayne if you so desire"

John putting his arm round Wayne and they all go walking up the hill to the top were they are over looking the plant.

"Lets drop this Sir bit, you see the plant at the bottom and all the containers coming out of the large building." John pointing towards the plant, with him still with his arm round Wayne.

"Yes Sir," then Wayne apologises and tells Derro that he did not know what to call him if he can not call him Sir.

"Call me John, and back to what I said have you wondered where all the raw material comes from if there is non going in."

"Yes Sir I have wondered about that and everyday when you look at the plant it seems to shimmer, just like it does when the heat rises off the ground on a hot day."

"Well they are bringing in goods from different Universe and disrupting time and space by doing so."

"How do you mean disrupting time and space." Wayne screwing up his face and looking at John and Merika.

"You see one off those Planets I live there and the time has stopped and the World and all the cosmos in my Universe is going to die for, the thinks that are going on down there are pulling my Universe and another into a black hole and billions and billions will lose their lives, unless I can put an end to Derro greed."

Wayne pulls back away from John and asks who he really is.

"My name is John Grant member of the British FBI on my planet the Earth." John pulls out a warrant card with a photo and all his details.

Wayne standing looking at John and John disappears in front of his eyes and appears behind him were John taps him on the shoulder. Wayne spins round and sees John for a second and John disappears again and he is in front of Wayne and John talks to him.

"You see Wayne I've not a lot of time to accomplish this and I would like your help in doing it."

"What good am I to you? You will be up against an army of Security Staff and they are armed and will kill and ask question after,

Why Me

that's if anyone survives to be interviewed. And what other magical powers do you have."

John explains all to Wayne and the other gadget that he had to get Derro to use, so he could be sent back to where he came from and stand trial for great misuse of there Government equipment.

Wayne thinks for a while and agrees to help, so long that if all went wrong he had to tell them that you had him under threat and you would kill him if he did not help you. John shakes Wayne's hand and pulls him to his chest and thanks him for his trust and bravery in this desperate situation.

Before they go any further John tells them the plan of action and what Wayne had to do, they are first going to go and have a look at the running of the plant and the machine that brings goods in from different Dimensions and Universes.

"Are you all sure what you have to do." They all tell John that they did, and John tells them to give him ten minutes. He goes into a building that served for incoming guests to the island to go to the toilet. John went in but Wayne and Merika were taken back when they thought he came out. John goes walking towards them when Wayne asked.

"Can I help you Sir." John laughs and tells him that it was him in disguise for he looks like Derro and does not won't to jeopardise the mission with Derro seeing him as he is. Wayne tells them that they will use the plant customers transport, he takes them round the corner and there is one of the transporters and when they approached the cigar shaped carriage with an all glass top and side for panoramic views Wayne voice activates the carriage and the top flips open and they get in, the driver at the front centre with the others sitting behind in a line, they will hold up to four and it looks like you are on a bike but with no wheels.

Just like a hover boat the craft goes about two feet into the air and glides off with very little noise for their tour of the compound, they approached a check point and they are pulled up by the security staff and the first thing they do is start to have a little banter with Wayne with him being a new recruit, they are laughing at him and poor old Wayne felt very embarrassed with him being with Merika and John, well John is used to handling nasty piece of work so these two should be easy play.

He storms out of the carriage and straight up to the two and starts to address them.

"Do you know who you're talking to shit faces; I'm Derro's adviser and top buyer. Anyone who gets in the way off me and my business can pay with the lattermost price their lives and you two are bordering on that. So get the fuck out of the way or I will come back with the biggest pair of gloves on and personally put my arm up you're arse and rip the fucking shit out of you."

John goes back to the carriage and if you could have seen the two security Staff they were adjusting them self's for I thing with what John had said they both were feeling their bum cheeks squeaking. Wayne sits there and looks at them both smiling and with the biggest grin as he asked them.

"Anything else before I go Gentlemen."

"No get gone now, go on go." Wayne pulls away and he is looking through the reverse mirror and tells John.

"You were bloody marvellous it's a wonder they both did not leave a pile were they where standing with a telling off like that." Wayne trying to contain himself with laughter.

Chapter 6

THE MACHINE FOR UNIVERSE SHIFFTING

Wayne pulls up at the building that contained the main work horse for the dimension and Universe transport of goods; he tells them that they will go to the observatory for guest's and buyers before they find Derro.

They enter by Wayne swiping his pass into an entry lift, for personnel only, the doors of the lift open and they enter. On the way up they hear the sound of humming and all of a sudden there on the lift when they looked at each other they seemed to be shimmering.

"What the hell is going off?" John looking at Wayne and Merika. And they are looking back with that unknown look that tells you that all is not normal. The lift doors open and Wayne takes them to the observation room and what they see makes them gasp. For down below they can see this great

Why Me

big machine with electric waves of lighting coming from it. And the entrance to the machine there is container after container coming from it.

"Now you now Wayne what I told you about this Derro the more he uses this thing the worst effect it will have on my Universe and the other, God I've got to stop him before it's to late." Then Wayne spots Derro at the front of the machine and pointing tells John to look.

"Down there, there is Derro and what is he doing." Wayne is looking at Derro then all of a sudden Derro changes and he his standing looking like another worker in white protective clothing.

"He's shape shifted, I wonder what for."

Then he sees why one of the workers is trying to open one of the containers that had come through the machine. Derro sees him and approaches and pulls out an atomisers and confronts the worker.

"No one steels of Derro." Then he lifts the atomiser and fires it at the worker who disappears with out trace. And he changes back to himself.

John Bolstridge

Derro is throwing orders here and there telling all that they had better stay on their toes or face the raff of Derro.

"My God that's the man I'm working for, if he did that to that poor guy what would he do to me if I step out of line."

"That's why we have to stop him is greed is taking over, and that is why we have to stop him."

They are looking at all the transfers going off and John stands and tells them.

"Right we have to go for the main aim and that is Derro, Wayne can you go and set up the meeting with me and Derro, tell him that you are showing us the running of the plant, and that I would like to purchase over 2 billion Gold bars and what price he requires."

"Will do and you just sit tight here and if anyone comes just mention my name, and tell them where I've gone." Wayne leaves the room to find Derro.

He's down on ground level and looking round and he did not have to look far for approaching him is Derro and he asks.

"What are you doing down here, where are you attached answer me now."

"Sir I'm showing John Guest around, who is interested in purchasing over 2 billion in Gold bars, and he would like to know what price."

"Bring him to my Office and I will entertain him there and be quick about it."

"Yes Sir straight away, I'm on my way." Wayne salutes Derro and comes back to John.

"How did it go Wayne all set up."

"Yes I've to take you to his office and he will entertainer you, but that is some short fused guy. You be careful and don't let him suspect anything or you will feel the full force of his temper." Wayne a little concerned about the meeting.

"Lead on Wayne lets get this ball on the road." Wayne takes them to his office and introduces John Guest and his wife Merika to Derro.

Derro is sitting behind his desk and John outstretches his hand in friendship but Derro just points to the chairs the other side of his desk and tells him to be seated.

"Don't think of me as rude but a man in my position can not be too careful." Derro telling John.

"No problem did the guard tell you my requirements and what will it cost me."

"Yes and straight to the point, I'm in the middle of negotiations to obtain a shipment from section 34, once I have delivered them the means of transferral. Hopefully straight after this meeting."

"And the cost would be." John trying to tempt Derro.

"2 billion in Gold bars would be, 1 billion to you."

"Fine soon as the Gold is here you will have the money delivered to where ever you require money transferred or cash."

Derro tells them that everything is in hand, and the Guard will show you back. Now I must be off, Derro sits and pulls out a gadget out of his pocket and starts pressing buttons and he disappears in front off them. John had seen his hand move and he pulls out the gadget that Zen of Great Thor gave him and John starts to press buttons, just as Wayne came in. he had just enough time to tell them that he would see them back in the room where they looked at the plant. Wayne is looking at John and he is about to say something when John disappears.

Why Me

Derro appears in a large warehouse that is full of Gold bars and John appears a short distance away next to a white overcoat rack. He slips one of the white coats on and picks up a board with paper on and starts to make is way to where Derro is with about five rather mean looking guys and Derro tells them to stand back and he dials some numbers and they all stand and look at an empty space that had been prearranged by Derro and one large Goods machine for transferring goods through time and universes appears.

"There is my transfer dimension transfer unit, simple to use when you have the goods to transfer all you have to do is follow the instructions on the screen and enter the goods for transfer into it. Any questions on the machine."

"They stand looking at the machine and tell Derro that they have the drift of it and don't worry us, we will have it up and running in no time. Excuse the pun."

"You will for within the hour you will transfer the Gold I require for a customer, and if you fail you will feel the full force of my raff, so be warned." With this Derro stands looking at them with a stern face and disappears in front of them to his own time and dimension.

The five men walk away from the machine and John still looking unnoticed starts to walk towards the Gold and puts a small disc that had appeared out off the device he had and put it in to the middle of the Gold.

He to disappear and he become visible back in the room with Merika and Wayne.

"What are you; you seem to have the same powers that Derro has, how do you do it." Wayne inquisitive with what John had done.

"It's a long story Wayne but trust me the people who won't him back have given me the same powers that Derro has."

"What will we be doing next, please it's going over my head with all this disappearing and difference appearances, who the hell will come through and start a conflict." Wayne by know is totally confused with the whole scenario, and just sits there with hand s on his head and shaking it side to side.

"Come on now Wayne you are the number one in this case you have all the keys and we would be know were with out you." John trying to pull Wayne together."

"I'm sorry but a lot has happened to me within the last few hours, I mean security Guard one minute and the next helping out on a massive Universe mission to safe billions of life's."

"And you're doing fine Wayne just keep it together, and What I won't you to do is get me back into Derro's office. For I won't to give him a surprise."

"OK let's go and this time just leaves the talking to me." Wayne leads off with John behind him and Merika staying where she is. The approach Derro's office and Wayne knocks on the door and there is no response, he opens the door and the room is empty. He turns to John to tell him but it's if John knew he tells Wayne to wait there and he enters. After about a minute John reappears and tells Wayne that's it everything is set.

Well poor old Wayne did not know what he was on about and they both go back to where Merika is.

Chapter 7

All three of them together and John is about to tell them something when the whole room around them is shimmering and everywhere they look the same affect.

"What's going on?" Merika looking at John and he looks like he his shimmering, John tells then to look at the dimension shifter and what is happening down on the warehouse floor.

The machine is at full power and the glow from it is starting to turn red. There are eclectic arc hitting the floor and then they look at the entrance to the machine which looks like a large circle with mist at the entrance and electric ace hitting containers that are emerging from the machine.

Then they see Derro throwing orders about like a man possessed, shouting and balling at the poor workers trying to move the containers from the entrance so more can come through.

"My God just look at it down there, what the hell people back home will going through and if I don't put a stop to him he will completely destroy my World and Universe." John looking at Merika and Wayne.

John looks at his watch and he had only 26 hours left to complete the mission, for he known that he will be turned back to his World and the end does not bear thinking about. Wayne tells them.

"I have to clock off in 10 minutes and they don't allow you to be on site after your time, but if you both would like to stay at my apartment your welcome. I could go and tell Derro that you are going to stop with me, and that I will bring you back in the morning to the plant for the completion of your sale."

"Go and do it we will wait for you here." John and Merika go towards the window and Wayne goes to confront Derro.

"You would not believe that this could affect so many people its beyond the imagination of what this could result in." John just steering down at the dimension machine still continuing with its work bringing goods in from other Worlds and dimensions. His hands on the glass looking at the continuation working down below. Merika tries to console him she stands behind him with her arms around him and she tells him.

"You will pull this off and there is only one outcome."

"What is that?" John turning and facing Merika.

"Tomorrow you will return to your World and your wife and I will be left here on my own."

"That's something I can not avoid, it's out off my hands. But you can rest a sure that when it happens and I sit in my garden looking up at the sky, there is only one thing that I will be thinking off and that is you. Will Merika sit there looking at the same sky and thinking of me? That is something that we both know we will not have the answer."

Merika spins John round and they are in a full kiss and the tears start to run down Merika face.

"A come on now we don't wont to lose it now, we have a lot to-do in the morning, and we still have to night." John wiping the tears from under her eyes. He is about to give Merika another kiss when the door opens and in walks Wayne.

Why Me

"That Derro is such a prick, I went up to him and the first thing he told me is, what the hell you won't. Then I told him about you and the first meeting and he then goes on and tells me to bring you to his office at 12.30 pm and that I better look after you well tonight our else. Then he just came straight out with it now get out of my face, what an arrogant man."

"That will leave it tight but it will leave me just enough time to say goodbye's to you both before I go back to my World." John squeezing Merikas hand. Wayne tells them to follow him and they go back to the hover bike that they came on and start to head out of the compound, they approach the check point and the two guards are on watch are the same as when they came in. well the difference when they see it was Wayne and John and Merika they straight away waved them on. For the both of them did not won't another confrontation with John.

They pull up at Wayne's apartment and they go into his lodgings and they are taken back by the view out of his living room, for it lead onto a veranda looking out across the water.

"You have a nice place here Wayne, how long have you had it." Merika asking Wayne.

"Only about two weeks with me being new here and having little experience this is where they put me."

"You telling me this Derro doe's have a heart after all." John looking around Wayne's apartment.

"No he only pays for it you would not catch him coming down here; this is just something he provides for his workers."

"Where are we sleeping then Wayne? Trying to look for the door to the bedrooms"

"The door where you are Merika you're welcome to stop in there. Merika opens the door and you would not believe what confronted her, only a Queen Size bed and the view was to die for.

"Oh my God how much do you pay for this then, Merika not believing what she was looking at?

"It comes with the job, so long as I work for Derro then it's mine but in the contract when I leave so do all the benefits. They go out onto the balcony and the night had draw in, John and Merika are looking at the view. They sit down on the balcony and the 3 moons are shining down on the sea and the gentle ripple of the waves crashing onto the beach.

Why Me

Wayne brings them drinks and all three sit looking at the view. Wayne asks John.

"What will happen to the plant after Derro has gone."

"I don't know Zen of Great Thor did not mention this before I came, but you can resets assure he will not leave it for someone else to start t up again. We will know the answers tomorrow. John smiles at Wayne but you could tell Wayne was not very happy about being out of work. Merika sees this and she turns to John and whispers something to John's ear. John tells Merika to do it.

"Wayne how would you like to come and work for me, in the same sort of game that we are in now."

"What catch criminals and fugitives, like the films you see on the 3d domes in the City."

"You've got it, and the rewards are good." telling Wayne.

"Thanks Merika you bet I would." Merika leans forward and gives him a kiss to seal the deal.

At about 11.30 John tells Wayne that they are going to retire to bed for they had a big day tomorrow. They say their goodnights to each other and John and Merika go to their room.

Merika showers and John comes into the shower room and asks if there is room for one more, come on in the waters fine. John steps into the shower and he gently soaps her back starting with her shoulders, and working down to her buttocks. John goes down to her legs his head is at the same level of Merikas buttocks, when she turns and faces him.

The water is running of his face and he slowly moves forward to her virgina and he starts to put his tongue onto her clitoris and starts to flick his tongue and Merika is moaning with pleasure, he is doing this for about 5 minutes when Merika can not stand it anymore she puts her hands under Johns arms and slowly pulls him up. She turns bends forward and grabs hold of the shower support arms and John mounts her from behind.

He is going at it for well over 20 minutes and he cannot hold it any longer and he ejaculates giving of one of the biggest pleasure groans you could imagine, Merika is doing the same and then it hits them, Merika stands facing John and they both burst out laughing out aloud.

"God hope Wayne did not hear us." John looking at Merika.

"Well if he did not hear that he must be stone deaf."

They go back into the bedroom and they are lying on their backs down on the bed and they tuck them self's in and the feeling off the Queen Size bed, really made them feel relaxed. Merika with her arm across John's chest tells him.

"I don't won't tomorrow to come round."

"Why's that then."

"You will be leaving me and what will I do knowing that I will never see you again."

"That's something that is not in our hands, anyway you will have Wayne. He's quit good looking you know, I bet if you met him first I would have not have not had a look in."

"That's a hypothetical question, which can not be answered. Course I would have Wayne and I would have not looked at you twice."

"What." John looking shocked at what she said.

"Only kidding, Merika laughing at John and at the same time giving him a little nudge in the side. They kiss each other goodnight and they both go drifting off to sleep.

The next morning they are woken by Wayne bringing them an early drink for he had to be back at the plant for his start of a new day. John looks at Wayne when he came into their room with the drinks.

"What time is it Wayne."

"6.30 John, come on let's have you up and get the show on the road."

"It's to early tell him to go away." Merika being disturbed from her sleep.

John and Merika are up and getting dressed and they are both a little under the weather, and we know why that is. They finally manage to come round and go into the dinning area and Wayne had made them a full breakfast.

"God he's not real 6.30am and facing a full breakfast." Merika sitting there looking back at John, who is tucking into the meal and looking back at Merika and telling her.

"Well try and eat something, I wish I had him back home on my Planet."

Wayne sits down with them and John tells them the plan for the day.

"We will go with Wayne back to the plant and we will go on a tour round the plant with

Why Me

being guest of Derro, you Wayne will carry out your daily duties and at 12.20pm you will come and find us to take us to see Derro in his office. With look it should all be over by 12.40pm."

They finish off their breakfast and are ready start to head back to the plant. The same transport that they came on, Wayne driving and John and Merika behind Wayne. They approach the gates and by chance it was the same guards that had confronted Wayne. He tells them that John Guest and is partner had a meeting with Derro; well straight away they wave him through and salute John when he went by.

"That's better Wayne a little talking to them made them realise that they are not the impotent ones but we are." John feeling a little important himself.

Wayne drops them off at the plant warehouse and they both make their way up to the room that over looked the dimension machine. Wayne in the mean time went on with his daily duties.

John and Merika are back in the room and they are looking down at the dimension machine and it is at full power and dimension shifting goods.

The room and the surrounding area are shimmering, when John tells Merika.

"If this carry's on like this then God help people back in my time and World they will not stand a chance." Merika reassures John.

"You will prevail over Derro's evil and save your World and Universe."

They stop in the room watching the events unfold below them and the time is approaching 12.00noon and John tells Merika that the time is approaching and that if anything goes wrong he will never forget the time we have had together.

"H'a come on now we don't wont defeatist, you will pull this off and save your World." Merika trying to reassure John.12.20 and Wayne is back.

"Are you ready for the meeting?" Wayne looking at John and Merika.

"Let's do it lead on Wayne." The time is approaching 12.30pm and Wayne knocks on Derro's door.

"Come who is there." Wayne starts to open the door and puts his thumb up to John.

Why Me

"Sir I've John Guest and his partner for their 12.30pm meeting with you Sir."

"Show them in and wait in the room with me with your sidearm ready." Derro tanking no chances.

Wayne brings them in and they sit on the other side of a large desk with Derro on the other side.

"Sir John Guest and his partner Merika."

"Yes you're the man who came and seen me yesterday about a shipment of Gold bullion, Have you the one Billion."

"Yes and No, you see my company have asked me to get your preference of payment." Derro throws across the table a card have you a con-ex communicator."

"Yes Sir."

"Well tell them that the numbers on the card will allow them to transfer the money and when it is done to contact me within the hour. This meeting is over, come back at one and if the money is transferred you will receive your goods."

Derro stands and leaves by a back door. Merika turns to John and asks.

"He is still here I thought that this was the time and place."

"Just one hour then fingers crossed it will happen." John looking at his watch for it is leaving it late for the dead line; for he had to leave this Planet is 3.30pm.

"Come let's have a drink before we return." Wayne takes them to the feeding mess, and the amount of staff and guards in the mess, just showed you how big Derro's set up is. They sit at the window that over looked the dock in the distance and there is a large container Hover craft bringing empty containers back to the compound, and Hover craft leaving full of container with goods that Derro had sold. Then John asks Merika.

"Where will you go when this is over?"

"To the otherside of the planet they are having a little trouble with crime and conmen. And there will be plenty of work for Wayne and myself to keep us in demand for a long time." Merika looking at Wayne and giving him a big smile. Then Wayne tells them that they had better get back. They rise and John pulls the gadget the Zen had gave him that enables him to stop time and travel in dimensions, and he presses a few buttons and gives it a kiss.

Chapter 8

"Already lead on Wayne they arrive back and Wayne knocks and they enter, Derro is pointing to the chairs and they sit, John noticed that there were two guards beside Derro and John asks.

"What is it with the two guards?"

"Nothing just the way I conduct things in business, have you in formed your so called company."

"Why have they not contacted you." And before Derro could answer him his con-ex rings and he pick it up and said.

"Derro here." Then Derro's face changes for this was not his con-ex and he looks straight at John, John smiles straight back at him and Derro tells him.

"You Bastard you're from ZEN of Great Thor. John never had time to answer him for Derro started to disappear into thin air. John turns to the two guards and tells them that they had better get out of there for there will be storm troupers trained to kill here any minute." Well the two guard's just drop there weapons and flee. Well poor old Wayne stands there and did not know witch way to turn and he asks John.

"What about me."

What are you on about?" Wayne looking out off Derro's window.

"Storm troupers armed to kill."

"That was just to frighten them away; I don't know what will happen next." Merika gives John a big kiss and all of a sudden a figure appears in a mist form. Merika and Wayne stand next to John at seeing the figure, a little frightened.

"Zen you have him back." John starts to talk to the mist.

"You have done well John; you have saved the two Universes. And the answer to your question, yes we have him back and he stood trial and he was sentence to life time to make his World a better place."

"What happens next Zen?"

Why Me

"Already my men have sent a little surprise to all the 34 machines that Derro set up and every one of them when the device goes through will send every last one of the machines back to Planet Unitze so no others can use them and the disc that you put on the gold will disappear of the transporters and will be used to fund events on my planet."

"Will I be going home soon." Asks John.

"One Earth hour from now and you will return and do not be shocked when you return, and once again thank you John and use you gadget wisely for good only." Zen fades away and Merika and Wayne stand looking at John.

"What do you won't to do for the last hour?" Merika tells him.

"Let's all three of us get of this island and go and walk along the shore at Point End Warf, it's only 3 miles away we will be there in time for at least 20 minutes before you depart."

"OK let's go." John pointing to Wayne to take charge and get them there.

They are off the Island and speeding to Point End Warf, they pull onto the beach and John is taken back by the view. Clear blue water white sands, the beauty of it all, the two Suns are beating down and the temperature is about 80f all three of them go along the beach hand in hand. Just general talk. John looks at his watch and the time is showing that there is only 5 minutes to go, he kisses Merika and he tell's her that he will think of her every time he looks up into the night sky and the stars shining back at him. He then looks at Wayne and tells him.

"Wayne Foden you look after Merika." He puts Wayne's hand into Merika's and he suddenly hears clack, clack and he suddenly remembers and spins round and running at full speed his feathered girl friend she comes to a sudden holt and starts her march off nodding like a pigeon.

well Merika and Wayne are killing them self's with laughter and the bird comes walking back clacking away when John fades away and he to had the biggest grin on his face.

He reappears in Sir Ralph's Ward office and he looks at Sir Ralph who is engrossed in is paper work, John tells him I'm back.

"Will you stop messing about John and go to wherever you are supposed to go and sort this mess out, you are starting to get to my nerves just go?"

"But Sir I'm back it's all over, the World should be back to normal."

Why Me

"What the hell are you talking about the time is still 3.30pm and you are still here." John stands and thinks for a moment and this is what Zen meant don't be afraid.

John stands looking round Sir Ralph's office and he suddenly notices that the Sun is no longer shining on his desk it had moved onto the carpet, witch confirmed that the Sun was moving and time was back to normal.

"Sir please look and sit and take notice." Sir Ralph drops his glasses onto his desk and tells John.

"This had better be good."

"Well Sir if I have not been yet, well please explain why the Sun is no longer shining on your desk but had moved and it is now shining on your carpet, it's over time is back to normal." Well Sir Ralph seeing this turns the TV on that he had in his office. And all the news is about the Sun moving and in Australia the dawn is breaking, and all the reports are the same. Time is moving again the abnormality is over.

"My God you're right how the hell you did it in a few seconds." Now Sir Ralph looks stunned.

"Believe it or not I have been there 3 days and you would not believe the people who helped me."

"Well how did you achieve this?" Sir Ralph sitting back in his chair and looking at John.

"Well Sir you remember the gadget I had and I was told that all I had to do is make Derro pick it up."

"Yes go on."

"Well Sir I went to his room early on and planted the gadget that he had to pick up and programmed my device to tell it to ring at a curtain time and he just picked it up and I had him."

"I don't believe it how the hell did you know that he would." Sir Ralph not believing it was that simple.

"Well you know that you have your Con-ex set for certain ring tone, you know let's say jingle bells. Well if you are on public transport and the tune jingle bells goes off everybody reaches into their pocket to answer their con-ex. Even that they know that it is not their ring tone. Human instinct they all go to answer it, this is how I got him."

"Well I'm dumb found I would have never thought of that you have done well, if you had been there that long you would be wonting to get back to your wife who If I'm right might need you by her side."

"Yes Sir I've missed her over these passed three days."

"Well you had better get off then, but remember she is just like me, don't start to tell her all that had gone before you in the last 3 days. She might think you're cracking up, for she knows you left this morning."

"Thank you Sir and I wish you well, John leaves Sir Ralph office and by the time he had sorted a few things out he be off home. The night light is starting to draw in and he is driving home he pulls up in his local when it is dark he gets out of his car and looks up to the stars but he has this strange feeling that he should know something special but he just can not thing what it was.

Do you think Zen had put things right and that John should not know, for he has a loving wife back home. And for Merika will we ever know if she it hit's it off with Wayne. And don't forget that John had the gadget that

John Bolstridge

Zen had gave him and he could you'se it in is work in the future.

Watch any bad guys in the future for you will not see John coming.

THE END

Lightning Source UK Ltd.
Milton Keynes UK
UKOW05f1223201213

223420UK00001BA/2/P